INTERNATIONAL BUSINESS ETIQUETTE

Europe

What You Need To Know To Conduct Business Abroad with Charm and Savvy

By
Ann Marie Sabath

INTERNATIONAL BUSINESS ETIQUETTE

Europe

What You Need To Know To Conduct Business Abroad with Charm and Savvy

By
Ann Marie Sabath

CAREER PRESS

Franklin Lakes, NJ

INTERNATIONAL BUSINESS ETIQUETTE: EUROPE

Cover design by Design Solutions
Printed in the U.S.A. by Book-mart Press

To order this title, please call toll-free 1-800-CAREER-1 (NJ and Canada: 201-848-0310) to order using VISA or MasterCard, or for further information on books from Career Press.

The Career Press, Inc., 3 Tice Road, PO Box 687, Franklin Lakes, NJ 07417

Library of Congress Cataloging-in-Publication Data

Sabath, Ann Marie.
International business etiquette. Europe : what you need to know to conduct business abroad with charm and savvy / by Ann Marie Sabath.
p. cm.
Includes index.
ISBN 1-56414-397-X (pbk.)
1. Business etiquette—Europe. 2. National characteristics, European. 3. Intercultural communication. I. Title.
HF5389.3.E85S23 1999
395.5'2—dc21

99-25036
CIP

Acknowledgments

My acknowledgments go to.....

That man of international vision, my publisher, Ron Fry.

My editor, Sue Gruber, for her attention to detail.

My father, who gave me the tenacity necessary for writing my fourth book.

My mother, who supported me with her very heart and soul.

My dearest Thomas Byron and schnauzer, Micah, for always being there for me.

My children, Scott and Amber, for their continued belief in my projects.

My assistant, Suzy, for holding down the fort as I was working on this book.

My research assistant, Julie Brigner.

My literary agent, Brandon Toropov, who made this book a reality.

Contents

Introduction

Europe! There are as many different customs and cultures on this continent as there are flavors of ice cream. When traveling to Europe, having a command of the language of the country you're visiting certainly is an advantage to getting to know others and being accepted. However, if you are not fluent in German, French, Spanish, Italian, Finnish, or any other European language, one way to successfully conduct business is to become knowledgeable about the country's customs and manners. This book has been written to assist you in doing just that. Besides giving you the do's and taboos of 25 European countries, it also provides you with the answers to questions you may be asking yourself as you prepare for your trip. These questions may include:

- How will the country's customs differ from what I am used to?
- What do I need to know about meeting and greeting others?
- What kind of gifts should I take and when should they be given?
- Which service people should I tip or not tip?
- When a tip is in order, what is the appropriate amount?
- What is the country's currency?
- Where will I get the best currency exchange rates?
- When I want to call home, what will the time difference be?
- On what days should I make a point of not scheduling appointments?
- Are there any special table manners I need to know?
- What should I wear?

With questions like these, you may not have all the time you need to prepare yourself for your trip to Europe. This book has been written to assist you in being well-prepared for the situations you will encounter on a daily basis, so that you can quickly overcome those "cultural shock jitters." This book's contents are designed to help you to think and act like a "local," based on the country in which you will be doing business. It will also help you to stop "interpreting" actions based on what they mean in your own country.

International Business Etiquette: Europe addresses the do's and don'ts of etiquette in 25 countries, including Austria, Belgium, Bulgaria, the Czech Republic, Denmark, England, Finland, France, Germany, Greece, Hungary, Ireland, Italy, Luxembourg, the Netherlands, Norway, Poland, Portugal, Romania, Russia, Scotland, Spain, Sweden, Switzerland, and Turkey. Each chapter begins with many vital facts and statistics, followed by etiquette tips addressing specific areas. Each country-specific chapter concludes with a section on "Whatever you do..." tips. These tips are meant to sensitize you to the nonverbal forms of communication that may be appropriate in your own country yet may be major *faux pas* in a European country.

Each chapter emphasizes the most important etiquette tips that are crucial for adapting to the customs and culture of the country you are visiting. While many countries are similar in their social mores, such as greetings, table manners, and gift giving, other customs are unique to their own country. You will learn in which countries you should seat yourself at a restaurant rather than wait to be seated, where to accept an alcoholic beverage prior to beginning a morning or afternoon meeting, and when to eat everything on your plate so that you are not perceived as being wasteful, among many other important things to know.

Following is a summary of the sections that will be covered in each chapter:

Statistics and Information

Air Travel

This section will familiarize you with the names of the main airport(s) of each country. It will also give you some tips on how to get from the airport to the heart of the closest city. Note: In most chapters, the airport(s) described is the closest to that country's capital.

Country Code

You may need to interact by phone or fax with a European client, so this section provides the country code and many of the city codes within that nation. You will find that some city codes consist of one, two, or even three numbers, depending on where you're calling.

Note: When making international calls, be sure to dial 011 first, followed by the country code, city code, and phone number.

Currency

This section describes the currency of each country and the various denominations of notes and coins. In addition, you will learn where to get the best currency exchange rates.

On January 1, 1999, the euro was introduced as the banking currency in Austria, Belgium, Finland, France, Germany, Ireland, Italy, Luxembourg, the Netherlands, Portugal, and Spain. Each of these country's own currencies has the same value as the euro. When doing business in these countries, you may conduct credit card transactions and write checks in euros.

The euro will be used as actual cash in the form of notes and coins beginning January 2002. At that time, the currency of each participating country and the euro will both be in circulation until July 2002, after which the euro will be used exclusively.

Dates

Throughout this continent, the European standard format is followed when writing dates. The number representing the day is listed first, followed by the number of the month and then the year (for example, June 24, 1999, would be written 24/6/99 or 24 June 1999). Because this format is different than the American standard format, in which the number of the month is listed first, it is advisable to write out the name of the month to avoid any miscommunication.

Note: When writing out the date in numbers and letters (for example, 13 February 2005), no commas should be used.

Ethnic Makeup

Many European countries are comprised of homogeneous populations, while others are very diverse. This section will tell you which nationalities you will encounter in the country you are visiting.

Holidays and National Celebrations

This section will assist you in knowing what holidays and national celebrations are pertinent to each country covered in this book. By becoming acquainted with these dates, you will know when *not* to schedule meetings or make calls to that country. You will also gain a working knowledge of which days you can expect government buildings, banks, offices, and many shops to be closed.

Language

Although English is one of the business languages spoken in many countries, you will find that Europeans are typically multilingual. By becoming acquainted with which languages you will hear, you will be able to bone up on those phrases (such as "Hello," "How are you," "Please," and "Thank you") that will start you off on the right "lingual" foot.

Religion

This section explains the main religion(s) that are practiced in each European country. While Roman Catholicism is widely practiced in many countries, you will also find pockets of people who are Evangelical Lutherans, Anglicans, Presbyterians, Calvinists, and other Protestant denominations, as well as such religions as Judaism,

Greek Orthodox, Romanian Orthodox, Russian Orthodox, Sunni Muslim, Sikhism, Islam, and Hinduism. This section will also identify those countries where religion is not practiced openly.

Time Zone Differences

When you are away from home, it may be more important than ever to reach out and touch someone—at least through the telephone wires. This section will assist you in determining the time difference between the country you're visiting and your home country so you'll know when to place that call.

Weather

Because climate is a very important variable to take into consideration when traveling abroad, this section will come in handy. It will prepare you for the weather you may encounter depending on the time of year you will be traveling and the part of the country you will be visiting. If you are planning to visit several European countries, it will be important to prepare for different climates by taking clothes that can be worn in layers. In addition, an umbrella should always be close at hand.

Etiquette

Business Attire

The way you are dressed is important in making a positive first impression, so you need to take care in packing the right clothes and accessories. In some countries, you will want to make a point of dressing elegantly, while in others, business professional attire will suffice. You will also find that in other European countries, people may not place a lot of importance on their appearance and dress in an understated manner. This section will guide you in making these distinctions, country by country, so that you can pack accordingly.

Finally, this section will assist you in learning about European color coordination and accessorizing. In what countries are dark colors worn more often? Where should one avoid wearing striped ties? Where is it acceptable for men to wear white socks with suits? This section will set you straight. Businesswomen will also learn in which countries tailored suits and business dresses will assist them in being taken more seriously and those nations in which it may be acceptable to wear slacks during the business day.

Business-card Etiquette

As in most countries across the globe, your business card is an important part of meeting and greeting others for the first time. It is always imperative to take more than an ample supply of business cards with you when traveling anywhere. This section will tell you in which European countries you should have your cards translated on the reverse side and into what language, as well as those countries in which it is acceptable to present your business cards in English. In many chapters, you will also learn what should be emphasized on your business card and to whom the card should be distributed.

Business Entertaining/Dining

This section will address how business entertaining is conducted throughout Europe. You will find that in some countries, people "live to eat." In these nations, the majority of entertainment centers on food. You will also find that in other countries, the inhabitants follow more of an "eat to live" philosophy. In these places, food may be part of the business-entertainment process. However, meals will not be offered in as lavish a manner as you will find in, say, Greece, Italy, or Turkey.

This section also shares information about when and where food will be served "family-style," what beverages you are likely to be offered, and some of the unusual foods you may have a chance to enjoy.

Many European countries have a particular etiquette to be followed when eating, from using the continental manner of holding utensils to keeping your hands in view above the table. This section covers some of the fine points of table manners in each country and may also touch on such subjects as when certain courses are served and how sandwiches should be eaten.

Conversation

This section will teach you in which countries "small talk" is an important part of the rapport-building process, and where "kibitzing" is a readily understood and accepted concept.

Each chapter will share safe topics of conversation and those areas that you may want to avoid. You will also learn the countries in which its nationals consider debating to be part of the conversational process.

By becoming acquainted with the conversational styles of Europeans, you will know what to expect, and therefore, avoid misinterpreting their behavior according to your own country's standards.

Gestures and Public Manners

Some Europeans are very expressive in their gestures and communication style. Others are more reserved and may be perceived as unexpressive or even standoffish. This section shares the do's and don'ts of spatial relationships, including beckoning, making eye contact, touching and patting, and body language in general. You will also avoid making major social gaffes by learning the gestures that may be considered acceptable in your own country but rude in other countries. In some chapters, you even will learn what to expect when queuing and the countries in which you should play down your hand gestures.

Gift-giving Etiquette

In most European countries, the gift exchange is a very important part of the business-relationship process. Thus, along with your personal belongings, you will want to pack some items that may be presented to others. The best gifts are usually ones that represent your organization and/or your city. This section will offer ideas on what to bring, as well as information on when to present your gift (such as when you first meet, after negotiations, or during the holidays). You will also learn in which countries practical gifts will be more appreciated than the lavish variety, and where you should expect to have the receiver open the gift in private rather than in front of you.

Greetings and Introductions

When first meeting an individual in any European country, the initial greeting typically consists of a handshake. In some countries, even after a meeting or two, the greeting may remain rather solemn and formal, whereas in other countries, once rapport has been established, you will be greeted with a hug and perhaps even a kiss on both cheeks.

This section will share with you in which countries you should expect a particular form of greeting and when. It also covers the sometimes sticky problem of who to introduce to whom first and the proper terms to use. Finally, this section emphasizes that you should address Europeans using their names, titles, and sometimes even both, unless you are invited to use their first names.

How Decisions Are Made

In some countries, decisions are made by consensus, while in others, these are made by the head person. This section will assist you in becoming acquainted with the decision-making process of each country so that you will have a working knowledge of the "internal" decision-making culture.

Meeting Manners

This is a very important section for anyone conducting business in a European country. You will learn when you should arrive at a meeting, when you will need an interpreter, in which countries you should make small talk before starting the meeting, and in which countries it is advisable to keep chatter to a minimum and get right down to business. You will also learn in which nations decision-makers are likely to be present and the ones in which the "messengers" will be sent to become acquainted with what you have to offer and then report back to the head person.

Punctuality

This section addresses in which European countries punctuality will be expected, and when the same respect for timeliness will be shown to you. You will also learn in which European countries time is perceived as fluid, meaning that you may be kept waiting 30 minutes or longer for a scheduled meeting to begin. You will also learn where *not* to acknowledge the tardiness of others and instead to take plenty of reading material with you so that you can use your time wisely as you are waiting for them to arrive.

Seating Etiquette

While there are no written rules for seating etiquette in some countries, there are some definite guidelines in others. This section will assist you in knowing where to sit and when in any given country. When seating etiquette rules are undefined, you may take your cue from your host.

Tipping Tips

Tipping is acceptable in some European countries and not necessary in others. It can also be tricky—how much do you give and when? This section explains when displaying your gratitude verbally will suffice rather than leaving a tip. It also tells you when giving a tip means rounding out a bill to the next highest figure or when a service charge is incorporated into your bill. (Note: In some countries, this charge may be higher on Sundays!)

When it is proper to give a tip, this section will tell you how much to give certain kinds of service personnel, as well as when it is appropriate to add on more in recognition of superior service.

When You Are Invited to a Home

In some European countries, being invited to someone's home is considered to be a great compliment. When it happens, these invitations may be extended several days to a week in advance, or in nations where the citizens are very spontaneous, you may be invited on a moment's notice. This section tells you in which countries you may or may not expect to be invited to a home and how to interpret or react to this personal hospitality. You will also learn what type of gifts to take, what to expect once you're there, and how long to stay without overextending your welcome.

Women in Business

Although many European women are climbing the business ladder of success, others haven't even had an opportunity to put their foot on the first rung of the ladder. This section will share information about the status of women in the country you will be visiting and how women traveling from abroad should act in order to be treated like the true professionals they are.

Some of the other sections may also help women to know what to order when they are out with men and when it may be better to prepay a bill so that their male European guest is not made to feel uncomfortable when the bill arrives.

Note: In addition to the common categories explained here, in some chapters you will also learn the specifics of hierarchy, toasting etiquette, taking taxis, and using public restrooms.

Chapter 1

Austria

Austria is a democratic republic located in central Europe. Its size is almost exactly that of the state of Maine. The country is bordered on the north by the Czech Republic, on the east by Slovakia and Hungary, on the south by Slovenia and Italy, and on the west by Switzerland and Germany. Because of its key position on the European continent and its history, Austria has often been considered to be the place where East meets West.

The country is very mountainous and is renowned for the beauty of its Alps. Vienna, located in the northeastern section of the country, is Austria's capital and has been a major cultural center in Europe for centuries. Other major cities include Graz, Linz, Salzburg, and Innsbruck. The majority of the population of more than 7.8 million can be found in the plains and lowland areas around Vienna and the Danube Valley.

The current democratic, federal government was established with the constitution of 1920 (amended in 1929) and allows for a division of power among the executive, legislative, and judicial branches. The country's president is elected by popular vote every six years. There are nine provinces in Austria, each with its own unicameral legislature.

Austria has a rich historical and cultural heritage. Its people are known for a strong work ethic, yet they also know how to play very well. This is a land known for its sumptuous architecture, art, and music, especially its waltzes. Mozart wrote some of his best-known operas in Vienna, including *The Magic Flute*, and Beethoven and Mahler achieved equal renown in that jewel of a city. Austria is known worldwide for such cultural trademarks as the annual Salzburg Music Festival, the Vienna Boys Choir, and the Lippizaner stallions. Austria is also where Sigmund Freud perfected the art of psychoanalysis.

Tourism is a major industry in Austria, as is the services sector, agriculture, and forestry. Its major exports include paper products, machinery and equipment, metal products, and textiles. Austria enjoys a very comfortable standard of living, a social insurance program covering all workers, and an excellent educational system, making it one of the most stable countries in Europe.

Statistics and Information

Air Travel

Austria's primary international airport is Vienna's Flughafen Wien Schwechati (the Schwechat Airport). This airport is modern and provides many conveniences. It is located about 10 miles southwest of Vienna. There are both buses and trains that run between the airport and downtown Vienna. You may also be able to take a taxi at a cost of approximately ÖS300 to 350.

Country Code

Austria's country code is 43. Key city codes are:

- 512 for Innsbruck.
- 662 for Salzburg.
- 1 for Vienna.

Currency

Austria's currency is called the *schilling* (abbreviated ÖS or AS). One *schilling* is equal to 100 *groschen* (g). Notes come in denominations of ÖS5,000, 1,000, 500, 100, 50, and 20. Coins come in units of ÖS20, 10, 5, and 1, as well as 50, 10, and 5 *groschen*.

You will find the best exchange rates for your currency and traveler's checks at post offices or the American Express office. The exchange offices located in airports and major rail terminals are open seven days a week between 8 a.m. and 8 p.m. (and often later in Vienna and certain resort areas).

Dates

Dates are commonly written with numbers rather than by writing out the day, month, and year in words. In Austria, as in other European countries, the proper way to write dates is to first list the day, followed by the month, and then the year. For instance, January 30, 1999, should be written as 30/1/99.

Ethnic Makeup

The majority of the population is of Germanic origin. A much smaller percentage includes Croatians and Slovenes. Many immigrants are also from Turkey and Yugoslavia.

Holidays and Religious Celebrations

The following are the holidays that are celebrated throughout the country. Because these are considered national holidays, it is wise to avoid scheduling meetings during these times.

January 1	New Year's Day
January 6	Epiphany
Late March/ April	Good Friday, Easter
May 1	Labour Day

Five weeks after Easter	Ascension Day
Eight weeks after Easter	Whitsunday, Whitmonday, Corpus Christi Day
August 15	Assumption Day
October 26	National Day
November 1	All Saints' Day
December 8	Immaculate Conception
December 25	Christmas Day
December 26	Boxing Day/St. Stephen's Day

Language

German is the official language of Austria. You will find that both accents and dialects may vary slightly, based on the region you are visiting. English is a frequently spoken second language. A tiny percentage of the population speaks Serbo-Croatian or Slovenian.

Religion

Roman Catholicism is the most widely practiced religion of 78 percent of Austrians. The remainder of the population observes the Protestant, Jewish, Muslim, and Orthodox faiths, or has no religious denomination.

Time Zone Differences

Austria is:

- One hour ahead of Greenwich Mean Time.
- Six hours ahead of U.S. Eastern Standard Time.

Weather

The climate will vary, depending on where you are. Highland areas stay cold all year long, with temperatures ranging between 10 and 40 degrees Fahrenheit. Temperatures in the low-lying areas are a bit warmer, depending on the season. The temperatures in Vienna can range from the low 30s in the winter to the high 60s in the summer.

Etiquette

Business Attire

Austrians take great pride in the way they dress, which you will find to be in a very simple yet elegant manner. Be sure to dress accordingly, because your attire provides an important first impression in Austrian eyes.

One way to be certain that you will pass Austrian dress inspection is by wearing high-quality clothes that fit well. Men will do well to wear dark suits with starched white shirts and conservative silk ties. Women are considered appropriately dressed in tailored suits with silk blouses or business dresses accented with quality jewelry.

Business-card Etiquette

Take plenty of business cards along to exchange with your Austrian counterparts upon your initial meeting. You will be expected to offer them to both the individuals with whom you are meeting and administrative personnel, including the company receptionist and secretary.

One way to get business relations off on the right foot is by having your cards translated in German on the back.

Titles are important in Austria, so be sure the name of your position is noticeably large and placed prominently beneath your name.

Business Entertaining/Dining

Although entertaining is an important part of the business relationship, you will find that Austrian business associates may wait until the negotiation process is close to completion before extending a meal invitation to you.

If you are invited to a business lunch, you will find it to be the largest meal of the day. Allow your host to set the tone by bringing up the topic of business first. Until this happens, be prepared to engaged in small talk unrelated to the business at hand.

If you receive an invitation to dinner, and your host's spouse is included, you can expect the invitation to be extended to your spouse to be part of the evening.

Depending on the formality level of your meal, you may or may not be served by a wait person. If the meal is less formal, the food may be offered "family-style," which means food is served in platters or bowls that are placed on the table. When this is the case, each person will be expected to serve himself or herself, rather than waiting to be served. Of course, the host or hostess should set the tone by extending the invitation for you to help yourself to the food. Do not begin eating until the hostess has started doing so.

Do not put your hands in your lap. They should be visible at all times and kept above the table. Never let your elbows rest on the table.

If the food is tender enough to be cut using the side of your fork, then do this rather than cutting it with a knife. Using a knife will be considered rude, as it insinuates that you don't think the food is tender enough. This is especially true with dumplings and potatoes. When you are served fish, be sure to use the special knife provided to you.

Rather than making a "bread and butter sandwich," the proper way to eat a roll is to break it with your fingers and eat it one piece at a time. When you are served a roll with lunch or dinner, do not expect butter to accompany it. However, when bread or a roll is served at breakfast, butter or Nutella (a hazelnut chocolate spread) may be offered with it. Another morning spread for bread and rolls is pâté or goose liver.

When you are in Austria, you may consider it safe to expose a hearty appetite and should try to eat everything that is served to you. Do not take large portions of food if you aren't certain you can eat it all. Otherwise, Austrians may perceive you as wasteful.

The way to signal to the server that you have finished eating is by placing your fork next to your knife diagonally on your plate in a 10 o'clock-5 o'clock position, with the serrated edge of the knife facing you and the fork tines up.

Unusual foods: Austrian cuisine is similar to German food. Rather than being light in texture, it tends to have a heavy consistency and is centered on meat. Sausage, ham, beef, and veal are popular entrées in Austria. Austria is especially famous for its *Wiener schnitzel,* which is a breaded and fried veal cutlet. Other popular Austrian foods are *Gulasch,* which is beef with noodles, and *Schweinsbraten,* which is pork that has been roasted.

Beverage etiquette: Wine and beer are usually served with the meal. Do not feel compelled to drink. If you choose to drink wine or beer, be sure to sip it rather than drink it in large gulps.

Conversation

You will find the Austrians to be a bit more formal than Westerners are in their personal conversations. However, a favorite pastime is to get together with friends to catch up with each other, as well as to discuss current events, family, and so on.

Taboo subjects for discussion include another person's salary or any topic that refers to money, divorce, separation, or religion. Also, be sure to avoid telling jokes. What may be considered humorous in one country may not be funny in Austria and could be misinterpreted as sarcasm or perhaps even making fun at someone's expense.

Gestures and Public Manners

Austrians conduct themselves in public with a great deal of formality. Therefore, whatever you do, be sure you do it with dignity and don't do anything that may draw attention to yourself.

Public displays of affection and even casual pats on the back are considered *faux pas* in Austria.

The proper way for getting another person's attention is by lifting your index finger with your palm open and facing outward.

Your hands should never be in your pockets when talking with others or even when standing alone. This is considered to be an offensive gesture.

Contrary to Western ways, hands should always be above board when sitting at a table. Hands under the table is considered impolite in Austria (as it is in many European countries).

The appropriateness of eye contact varies by continent. In Europe, and specifically in Austria, looking at another person directly in the eye is the proper thing to do both when listening and when talking.

Toilet etiquette: Be sure to go with change in hand when entering a W.C. ("water closet" or toilet). You will either find a washroom attendant who will unlock the door of the stall after you've paid or you will be required to insert a coin in the door to enter the stall.

Queuing: Although you will find that Austrians try to be patient when waiting in line, you will also find that queuing does not come naturally to them. If they edge forward and make you feel as though they are closing in behind you, conceal your annoyance.

Gift-giving Etiquette

Gifts are not generally exchanged casually in business. However, in the event that you are presented with a gift by an Austrian, you should have one or more small presents with you, so that you can reciprocate immediately.

Your gift will be opened in front of you, rather than in private. Thus, you may feel free to do the same when you receive something.

Gifts should be moderate and unassuming. Books describing your city, quality pens, calculators, or nice pictorial coasters all make good gifts when exchanged in an office or home setting.

When you are invited to an Austrian's home, you should go with a gift in hand for the person's spouse and children. Quality chocolates or an uneven number of flowers (other than roses) are suitable gifts for your contact's spouse. Recommended gifts for children include calculators or other electronic gadgets. A quality bottle of wine or liquor will make a good gift for your host.

Greetings and Introductions

Try not to introduce yourself to others. When possible, wait to be introduced by a third person.

When shaking hands, be sure to give a quick yet confident handshake. Men should wait for a woman to initiate any handshake.

You will find that it is common in Austria for a man to kiss a woman's hand as the greeting, rather than shaking hands. Western men should wait for Austrian women to initiate this gesture.

Just as in many countries, a handshake should be extended when leaving as a way of solidifying what was discussed.

Austrian etiquette dictates that you acknowledge people with a greeting before jumping into conversation. This includes any and all individuals in the room besides your primary contacts. If you know the positions of the people with whom you're meeting, be sure to extend your hand to the most senior individuals first.

Proper forms of address: You will notice that Austrians will address you by your last name. You should do likewise unless you are asked to do otherwise.

You will find that status and hierarchy are an important part of Austrian culture. In fact, it is so important that when someone holds a title of professor, doctor, or lawyer, for example, be sure to address the person using both the equivalent of Mr., Mrs./Ms., or Miss, *plus* the person's title and last name. For example, the appropriate way to address an Austrian who holds the title of professor would be Herr Professor Scheer.

During subsequent conversations with Herr Professor Scheer, you should still maintain formality by continuing to use his title of professor preceded by *Herr*. However, at this point you may drop the person's last name, and simply address him as Herr Professor.

Here are a few Austrian titles to remember:

- *Herr*: Mr.
- *Fräu*: Mrs./Ms.
- *Fräulein*: Miss.

How Decisions Are Made

You may find that the decision-making process will take more time than you want it to take. One reason for this is that Austrians are not risk takers and make decisions carefully and thoroughly. Companies are vertical in structure and decision-making power lies only with those at the very top.

It won't take long for you to realize that decisions are made by the bosses rather than by consensus. For that reason alone, it is important to understand that the person with whom you are meeting may not necessarily be the person who has the final authority.

You will also find that your attention to detail will be a factor taken into consideration when a decision is finally made to do business with you.

Meeting Manners

Always arrive on time to meetings. Austrians plan their schedules weeks and even months in advance and try to abide by what they have on the books. If you must reschedule an appointment, be sure to do so as soon as you know of the change.

Meetings with Austrians usually begin with a short period of small talk. Be sure to brush up on current world events and perhaps even a tidbit or two of Austrian history and culture. By doing so, you will get the meeting off on the right foot.

Your presentation should be concise and well thought out. As in most countries, make your facts and figures also available in a point-by-point written form to support your presentation. Besides avoiding any miscommunication, this documentation will also assist your Austrian counterparts in sharing information about your presentation with others in the organization who were not present yet may be instrumental in coming to a decision.

Punctuality

Just as with most Western Europeans, Austrians are keen on punctuality and expect it to be observed at all times. Austrians view people who can manage time as also being able to handle projects with attention to detail—something that is of great importance to them.

Seating Etiquette

The host and hostess of an event should arrange the guests in any way they see as suitable. Traditionally, the male guest of honor will sit to the right of the hostess and the female guest of honor will sit to the right of the host.

Taxi Etiquette

Taxis cannot be hailed on the street. The best way to get a taxi is to go to one of the designated stops. When you are leaving from a hotel, ask the bell captain to call one for you.

Tipping Tips

Many restaurants will include a 10- to 15-percent gratuity in the bill. If this is the case, round the bill up for an additional tip. If a tip is not included in the total, give 10 to 15 percent more.

Porters at airports and railway stations, as well as hotel porters, should be given ÖS15 per bag handled. When traveling by taxi, an appropriate tip is 10 percent of your fare. If the driver assists you with luggage, be prepared to give a little more in your gratuity. Washroom attendants and coatroom clerks should be also given a small tip—ÖS5 is appropriate.

Toasting Etiquette

Austrian etiquette dictates that the host of the meal or event initiate the first toast. Until then, no one should lift a glass.

You will know when a toast is being proposed. The host will lift his or her goblet while making eye contact with the most senior guest and say, "*Prost.*"

After the first toast has been made, the guest of honor (male or female) should offer a toast of thanks. This should be done sometime prior to the end of the meal.

When You Are Invited to an Austrian Home

Austrians do not usually entertain business associates in their homes, so if you do receive an invitation to an Austrian home, consider it an honor. Arrive on time and take a gift for the hostess, children, and host.

Typically, the meal will be preceded by drinks and appetizers. After dinner, expect to engage in conversation and be served an after-dinner brandy. Be sure to practice good guest etiquette by departing within an hour after dinner has ended.

Women in Business

Traditional attitudes towards women and their roles in society still abound in Austria. However, Austrian women are making great strides. Western women will be welcomed as decision-makers and will be treated with the utmost respect.

Whatever You Do...

- Don't refer to Austrians or their culture as German. The only thing that is truly German in Austria is their language.
- Don't make promises you don't intend to keep. Americans are very casual in making promissory statements, such as "Let's have lunch next week" or "I'll drop that book off soon." Austrians take people at their word and you will be expected to deliver on any or all statements you make.
- Don't wait to be seated at a restaurant. Many restaurants expect you to seat yourself.
- Don't plan to schedule business meetings in the month of August or any time near the Christmas holidays. Many Austrians schedule lengthy trips around these times.
- Don't ask where the "bathroom" is when you need to use the restroom. The term "bathroom" describes the room for showering and bathing and it may not have a toilet. The correct way to identify your need for toilet facilities is to ask for the "W.C."

- Don't arrive late for any function. Austrians are sticklers for punctuality. Whether the function is business or social, promptness is crucial.
- Don't be flamboyant in your mode of dress or in dispensing compliments. Conservatism is key for business success in Austria.
- Don't address people by their first names until you are invited to do so. Use the formal *Herr*, *Fräu*, and *Fräulein* with their last names, and if they have a title such as doctor or professor, use this, as well (for example, "Herr Doctor Schmidt").

Chapter 2

Belgium

A constitutional monarchy and centerpiece of the European Union, Belgium is a beautiful and unusual nation in western Europe, sharing boundaries with the Netherlands and Germany on the east, Luxembourg on the southeast, and France on the south and southwest. Its northern border lies on the North Sea. The country is divided into three geographical areas: the western section, called Lower Belgium, the central plain in the middle, and the Ardennes tableland in the southeast. However, one might more accurately describe the country as divided into northern and southern sections, called Flanders (where Flemish is spoken) and Wallonia (where the language is French), respectively. There is also a third, German-speaking section in the eastern part of the country. This sets Belgium apart from its European neighbors, because when you visit here, you will feel that you are visiting three countries in one.

Belgium has a population of more than 10 million people, and its ethnic division dates back many centuries, when invaders and settlers from France, Germany, the Netherlands, Rome, Austria, and even the ancient Celts all left their cultural and linguistic marks in specific areas. Flanders, Wallonia, and the small German section eventually evolved into the distinctive regions they are today—and have been for the last 1,400 years. While French is the country's business and administrative language, Brussels, the country's capital, is a bilingual amalgam of north and south, and public signs there are in both French and Flemish. Otherwise, you will always know what part of the country you are in by what language you see and hear. Despite this ethnic and linguistic diversity, overall, the citizens of Belgium do not think of themselves as Flemish or Walloon, but as Belgian.

Belgium's geographic position in Europe has made it both a major trading center and a battleground in wars throughout the centuries. (Its best known battleground is Waterloo, where Napoleon was defeated in 1815.) In more recent years, its key location has also made it the centerpiece of both the European Union and of the North Atlantic Treaty Organization (NATO), with both organizations headquartered in Brussels. For this reason, Brussels is considered by many to be the capital of Europe and Belgium itself as a model for peaceful coexistence with its European neighbors.

Belgium is known for the beauty of its countryside, as well as for the modernity of its urban areas. Besides Brussels, these include the great art cities of Antwerp, Bruges, and Ghent in Flanders, and the richly historical cities of Liege, Namur, and Tournai in Wallonia. Belgians enjoy a very high standard of living. The nation's industries center primarily on manufacturing, and they are one of the world's primary producers of flax fiber. Belgian glass is also a renowned export. Like most of the country's industries, ore mining (which has declined in recent years) has been controlled by at least one of six major trusts. The largest and most important of these is the Société Générale, founded in 1822. Others include the Groupe Solvay, Confinindus, Empain, the Groupe Coppé, and the Banque Lambert.

Long controlled by other countries, Belgium finally became an independent nation in 1830, forming a constitutional monarchy. The Belgian government rarely, if ever, interferes in the country's business. The prime minister heads a bicameral parliament, and the king of the Belgians is head of state.

Statistics and Information

Air Travel

The Brussels National Airport at Zaventem is less than 10 miles away from the business district in Brussels. Transportation from the airport into the city can be obtained by way of taxi, bus, or rail service.

Country Code

Belgium's country code is 32.

City codes include:

- 3 for Antwerp.
- 50 for Bruges.
- 2 for Brussels.
- 9 for Ghent.
- 4 for Liege.
- 65 for Mons.

When calling the United States from Belgium, first dial 00 + 1, then the area code and phone number.

Currency

Belgium's currency is called the *Belgian franc* (abbreviated BF or BEF). One *franc* consists of 100 *centimes*. The *franc* is available in denominations of BF5,000, 1,000, 500, and 100. You will find coins in 50, 20, 5, and 1 *francs*, and also in 50 *centimes*.

You may exchange your currency at any bank or at a foreign exchange office (many of which are open on Sundays). Keep in mind that banks close at 4 p.m.

Dates

When writing dates, use the European style, listing the day of the month first, followed by the month, and then the year. In other words, May 10, 1999, should be written as 10/5/99.

Ethnic Makeup

The majority of Belgium's population consists of Flemings and Walloons. More than half of the population in northern Belgium (Flanders) consists of Flemings. Approximately one third of the population in southern Belgium (Wallonia) is comprised of Walloons. Under one percent of Belgium's population in eastern Belgium consists of Germans. This ethnic mix has made Belgium both a multilingual and a multicultural country.

Helpful Hints for Travel

The workday usually begins at 8:30 a.m. and ends at 6 p.m.

Most government offices are closed between noon and 2 p.m.

Most offices are closed on Saturdays, while stores remain open until 6 p.m.

When traveling by car:

- Paris is less than 200 miles from Brussels.
- Luxembourg is less than 150 miles from Brussels.

Holidays and Religious Celebrations

The following are the holidays that are celebrated throughout the country. Because these are considered national holidays, it is wise to avoid scheduling meetings during these times.

January 1	New Year's Day
March/April	Easter
May/June	Whitsunday (49 days after Easter)
May/June	Whitmonday (50 days after Easter)
June/July	Corpus Christi (60 days after Easter)

July 21	Independence Day
August 15	Assumption
November 1	All Saints' Day
November 11	Veterans Day
December 25/26	Christmas Day

(All holidays that fall on a Sunday in any calendar year are celebrated on the following Monday).

Language

What language you hear in Belgium will depend on what part of the country you are in. In Flanders, Flemish is the language of choice, whereas in Wallonia, French is spoken. German is spoken in a small eastern section of the country. In bilingual Brussels, both French and Flemish are spoken, with French being used for business. English can also be heard, primarily in Brussels.

It is important to remember that language is a sensitive subject in Belgium, especially in Wallonia.

This multilingual characteristic can sometimes lead to problems. For instance, when you are in northern Belgium and are inquiring about a city in the eastern section, the city name under discussion may be different from the information you have, depending on whether you are speaking to a Flemish-speaking or a French-speaking individual.

Religion

The vast majority of the population practices Roman Catholicism, although the Walloons are more liberal in their attitudes, while the Flemish adhere closely to doctrine. A very small percentage of the population practices Protestantism, Anglicanism, or Judaism.

Time Zone Differences

Belgium is:

- One hour ahead of Greenwich Mean Time.
- Six hours ahead of U.S. Eastern Standard Time.

Weather

This country has a very temperate climate during the summer months, with the temperature reaching only into the low- to mid-70s. During the winter, the temperature rarely goes under 40 degrees Fahrenheit. If you like to ski, the Ardennes mountains provide the best places to go.

Etiquette

Business Attire

During business situations, men should wear suits and ties. Professional attire for women consists of suits or business dresses.

When invited to someone's home, you may dress one notch down and wear business casual. A man should wear a sport coat with a shirt, tie, and trousers, while a woman may wear a tailored pair of slacks and an attractive blouse.

Business-card Etiquette

Just as in most parts of the world, the business card exchange is an important part of initiating a business relationship in Belgium. Because English is spoken, you need not have your cards translated.

Business Entertaining/Dining

Most business entertaining is conducted over lunch. Belgians prefer to reserve the dinner hour for their families, so do not expect to do business at that time, although a dinner invitation may be extended to you.

In some countries, prevailing etiquette recommends that you leave something on your plate to show that you are satisfied. However, this is not the case when eating in Belgium. Short of licking the platter clean, you may eat everything.

While bread is a common part of most meals, this is not the case when you are in northern Belgium, where only one starch is served. Thus, bread will not be offered if potatoes are part of the meal. On the other hand, bread is a standard part of the meal in southern Belgium. However, butter may not be offered with your bread. If this is the case, let it go, and do not ask for any.

The proper way to hold utensils is European-style, with your fork held in your left hand, tines down, and your knife in your right hand at all times, whether cutting or eating the food. When you need to put your knife and fork down, they should rest on the plate in an "X" position, with the fork's tines placed over the knife. When you are finished with your meal, the knife and fork should be placed in a 10 o'clock-4 o'clock position, with the fork tines facing up.

While wine is commonly taken with lunch and dinner throughout Belgium, mineral water is also available. If you would like coffee or hot tea during either of these meals, be sure to request it following the entrée.

As in other European countries, salad will be served *after* the main course, rather than before it.

Be prepared—smoking is commonplace in Belgium. If you are a smoker, take your cue from your host. Always offer a cigarette to another before lighting up yourself. At the beginning of a meal, you may smoke only until the first course has arrived, then not until the last course, including desert, has been removed.

Conversation

As in most countries, good topics of conversation include the part of Belgium you are in and other parts of the country you may have visited. Other possibilities for discussion include sports, such as bicycling and soccer, along with the excellent food and beer you've enjoyed in this country.

Whatever you do, do not bring up the subject of politics or the different languages spoken in Belgium. This would be considered as offensive as discussing social class differences in other countries.

Be sure to speak in a low, controlled voice at all times, no matter what you are talking about. Getting too excited or animated is not acceptable.

Gestures and Public Manners

Do not snap your fingers. This is considered to be an obscene gesture in Belgium. Patting someone on the back is also a "no-no."

Pointing with your forefinger is seen as rude in this country. Use your whole hand when you wish to point at something.

Try to keep yourself from yawning. While we may think nothing of it in the West, yawning is another gesture perceived as rude in Belgium.

Be sure to keep an arms' length distance when talking to another person. Anything closer may invade that individual's space.

When you are interacting with the French-speaking Walloons, don't be surprised to see people who know each other kissing the French way, with alternate kisses bestowed three times on each cheek. It is also common for men who know each other well to embrace.

Men should be sure to stand when meeting and greeting a woman. Similarly, a junior executive who is seated should stand when being introduced to a more senior executive.

Don't slouch! Good posture is considered very important both when sitting and standing.

As in most countries, gum chewing is not an appropriate thing to do in Belgium.

When staying in a hotel, don't be alarmed if the person checking you in requests that you leave your passport at the front desk while the paperwork is being completed. If you know you will need your passport for exchanging currency at a bank, let the clerk know this, so that any forms the hotel needs to complete can be seen to promptly.

Note that Belgian hotels require you to leave your room key at the front desk each time you leave. You must then request it upon your return to the hotel.

Gift-giving Etiquette

When you are visiting a home, quality chocolates and flowers are appreciated. However, you should avoid giving chrysanthemums, as these flowers are equated with mourning.

When you are presented a gift, be sure to open it in front of the person rather than in private, and express your appreciation. You may also expect your gift to be opened in front of you.

Greetings and Introductions

The handshake is the only acceptable form of public touching in Belgium, so you should be sure to extend your hand to whomever you meet and introduce yourself by name. When bidding others "adieu," extend your hand once again. In a business setting, be sure to shake hands with everyone, including administrative personnel.

Do not prolong your handshake or make it too hearty. Your grip should be light and it should last no more than five seconds. Maintain steady eye contact and do not look away as you are shaking hands.

Men should wait for women to extend their hands first. This is an old-fashioned custom that is still adhered to in Belgium.

Common sense dictates that formality overrules casual behavior when meeting and greeting. Thus, always use last names preceded by Mr., Mrs., or Ms., unless you are invited to do otherwise.

Hierarchy Is Important

Doing business in Belgium is like conducting it in two totally separate countries. Flanders and Wallonia take separate routes not only in their chosen language, but also in the way they do business. For instance, hierarchy is of the utmost importance in Wallonia, whereas there is not as much importance placed on your business title and position in Flanders.

How Decisions Are Made

When you are doing business in Flanders, you will notice that decisions are made by the group as a whole. However, the decision-making process is very different in Wallonia, where the final word will come from the head person in more of an autocratic manner.

Meeting Manners

Start your meeting the right way by engaging in some small talk before actually getting down to business. Allow your Belgian client or associate to set the tone of the meeting and make the transition to business.

If you are spearheading the meeting, be sure to go with an agenda in hand for each person. The Belgians present will appreciate this, and it will also help the meeting to stay on target.

Be sure to have written documentation to support any material you are presenting. Make copies available for each person in the meeting.

Be sure to keep interruptions to an absolute minimum. Thus, do not excuse yourself to make or accept telephone calls or do anything else that detracts from the flow of the meeting.

Punctuality

Belgians respect time and expect punctuality. Therefore make sure you are prompt for all meetings.

Seating Etiquette

When you are in a meeting or in a restaurant setting, your host will usually tell you where to sit. When you are in any other situation, simply wait for a seat to be offered to you before sitting.

If you are hosting a meal, be sure to sit at the head of the table. If your spouse is with you, that person should be opposite you. Just as in the West, seating etiquette dictates that the most senior woman sit to the immediate right of the host with the most senior man seated to the immediate right of the hostess.

Tipping Tips

Service charges and value-added taxes are included in most bills (usually 15 percent), so tipping is not expected or necessary. However, when individuals in the service industry do you a special favor or have provided you with additional amenities, an extra gratuity is certainly in order.

It is not necessary to tip a sommelier or wine steward. If a maitre d' has extended a special favor to you (for example, seated you at the table of your choice), a 50 to 100BF tip is in order. Hotel and railway porters, ushers, and chambermaids should be tipped 25 to 50BF. Cloakroom attendants may be tipped 50 to 100 BF per coat. Washroom attendants may be tipped at a lower rate, 10 to 20BF. Hotel shuttle drivers are often not tipped, but they should be. Their tip should be a minimum of 15 percent of what it would have cost you if you would have taken a cab to the hotel. If the person assists you with your luggage, be sure to add an extra tip for this assistance.

Toasting Etiquette

Toasting etiquette dictates that you wait to sip your beverage until after your host has initiated a toast. If your host stands when proposing a toast, you should follow suit.

When You Are Invited to a Belgian Home

Belgians are a rather private people and prefer to retain the dinner hours for time with their families. If you are extended an invitation to a home in Belgium, it will be most likely be a Fleming in northern Belgium who has invited you. Consider this to be an honor!

Don't be surprised if you are invited to the home later than you might expect, because the dinner hour in Belgium typically begins around 7:30 p.m. or later.

Be sure to keep business out of the conversation and enjoy the company and conversation of your host and his or her family.

After-dinner conversation may take place in a living room with an after-dinner drink. Be sure to act like a good guest and take your leave within an hour following dinner.

Women in Business

While Belgian working women may often be in positions that are more administrative than managerial in nature, businesswomen traveling to Belgium will be accepted and treated with the same respect as their male colleagues.

Whatever You Do...

- Don't make jokes about the Flemings to the Walloons, and vice versa.
- Don't comment on the linguistic diversity in Belgium.
- Don't drink and drive. If you are caught and do not pass the breathalizer test, you can be thrown in jail for 365 days.
- Don't blow your nose in public. This gesture is considered offensive.
- Don't touch or invade the "private space" of another person.
- Don't put your hands under the table during a meal. It is perceived as very rude.

Advice From the Experts

"Stay away from commenting on the difference between the Flemish-speaking (in the North) and the French-speaking (in the South). It's a very complicated situation, with lots of pitfalls for the uninformed."

—Paul Allaer, Partner, Thompson, Hine & Flory Law Firm, Honorary Consul of Belgium

Chapter 3

Bulgaria

At one time a Communist-controlled nation, and now a socialist republic struggling to achieve economic and democratic success, Bulgaria is located in the eastern half of the Balkan Peninsula. It is bordered on the north by Romania, on the west by Serbia and Macedonia, on the south by Greece and Turkey, and on the east by the Black Sea. Its capital, Sofia, is located in a valley near Mt. Vitosha in the west. With a beautiful, varied coastline, the abundant plains of the Danube region, and the impressive Balkan Range in its heartland, Bulgaria is an up-and-coming nation with a great deal to offer both businesspeople and tourists.

The country was founded in 681 by a tribe from Central Asia called the Bulgars. Over the centuries, it has been occupied by the Byzantine and Ottoman Empires, and the Eastern influence can still be seen and felt throughout the land, in both its architecture and its culture. Bulgaria was liberated from the Turks during the Russo-Turkish War of 1877-1878, but did not become fully independent until 1908. During that time, and subsequent to the first Balkan War of 1912-1913, it entered into numerous disputes over its borders (among other things, laying claim to Macedonia). An Axis supporter during World War II, Bulgaria came under Communist influence late in the war, and the government was eventually taken over by a pro-Soviet Communist leadership that remained in power until 1989. Along with the changes taking place in the Soviet Union came uncertainty and insecurity in the countries it used to protect, including Bulgaria. In 1990, free elections were held for the first time, followed by a period of economic and political instability. In 1991, a new constitution was put into effect and the first presidential election took place in January, 1992, at which time the Union of Democratic Forces (UDF) took power (and has retained it ever since). The central government is headed by the president, assisted by the prime minister and a 14-member cabinet called the Council of Ministers. Four hundred seats in the unicameral National Assembly are filled by party members of the UDF and the Bulgarian Socialist Party (BSP). Nine provinces in the country are run by people's councils with limited authority.

An agrarian society for centuries, Bulgaria is now making the leap into the modern world of international commerce and enjoying the privileges of a democratic ethic. This task has been made more difficult for the nation with the loss of Soviet support, but it is slowly finding its footing. Primary exports include machinery and equipment, agricultural products, consumer goods, and raw materials. Bulgaria is a member of the United Nations, the International Monetary Fund, the World Bank, and the General Agreement on Tariffs and Trade.

Statistics and Information

Air Travel

Bulgaria has three airports. The main one is the Sofia International Airport, located in Bulgaria's capital. The other two are in the country's third and fourth largest cities, which are Varna and Burgas. Balkan Airlines offers flights within Bulgaria.

Country Code

Bulgaria's country code is 359.

City codes include:

- 073121 for Blagoevgrad.
- 056 for Burgas.
- 0997437 for Melnik.
- 032 for Plovdiv.
- 02 for Sofia.
- 52 for Varna.

Currency

Bulgaria's currency is called the *lev* (*leva* in plural). One *lev* equals 100 *stotinki*. The *stotinki* is available in coins of 50, 20, 5, 2, and 1. The *lev* is available in notes of 2,000, 1,000, 500, 200, 100, 50, 20, 10, 5, 2, and 1. *Leva* is also available in coins of 10, 5, 2, and 1.

When going to Bulgaria, be sure to go with cash in hand. While you will be able to exchange your currency in *leva*, many locations will charge a 5-percent commission to exchange traveler's checks.

Dates

Dates are written in the standard European format—that is, the day of the month should be listed first, followed by the month, and then the year. For example, May 25, 1999, is written as 25/5/99. If you want to be sure to avoid any miscommunication, write out the date in full rather than in number format.

Ethnic Makeup

The majority of Bulgaria's population is native Bulgarian. Less than 15 percent is comprised of other ethnic groups, including Turks, Gypsies, and Macedonians. There is also a tiny percentage of people of Armenian descent.

Holidays and Religious Celebrations

January 1	New Year's Day

March 3	Liberation Day (also known as Independence Day)
April 19-21	Orthodox Easter
May 1	Labor Day
May 24	Bulgarian Culture Day
December 24-26	Christmas

Language

Bulgarian, a South Slavic language, is the most commonly spoken language in this country. It is made up of the Cyrillic rather than the Latin alphabet. While you may hear a few people speaking English, Russian is the second most commonly spoken language, followed by German and French. Turkish is also spoken. When you are conducting business in Bulgaria, you will find that many people will make an effort to speak English, because it is becoming the language of business in today's world.

Religion

More than three quarters of Bulgarians are Bulgarian Orthodox, while approximately 13 percent is Muslim. You will also find a very small number of Jewish and Roman Catholic practitioners.

Time Zone Differences

Bulgaria is:

- Two hours ahead of Greenwich Mean Time.
- Seven hours ahead of U.S. Eastern Standard Time.

Weather

If you travel to Bulgaria during the winter months, expect to experience cold, wet weather. During the summer months, it will be very hot with little rain. Precipitation is highest during the months of March and April.

Etiquette

Business Attire

Appropriate business dress is similar to most other European countries—that is, conservative suits are best for men and suits or business dresses are considered acceptable for women.

Business-card Etiquette

As in other countries, it is important to take plenty of business cards with you to exchange with your Bulgarian colleagues. However, because English is the language of business in this country, you need not have your cards translated into Bulgarian on the reverse side.

Business Entertaining/Dining

If you are eating a food that has a sauce on it, it will not be considered gauche to dunk your bread in the sauce.

Conversation

Family is very important to Bulgarians, so it will be appreciated if you inquire about a person's family.

As in many other countries, the topic of politics should be avoided in Bulgaria. You should also avoid making remarks about how different Bulgaria may be from your homeland.

Gestures and Public Manners

You will quickly learn that when a Bulgarian gestures "*da*" (or "yes"), that person will shake his or her head from side to side. On the other hand, when a Bulgarian says "*neh*" (meaning "no"), then you will see him or her nod, in the same way most cultures say "yes."

As in many European countries, when you are using a public restroom, you should expect to pay to get into the stall. This is true whether you are at a restaurant, in a theatre, or even in your hotel lobby.

Be sure to know what you are getting into before you enter a bathroom in Bulgaria. Go with tissue in hand—and be prepared to squat.

Gift-giving Etiquette

When visiting a home, take a bottle of wine for the host and a box of candy or unwrapped flowers for the person's spouse. However, do not take lilies or gladiolas, because they are given for formal functions.

Appropriate gifts to exchange with a business colleague in Bulgaria include whiskey and items for a desk (a pen, a paperweight, and so on).

Contrary to what is appropriate in the United States, cologne and perfume are considered acceptable gifts and will be appreciated by Bulgarians.

Greetings and Introductions

Address individuals by their last names and remain formal at all times, unless you are invited to use their first names.

How Decisions Are Made

Bulgarians will take their time to consider all the facts. Thus, prepare for the decision-making process to take a long time and don't be too disappointed at having to wait.

Meeting Manners

While coffee is commonly offered as a meeting beverage in many countries, hard liquor such as vodka may be offered to you prior to the start of a business meeting in Bulgaria. Even if you prefer not to take it, display your appreciation for the offer.

As when developing business relationships in other countries, patience will be a much-needed virtue regarding the length of time it takes for decisions to be made in Bulgaria.

Punctuality

Bulgarians will expect you to respect time by being punctual. However, if they are a bit late, don't be alarmed.

Seating Etiquette

The most senior seat at a table is the one in the center rather than at the head. If you are hosting a meal, be sure to defer that seat to your guest of honor.

Tipping Tips

While tipping is not expected, it certainly is appreciated by service personnel. An acceptable tip would be 10 percent of the total bill (or *smetka*).

Toasting Etiquette

When you are at a table with one or more Bulgarians and someone lifts his or her glass and says, "*Na sdrave*," know that this person is proposing a toast to you.

When You Are Invited to a Bulgarian Home

Be sure to go with gifts in hand (see the gift-giving section). Bulgarian etiquette dictates that it is far better to arrive at a party a little late than early. Let the host and hostess set the tone about where to sit, when to talk during the meal, and so on.

Women in Business

Although Bulgarian women are rarely found in managerial positions, businesswomen traveling to Bulgaria will be treated respectfully, both professionally and from a personal standpoint.

Whatever You Do...

- Don't be surprised if you are asked how much money you make. It is considered all right to ask personal questions in Bulgaria.

- Don't be surprised if you hear Bulgarian politics discussed and even criticized in your presence.
- Don't make a point of telling Bulgarians how many more resources you have in the United States than they have in their country.
- Don't go for a drink with a stranger. You may be in the company of a thief who may try to drug you before stealing your valuables.
- Don't be surprised if you are offered an alcoholic beverage prior to the start of a morning or afternoon meeting.

Chapter 4

Czech Republic

The Czech Republic was formed in 1993, when the nation of Czechoslovakia, which had been under Communist control for 40 years, was split in two, resulting in this country and Slovakia, now its neighbor on its southeast border. Completely landlocked, it is situated in almost the geographical center of Europe. Poland lies on the north and east borders, while Germany borders on the north and west and Austria lies due south. The majority of the Czech Republic is composed of the provinces of Moravia and Bohemia. Its land runs between two large mountain systems, giving the topography a variety of hills, plains, and mountains.

The Czech Republic has a population of approximately 10.3 million, three quarters of whom live in urban areas. This democratic country is governed by a bicameral parliament that elects its head of state, the president, for a five-year term. The president appoints the prime minister and other members of the government, as well as judges. The Czech Republic is highly industrialized, manufacturing machinery, automobiles, chemicals, textiles, and beer, among other exported products. Agriculture forms only a very small part of the economy, which has been making a gradual transformation, thanks to a privatization program begun in 1990. The United States is a large investor in the Czech Republic.

Rich with history, but also ravaged by wars and dissension over the last half century, the Czech Republic has been gradually reclaiming its historical and cultural heritage. This is a country that can lay claim to many "firsts"—the first dollars in the world were minted in Jachymov, the first modern plow was invented by a Czech, and the Czechs were the first in the world to brew beer. The country also boasts many magnificent pieces of architecture—still standing from the Gothic, Baroque, and Art Nouveau periods—and beautiful towns and castles throughout the land, especially in Bohemia.

Commercialism is on the rise in the Czech Republic, as evidenced by an increasing number of billboards and signs on trains. Much splendor and craftsmanship can be found on sidewalks and in shopping centers, particularly in Prague, the country's capital. Prague itself, the city where Kafka wrote masterpieces and Mozart triumphed in opera houses, is once again becoming a mecca for artists, writers, and musicians. Improved services are also helping to increase tourism.

Statistics and Information

Air Travel

The Czech Republic's main airport is the Ruzynê Airport, located 20 kilometers northwest of Prague. While a shuttle is available for getting to the city, you can also take a taxi (but be sure to find out how much you should expect to pay before getting in the cab, as drivers have been known to attempt to exploit individuals from abroad).

Country Code

The Czech Republic's country code is 420.

City codes include:

- 5 for Brno.
- 68 for Olomouc.
- 19 for Plzen.
- 2 for Prague.

Currency

The Czech Republic's currency is the *koruna* (plural *koruny*; abbreviated Kc or Kcs). One *koruna* is equal to 100 *haléru* (plural *hellers*; abbreviated h). Bank notes are available in denominations of Kcs 1,000, 500, 100, 50, and 20. Coins come in 50h, 20h, and 10h, and Kcs 50, 20, 10, 5, 2, and 1.

Banks provide the best rates for exchanging your money. Avoid the private exchange offices you will see everywhere in cities such as Prague, as their exchange rates are very steep.

Before leaving the Czech Republic, be sure to spend or exchange your *koruny*, because you will find that many other countries may not exchange it or will choose only to exchange *koruny* in denominations of 100 or higher.

Dates

Dates are written in the typical European fashion, with the day preceding the month, followed by the year. For example, January 30, 1999, would be written as 30/1/99.

Ethnic Makeup

About 94 percent of the population is comprised of native Czechs (and depending on the area, many refer to themselves as Moravians). Another 4 percent is of Slovakian descent. There are also ethnic minorities of German, Polish, and Hungarian (or Romany) extraction.

Holidays And Religious Celebrations

Below is a list of the Czech Republic's celebrated holidays. While many businesses may remain open on the days of religious celebration, they do close for public holidays.

January 1	New Year's Day
Late March/ Early April	Easter Monday
May 1	Labour Day

May 8	Liberation Day (1945)
July 5	The Feast of St. Cyril and Methodius
July 6	Jan Hus Day
October 28	Independence Day (Establishment of Independent Czechoslovakia in 1918)
November 1	All Saints' Day
November 17	Velvet Revelation Day
December 6	St. Nicholas Day
December 25	Christmas Day
December 26	Boxing Day/St. Stephen's Day

Language

The country's official language is Czech. It is made up of the Roman alphabet and is similar to Russian. German is the second most commonly spoken language in the country. You will also find that some Czechs speak and understand English, especially those working in commercial areas.

Religion

Because religious observations were discouraged under Communist rule in the past, many Czechs do not outwardly practice any religion. In the most recent census, half the country's population claimed to be atheist. Of those who have adopted a religion, Catholicism is practiced most widely, followed by Evangelism. Some Czechs follow Judaism, while the rest practice a variety of other religions.

Time Zone Differences

The Czech Republic is:

- One hour ahead of Greenwich Mean Time.
- Six hours ahead of U.S. Eastern Standard Time.

Weather

The Czech Republic lies in a very temperate area in Europe, so it is generally subject to very pleasant, mild summers and moderate winters, except in mountainous areas where it gets colder. There is heavy rainfall in many places, but less so in Prague.

Etiquette

Business Attire

The key word to dressing appropriately for doing business in the Czech Republic is *modest.* While the Czechs are well-groomed, hygienically sound, and always appear presentable, they are not overly concerned with their personal appearance.

Men should wear suits with starched white shirts and ties. Women should wear flattering yet conservative dresses or suits. Choose deep, dark shades—blues, browns, and grays are good choices.

Keep your accessorizing, especially lavish jewelry, to a minimum. Czechs are not accustomed to wealth and pomp. In fact, they are suspicious of people who dress in such a manner.

Business-card Etiquette

Be sure to pack an ample supply of business cards (also called visiting cards). The Czechs pass cards out to virtually everyone they meet.

It is a good idea to have your cards written in English on one side and Czech on the reverse side.

Business Entertaining/Dining

Entertaining is not a common part of business in the Czech Republic and should only be done between parties involved in negotiations. Invitations should be extended far in advance, as the Czechs are planners and dislike last-minute engagements. Including spouses at evening functions is optional.

If you are initiating an invitation to a restaurant, be sure to make a reservation in advance. Frequently, there are more guests than seats and patrons cannot be accommodated.

Business luncheons are usually enjoyed by colleagues who may go out together to get a quick bite to eat. This meal also acts as the main meal of the day. Lunch typically consists of soup and an entrée. Expect to be served hearty portions.

Czech cuisine usually consists of meat (pork, beef, or sausage) and potatoes, as well other starches, such as dumplings. Because the main course is usually a rather large portion, Turkish-style coffee or *kava* will likely be served without dessert. If dessert is offered, it may consist of something that contains a fruit or jam.

If you are eating with Czechs during an informal meal, don't be surprised if you see them keep their napkins on the table rather than in their laps. When they are finished eating, they may use the napkins and then place them on their plates. In more formal meals, however, you will find that napkins are kept on the lap and then placed to the right of the plate after the meal has been completed.

Czechs eat continental-style—that is, the knife is held in the right hand and the fork stays in the left hand, as both utensils are used simultaneously.

It is considered good manners to politely refuse second helpings when they are first offered to you. When your host or hostess insists the second time, you may accept.

When you have finished eating, place your fork and knife together on one side of your plate. Utensils that are crossed in the center of your plate means that you plan to continue eating.

As throughout Europe, smoking is common in this country, and you can expect it at meals. If you are not a smoker, you may want to bring something with you to help you tolerate the smoke.

Beverage etiquette: Prepare to consume beer or wine with your Czech meal. American businesspeople who prefer to drink nonalcoholic beverages can request a tasty drink called *pito*. Fruit juices or cola beverages may also be available for you if you ask. If you like, it may even be possible to obtain a nonalcoholic beer. (See also Toasting Etiquette.)

Conversation

Czechs may appear rather shy, reserved, or even unfriendly upon first meeting, but in fact the reverse is true. Unfortunately, having been under Communist rule for so long, many Czechs have a hard time trusting others and are not initially outgoing with strangers. However, once you have "broken the ice" and made it through the initial greeting, you will see that the Czech people are excellent conversationalists and are intrigued with individuals from abroad.

Czechs are very open to asking and answering personal questions. It is likely you will be asked about your family, your religion, and even your income very soon after making an acquaintance. Good topics for discussion are politics, travel, and sports.

You may be very curious about what life was like during the Communist years, but *do not* introduce this subject in conversation. Many people have no problem discussing it, but you should wait for a Czech to bring up the topic first.

It is not a good idea to use a lot of humor or to joke with those you do not know well. Czech humor is different from that of most Americans and they may not understand your attempts to be funny.

Gestures and Public Manners

Czechs do not rely on body language and gestures to play a large role in communicating. For this reason, you should refrain from using large hand movements and a loud voice. It is not wise to draw undue attention to yourself.

Never wave or yell to get someone's attention. The correct way to get another person's attention is to raise one hand and extend only your index finger.

You may feel that Czechs stand uncomfortably close to you. They do not have the same need for "personal space" as Americans do. However uncomfortable this may make you, try not to back away, as it would be insulting.

You will note that a common gesture for many Czechs is to throw their arms up in the air. This indicates frustration and exasperation.

If you must cross your legs, do so at the knees and keep your feet down, rather than resting the calf of one leg on the other knee. It is improper to allow the bottoms of your feet to show in public.

It is important to maintain good posture at all times and never speak to someone with your hands in your pockets.

After entering a public location, such as a theater or restaurant, check your coat rather than wearing it or taking it with you to your seat.

Gift-giving Etiquette

Having been closed off from much of the world for so long, the Czechs delight in receiving gifts, especially those from abroad. It is therefore in order to present a small token at the beginning of a relationship. Recommended items are pens, cigarettes, and lighters, or items bearing your company logo.

Once a business deal has been completed, a gift of greater value should be given. Suggested gifts include electronic devices, such as calculators and radios. Whatever the case, be sure to give gifts that are practical and useful in everyday life.

Greetings and Introductions

Shaking hands is an important part of interacting in the Czech Republic and should be used as part of both the greeting and the farewell. Men may initiate a handshake with a woman before she extends her hand.

When you are meeting a Czech, be prepared, as he or she will stand very close to you—most likely less than two arms' lengths away. While this spatial distance may not be to your liking, simply deal with it rather than taking the chance of insulting the person by backing off.

Proper forms of address: Always address a Czech by his or her last name and an appropriate title until you yourself have been addressed by your first name or invited to use a more informal address. Calling people by their first names is rare in the Czech business world.

Titles are a must for the Czechs. The following are the most commonly used forms of address:

- *Pan*: Mr.
- *Paní*: Mrs.
- *Slecna*: Miss

The appropriate one of the above terms should be followed by the person's last name. If he or she holds a professional title of professor, engineer, doctor, or the like, you may substitute the title in place of the person's last name. For instance, a man who is either a medical doctor or has earned his Ph.D., should be addressed as *Pan Doktor*.

You can determine the gender of a Czech by the suffix attached to last names. Males' last names will usually end in a consonant or the letter "a." Females with the same last name will have the suffix "ová." If the male form of the name ends in a "y," it is made feminine by changing the "y" to an "a."

How Decisions Are Made

The length of time taken to make decisions will often depend on how eager the Czech team is to do business with your company. Decisions ultimately lie with top management called "directors." However, employees at lower levels will be part of your initial meetings.

When you are in a decision-making situation with a Czech team, be prepared for them not to be completely forthright. This may occur if a Czech is in a situation for the first time and is unsure of what the end result may be, yet may not want to admit it. Be patient and do what you can to earn their trust.

Hierarchy Is Important

In the Czech Republic, a company director is equivalent to the Western world's company president, and therefore is usually the top person in the organization. Therefore, if you are meeting several people and a director is part of this group, acknowledge that person first.

Meeting Manners

The foremost thing to keep in mind in the Czech Republic is the newness of the free economy and the privatization of business there. Although the Czechs have made amazing strides to bring their market up to speed with the rest of the free world, there are still glitches. They are by and large hard-working people who think in a logical, realistic way. You will need to be patient, as things move at a much slower pace than in most Western countries. This is partly because of the Czechs' casual view of time, but also because they are still new at negotiating deals and working within government laws that have only recently been established.

Always arrive on time for your meetings. Meetings usually begin with beverages and conversation.

The best way to succeed professionally is to win the Czechs over on a personal level. Never speak with a tone of condescension. Come across as sincerely interested in making the mutually best deal. Your presentation should be well-articulated and precise.

You will most likely need to employ an interpreter. Although many businesspeople speak English, they are often not up to speed and this can make negotiations difficult. If you use visual aids, keep them basic. Czechs are not yet fully computerized and may not understand hi-tech charts and graphs.

Punctuality

The Czechs are not overly concerned with time and schedules. They have a much more relaxed attitude toward appointments than many Westerners. However, you should be flexible. Simply arrive on time and take reading material with you to occupy yourself if you have to wait.

Seating Etiquette

There are no strict guidelines regarding seating at a Czech dinner function. Take your cue from your host as to where you should sit.

Taxi Etiquette

Taxi service is not regulated by the government. Many taxi drivers will seek out foreigners and charge them an outrageous fare, so play it safe and set a fare with the drivers before you agree to accept a ride. (Rates should be posted on the cab's door.) Asking for a receipt is one way to ensure that you are charged an appropriate amount.

It may be difficult to hail a cab off the street. To make certain that you are on time for appointments, call ahead for a cab.

Tipping Tips

In the Czech Republic, tipping consists of rounding out the bill to the next highest figure. For instance, if your bill is 134 *koruny*, you should leave 140 *koruny*.

If a porter has assisted you with you luggage, 8 *koruna* should be given. Chambermaids can be tipped in gifts of toiletries rather than money.

Toasting Etiquette

Czechs are without question the world's largest beer consumers. As the first nation to brew beer, the Czechs have contributed words such as "Pilsner" and "Budweiser" to the global lexicon. You will find that Bohemia is best known for its beer, while Moravia is better known for its wine. Beer and wine will be served with every meal. If you do not want to drink, be very polite in how you decline it.

When you are a guest at a gathering, always wait to drink until everyone's glass has been filled and a toast has been offered by the host.

When you are hosting a meal, be sure to propose a toast and make a point of looking at your guest rather than at the beverage as you take the first sip.

Toilet Etiquette

You may run into problems finding toilets for public use. You will be further troubled when you see how unclean most public toilets are.

If nature calls, your best bet is to look for a facility in a restaurant, hotel, museum, or train station. You should carry your own tissue.

Be prepared to be charged about 2 *koruna* for the use of any public facilities.

When You Are Invited to a Czech Home

Invitations to a Czech home are not common. If you receive such an invitation, you should feel honored and plan on having a wonderful experience. Czechs are among the world's greatest hosts. They will go out of their way to see that you receive the utmost in hospitality.

For dinner invitations, be sure to arrive on time and bring a small gift, such as wine, flowers, or chocolates, for the hostess. If children are part of the family, toys would be appropriate.

You may be asked to remove your shoes before entering a Czech house. It is likely that your host will give you slippers to wear.

Your visit will probably begin with drinks and snacks. Depending on the time of day, a meal will follow. If you are invited to someone's house for appetizers, prepare to eat lunch meat and cheese.

It is good form to extend your compliments on the meal and the gracious hospitality you have received. Do your best to take seconds (wait until they have been offered a second time before you accept) and finish everything on your plate. After the meal, plan on staying for at least an hour to enjoy coffee and conversation.

Women in Business

While there are women in the business arena, few are in leadership positions. Women in decision-making roles from abroad will be accepted, as long as they are conservative in both dress and behavior.

Whatever You Do...

- Don't give a bouquet of flowers if you are unsure of how they will be perceived. Flowers have highly romantic overtones for many Czechs.

- Don't refer to anything in the Czech Republic as being German.
- Don't leave the country with *koruny*. It is difficult to exchange in other countries.
- Don't arrive in the Czech Republic without having confirmed your hotel reservation. There is often a shortage of hotel rooms, which may cause your reservation to get "bumped."
- Don't take your room key with you when you leave your hotel for the day. As in many other European countries, guests are expected to leave the key at the hotel's front desk, even when they are going out for just a short while.
- Don't schedule business trips to the Czech Republic between late July and early August. Many Czechs go on holiday at this time.
- Don't get into a taxi without first learning from a concierge or bell captain the approximate fare you should expect to pay to reach your destination. Confirm this fare with the driver before actually taking off.
- Don't make any references to a Czech's tardiness.

Chapter 5

Denmark

A beautiful peninsula on the North Sea accented by scores of lovely green islands, Denmark is a country famous for both its strategic geographical position in Europe and the friendliness of its people. Approximately one-ninth the size of California, its only border on the continent is shared with Germany. Its closest Scandinavian neighbors are Sweden and Norway. Amazingly, despite its modest size, Denmark's length of coastline created by its peninsula and islands adds up to one sixth of the earth's circumference. At one time, Denmark also laid claim to Iceland, which, along with Greenland, had been settled largely by Danes.

About 70 percent of Denmark's population of 5.1 million live in urban areas—1.4 million are located in its capital, Copenhagen, alone. This country boasts the oldest capital city and the oldest flag in Europe. The land is dotted with magnificent old castles and manor houses that speak of a royal and tradition-laden history. Not as immediately evident is Denmark's Viking past, when the Danes invaded and conquered other countries, including England. Now a constitutional monarchy with a strong social welfare system, the country's current sovereign (since 1972) is Queen Margrethe, whose lineage dates back to the early 900s.

Only 90 of the country's 406 islands are inhabited. Most are linked together by bridges or ferries. The largest island is Zealand, where Copenhagen is located. The land varies throughout the country, but mostly, there is the green countryside for which Denmark has been celebrated in story and song. It is a nation that has long depended on its agriculture and on the famed navigational skills of its people.

Denmark has been home to many of the world's great writers, including Hans Christian Anderson, Isak Dineson, and Søren Kierkegaard. It has long been a cultural epicenter. Among other Danish achievements in the arts, the Royal Danish Ballet is known throughout the world.

Statistics and Information

Air Travel

Denmark's major airport is Kastrup International Airport. It is located less than 20 miles from the center of Copenhagen. There are several ways to reach the city, including taxis, shuttles, and trains.

Country Code

Denmark's country code is 45.

Copenhagen does not have a city code. When calling someone in this city, simply dial 01145, followed by the eight-digit local phone number.

Currency

Denmark's currency is called the *Danish krone* (abbreviated DKK). One DKK is equal to 100 *øre*.

Notes come in units of DKK1,000, 500, 100, and 50. Coins come in units of DKK20, 10, 5, and 1, while *øre* are available in 50, 25, and 10.

Banks and ATM machines provide the best rates for exchanging your money.

Dates

Dates are written in the standard European manner, with the day preceding the month, followed by the year. For example, January 30, 1999, would be written as 30/1/99.

Ethnic Makeup

Native Danish account for all but 1 percent of the population.

Holidays and Religious Celebrations

The following is a list of Denmark's celebrated holidays. Because all are either national holidays or religious celebrations, it is wise not to schedule meetings for these days.

January 1	New Year's Day
Late March/ April	Maundy Thursday, Good Friday, Easter
40 days following Easter	Ascension Thursday
56 days following Easter	Whitmonday
April 16	Birthday of the Queen (not a public holiday)
June 5	Constitution Day
June 23	St. Hans' Eve
December 24	Christmas Eve
December 25	Christmas Day
December 26	Boxing Day
December 31	New Year's Eve

Note: In June and July, it is common for the Danish to go on holiday with their families. For that reason, avoid scheduling appointments around this time.

Language

The country's official language is Danish. English is taught throughout the school years and is the dominant second language. A large portion of the population also speaks German.

Religion

Evangelical Lutheran is the country's official religion and is practiced by the vast majority of the population.

Time Zone Differences

Denmark is:

- One hour ahead of Greenwich Mean Time.
- Six hours ahead of U.S. Eastern Standard Time.

Weather

Denmark is relatively cold, yet it benefits from the Gulf Stream, which brings moderate winters and summers. The average winter temperature is in the mid-30s, while summer temperatures average in the low to mid-60s.

Etiquette

Business Attire

When you are in Denmark, make a point to dress in a smart yet understated way. The Danish have a strong sense of equality and that is reflected in people's appearance. You are expected to appear professional and well-dressed, and you should keep it low-keyed.

Men do well by wearing suits with starched white shirts, ties, and well-kept shoes. Women should wear stylish yet modestly cut suits and pumps. Accessories should be kept to a minimum. Be sure to pack clothes for cool, rainy weather, which you are sure to encounter.

Because you may be invited to a black-tie function, men should take a tux with them, while women should pack an evening gown.

Business-card Etiquette

As in other countries, business cards are a must. However, in Denmark, it is unnecessary to have them translated into Danish on the reverse side, because many people have a command of English.

If the company you represent has been in existence for 10 or more years, be sure to list that fact on your business card. Stability is an important trait to the Danes.

Business Entertaining/Dining

Danes usually take breakfast at home with their families, so do not expect to conduct any business at this time of day.

If you are invited to a business lunch, it will take place somewhere between noon and 2 p.m. A typical Danish lunch may consist of an open-faced sandwich called a *smørrebrød.*

On other occasions, prepare to enjoy a *smørgäsbord*, a Danish buffet also called *det store kold bord*. This popular way to serve a meal consists of a huge table of breads, meats, vegetables, seafood, and desserts served buffet-style. These spreads are often seen at dinner parties.

Take care during meals not to discuss any business, unless your host brings it up. In general, meals are reserved for lively discussions that do not include work topics.

The Danish eat continental-style, so you should, too. Cut your food with the knife in your right hand, and keep your fork in your left hand to hold the food and bring it to your mouth with the tines pointing down.

It is very common for dinner to be served "family-style," which means that platters will be passed around the table from which you may serve yourself. You will be offered "seconds," so prepare yourself in advance by taking only a small helping the first time around.

Wait until everyone has been served and take your cue from your host before you begin eating.

You may not find everything to your taste. Nevertheless, you should try your best to eat it, to avoid appearing wasteful.

After you have completed your meal, you may indicate that you are finished by laying your fork and knife together on your plate at a 90-degree angle.

It is considered good manners to wait for the host to rise after the meal has come to an end and table talk is over before you leave the table.

Conversation

While you may get the impression in conducting business that Danes appear to be unfriendly and uncaring, in fact they are very warm people who enjoy lengthy conversations and being with friends. They are especially at ease at home and in other social settings.

Once you are introduced to a Dane, the likelihood is that you will have an instant friend. Safe topics to discuss are Danish culture, current events, and your home state or town.

It is considered rude to get too "chummy" with someone with whom you have only a casual acquaintance and to ask personal questions about him or her. This includes anything about the person's private life (such as questions or comments about family, salary, or religion). Allow your new Danish acquaintance to set the tone of the conversation by choosing the topics of discussion.

While many people are flattered by compliments about how they look or about an outfit they're wearing, this is not the case with Danes. Instead, what we perceive to be kind words are considered improper in Denmark.

Gestures and Public Manners

The Danes are unexpressive people in public. Their communication style, body language, and voice inflections tend to be low-key. In order to "mirror" their behavior, power down a bit, especially if you are animated by nature. Rather than flaunting what you do or the financial freedom you may have worked hard to attain, the key to being accepted and respected in Denmark is to blend in rather than stand out. When in Denmark, do as the Danes do—and you will avoid drawing attention to yourself.

When talking to a Dane, stand at least two arms' lengths away to give him or her enough space.

Being categorized in a social class is not an important quality to the Danes. One reason is that Denmark has a strong sense of equality among its people. In fact, surprisingly, many professionals and blue collar people actually earn similar salaries.

Taking the direct approach: Like the Germans, the Danes are very blunt in their approach. They make a point of being direct about others' faults. If you criticized by a Dane, you will get further ahead by remaining low-keyed rather than flaring up and telling the person how undiplomatic he or she is. If you choose to express your feelings, it won't change the person—so save your energy.

Gift-giving Etiquette

Danish etiquette does not encourage you to have a gift in hand at a first meeting. However, if it looks as though business is moving forward, then a small gift may be given to your contact after agreements have been signed. If you happen to receive a gift in return, feel free to open it in front of the person rather than waiting.

Because Danes enjoy alcoholic beverages, wine, whiskey, or the like make good gifts. Other possible gifts include a good pen, a paperweight with your company logo, or a book depicting the city you represent.

Greetings and Introductions

Danish business introductions consist of a formal and solemn exchange. If you are sitting and being introduced to a new contact or associate, be sure to stand up before extending your hand. Offer a firm handshake as you make eye contact. Any effort that you make to incorporate a Danish greeting into your introduction (for example, "*Goddag*," meaning "Good Day") will be appreciated.

Men may initiate a handshake with a woman rather than waiting for her to do so. Of course, handshakes should also be exchanged when leaving.

Proper forms of address: It is considered good manners to address Danes using their last names until you have been invited to be more informal. The trend in Denmark today is to call people by their first names once rapport has been established. Still, you must wait for the word from your Danish acquaintances. Use professional titles when applicable. Otherwise use the following Danish courtesy titles:

- *Herr*: Mr.
- *Fru*: Mrs.
- *Froken*: Miss

How Decisions Are Made

In many Danish companies, bosses are seen more as team leaders than as the sole decision-maker. For that reason, during meetings and when making decisions, everyone is encouraged to express an opinion in order to give consideration to many perspectives. However, remember that the final decision lies with a team of top leaders.

Danes are people of their word. Thus, once an agreement is signed, you can count on the project moving forward.

Meeting Manners

The Danes want every minute spent on the job to be productive and used effectively. It is important to arrive on time and to have your presentation rehearsed and up to "show" quality. Meetings move quickly and will start and end on time.

Depending on the tone set by the person leading the meeting, it will either start with a few minutes of "small talk" or the leader will get right down to business.

When it is your turn to have the floor, be sure you are clear and get straight to the point. Use charts, graphs, and literature to enhance your presentation. Besides clarifying the points in your presentation, you will be taken more seriously because of the attention you paid to detail.

The Danes have no problem letting you know how they feel. You may find them blunt and highly undiplomatic, but that's the way they get things done. You should accept their comments and respond in a positive tone.

Punctuality

Danes are very business-oriented during the workday. They take their work seriously and are strict about following schedules and appointment times. In other words, the Danes value promptness, so make a point of arriving on time for all business and social engagements.

Seating Etiquette

Danes follow the traditional western seating arrangement. The host and hostess will sit at opposite ends of the table. The female guest of honor is offered the seat to the right of the host, and the male guest of honor will be seated to the right of the hostess. Name cards are often placed at each place setting.

Taxi Etiquette

Although taxis can be hailed on street corners, you can ensure yourself of getting a cab by calling for one to pick you up at your starting point. By doing so, you will be certain to arrive at your meeting on time rather than risk being late.

Tipping Tips

You should not feel obligated to tip in Denmark. Typically, taxi fares include the gratuity. However, hotel porters commonly receive DKK5 per bag.

Restaurants include a 12- to 15-percent gratuity in all bills. Many people choose to round the bill up to the nearest DKK so the server receives a small additional tip.

If you use a public restroom with an attendant, he or she should be tipped DKK1 or 2.

Toasting Etiquette

Beer (or "*ol*") is the prized beverage of Denmark and may be considered the country's official drink. Beer or wine will be served with every meal.

Do not begin drinking until your host has proposed a toast to the entire party. If your host stands when proposing a toast, so should you. A common toast is "*Skäl!*"

The male guest of honor should propose a toast to the hostess at the end of the meal. One way of getting others' attention is by lightly clinking your spoon on the side of your glass.

Toilet Etiquette

Public toilets are easily accessible in restaurants, pubs, museums, and office buildings. The best part is that they are free. If you see a door labeled "*Maend,*" this is the Men's Room. The door labeled "*Kvinder*" is the Women's Room. Many public restrooms have attendants (who should be tipped).

When You Are Invited to a Danish Home

It is common for Danes to extend invitations to their homes. If your spouse has traveled to Denmark with you, the invitation will most likely include him or her.

Contrary to what is considered inappropriate in many other countries, roses are acceptable as gifts for your host or hostess. However, be sure you don't give white roses, because this color is associated with mourning. If you do give flowers, be sure they are presented wrapped. Other suitable items include a box of fine chocolates or desk items with your company's logo.

Once again, promptness will be both expected and appreciated. Besides being the courteous thing to do, the hour you have been asked to arrive will most likely also be the time dinner is scheduled to be served.

Follow the lead of the host, hostess, and other guests in eating and drinking. After the meal, plan on staying for a while for drinks and conversation. It is common for dinner parties to continue until 1 a.m. in Denmark.

Women in Business

If you compare Denmark with other European countries, you will find that it is one of the most progressive countries when it comes to equality between men and women. In fact, Denmark ranks number one when it comes to the greatest percentage of women working outside the home, and many women hold top positions in Danish companies.

Women from abroad will find that it is a pleasure to do business in Denmark. They can feel free to initiate meetings and even social engagements with men.

Whatever You Do...

- Don't introduce a business plan that will have detrimental side effects for the environment. Danes are committed to preserving the environment.
- Don't leave food on your plate. Danes are strict followers of the "clean plate club." In fact, you will greatly offend your hostess if you leave food untouched on your plate.
- Don't give preferential treatment to anyone. Denmark is such an equality-based society that you are expected to give the same preferential treatment to a company janitor that you would to the organization president.
- Don't pry into the personal life of someone you've just met. The Danish are not comfortable discussing their occupation, family, or private beliefs with people they barely know.
- Don't be surprised if you have a difficult time scheduling a meeting in the summer. This season is a common holiday time for Danes.

- Don't assume that local telephone calls are free, as they are in your homeland. There is a charge for calling within cities in Denmark—even if you are calling from a home.
- Don't go into a meeting and begin making small talk. Danes hold to the axiom that time is money and believe in getting down to business.

Advice From the Experts

"Do not leave your host's house too soon after dinner. It is considered impolite. Never get up from the dinner table until your host or hostess does."

—Barbara G. Toms, Traffic Manager, Goettsch International, Inc.

Chapter 6

England

As the largest country in the United Kingdom, England is often considered the cultural capital of Europe. This country takes up more than half of the island of Great Britain and accounts for four-fifths of the U.K.'s population (more than 48 million). It is bordered on the north by Scotland and on the west by Wales. The waters that surround the island consist of the Irish Sea and the Atlantic Ocean on the west, the English Channel on the south, and the North Sea on the east.

England's topography consists of a 2,000-mile coastline containing a rich variety of hills, plains, and farmland. It is also well-known for its moors, many of which are contained in the area of the country located above the Pennines. The nation is geographically divided into eight sections, the most dominant being the South East, where the capital, London, is located. Other districts include the South West, where the darkly beautiful Cornwall is found and tourism has been on the increase; the West Midlands, home to Birmingham and Stratford-on-Avon; the East Midlands, which supports manufacturing and farming; East Anglia, which is primarily agricultural in nature; the North West, where the manufacturing city of Birmingham and the key port city of Liverpool are found; the North region, which reaches to the Scottish border; and Yorkshire, made famous by the James Herriott stories about veterinary life in England.

England is a country steeped in history and tradition. Its people are celebrated for their "stiff upper lip" and courage under fire, enduring and surviving such trying times as the German Blitz during World War II. From its Celtic origins, through centuries of growth, to its present status as a global power, England has set standards other countries have learned to follow in numerous areas, including political, artistic, and intellectual life. Many of the world's greatest leaders, thinkers, scientists, architects, and creative artists have been from England. At one time, this nation had colonized so much of the world that it was said that "the sun never sets on the British Empire." While this is no longer the case, England continues to exercise a strong influence on international affairs.

England's form of government is a constitutional monarchy with a parliamentary system headed by a prime minister, which has been copied by numerous governments. The current monarch is Queen Elizabeth II of the House of Windsor. The English are known for their fascination with all things royal and the pomp and circumstance that goes with it. Thus, despite frequent calls to dissolve the monarchy, the likelihood is that England will always have a sovereign, in keeping with the tradition of centuries.

Statistics and Information

Air Travel

England has four major airports. Heathrow International Airport, located west of London, is the airport for most international flights. While taxis may be taken into London from Heathrow, the underground subway is also accessible and much less expensive, so this is the best way to go if you are traveling light. If you prefer to travel by taxi, prepare to pay a hefty sum.

Country Code

England's country code is 44.

City codes include:

- 121 for Birmingham.
- 151 for Liverpool.
- 171 for inner London.
- 181 for outer London.
- 161 for Manchester.

Currency

England's currency is the *pound* (£). One *pound* is made up of 100 *pence* (p). The *pound* is available in denominations of £50, 20, 10, and 5. Coins come in £1, and also 50, 20, 10, 5, and 2 *pence.* To exchange your currency, you will find the best exchange rates are offered by the "bureaux de changes" in various parts of the city. Banks and post offices will also offer you competitive rates.

Dates

The British follow the European standard when writing dates—that is, the day is written before the month, followed by the year. For instance, September 20, 2005, would be written 20/9/05.

Ethnic Makeup

England has an historically mixed ethnic heritage. Although insulated in earlier centuries by its island status, it was later invaded by Vikings, Romans, and French. Descendants of these invaders, as well as of the ancient Celts and Anglo-Saxons, make up the vast majority of England's Caucasian population. The balance of the population is comprised of Indians, Africans, and other European ethnic groups.

Holidays and Religious Celebrations

Below is a list of England's celebrated holidays. Because these are national holidays, it is best to avoid scheduling meetings on these days.

January 1	New Year's Day
March 1	St. David's Day

Late March/ Early April	Easter Monday
April 17	St. George's Day
First Monday in May	May Bank Holiday
Last Monday in May	Spring Bank Holiday
Last Monday in August	Summer Bank Holiday
December 25	Christmas Day
December 26	St. Stephen's Day/Boxing Day

Language

The country's official language is British English, a language that has evolved from the old Anglo-Saxon and has been influenced heavily by Latin, French, and German. Although there are many similarities between British English and American English, many words also have different meanings in the two countries (for example, a lift in British English refers to an elevator, whereas in American English a lift is defined as picking up something or someone). If you are even slightly unsure of what a term means in British English, be sure to ask.

Individuals from the United States frequently make errors in the pronunciation of British words, particularly names and places. For instance, a rather common mispronunciation has to do with words and terms ending in "cester." For example, Leicester is typically mispronounced as "Lie-chester," rather than given its correct pronunciation of "Lester."

Religion

Of all the European countries, the British attend church the least. Those who do go are likely to attend Anglican, Catholic, or Protestant services. The Anglican church, of which the Queen is the head, is the predominant religion in England. Eastern religions are on the rise and a small percentage of the population practices Buddhism, Sikhism, Islam, and Hinduism. Also, there is a small percentage that practices Judaism.

Time Zone Differences

England is the home of Greenwich Mean Time. The country is five hours ahead of U.S. Eastern Standard Time.

Weather

The English weather is rather moderate and similar year round. However, be sure to take an umbrella with you, because precipitation is common. Winter temperatures typically range in the 40s (colder in the northern elevations), while summer temperatures usually hover in the 60s.

Etiquette

Business Attire

You will find that British fashion runs the gamut, and everyone tends to sport a personal style. On the whole, you will find business attire in the major cities (especially London) to be more formal, even in casual settings. Business dress follows an American tradition. However, dark colors and heavier fabrics are more the norm than the exception in England.

For men, appropriate business attire usually means suits in dark colors with starched shirts and ties. Leave your striped ties at home; this will prevent your making a *faux pas* and accidentally wearing one that may be the stripe of the regiment to which your British contact belongs.

Businesswomen should be dressed appropriately by wearing conservative yet fashionable suits with pumps. Note that slack suits are not worn as much by women in England as they are by their American counterparts.

Business Entertaining/Dining

Because England is the home of polo and cricket, you may want to bone up on the rules of these sports. This way, if you are invited to an event in which you will be watching either sport, you will be able to follow the game. Note: If you are invited to watch a *football* match, don't expect to see what you would in the United States. Instead, you will be watching individuals playing soccer.

You will find that lunches and dinners are popular forums for discussing business and establishing personal relationships with your British counterparts. In addition, most business entertaining is done in restaurants.

If you are invited to "tea," note that this is the term used for the evening meal that Americans typically refer to as dinner or supper.

There are noticeable differences between the way utensils are handled by Americans and the British. While individuals in the United States typically follow the "American" style of dining (cutting the food, then switching the fork from one hand to another), the British, like most other Europeans, follow the "continental" or European method. This consists of keeping the knife in the hand with which you write and the fork in your opposite hand, and using them simultaneously, without switching. After cutting a bite-sized piece of food, the fork and knife (serrated edge down) may remain in your hands, while the fork (with food attached) may be taken to the mouth with the tines down.

When sitting at a table, make sure your hands are showing at all times. To do anything else would be considered impolite.

When eating in more casual environments, British food is often served "family-style"—that is, it is placed on platters in the middle of the table. When this is the case, it is appropriate for you to serve yourself rather than to wait for another person to serve you. However, take the cue from your host before serving yourself.

Always wait for your host and hostess to take the first bite before you start eating.

Rather than belonging to the "clean plate club," it is considered proper to leave a few bites on your plate at the end of the meal. By doing so, you will be showing that the meal was very satisfying.

When you have completed your meal, the "finished" continental style is to place your knife and fork diagonally on your plate with the fork tines facing up. Also make sure that the fork is closest to you.

Beverage etiquette: Tea is definitely the beverage for which the British have the strongest passion. You can be certain that you will be served many cups of tea while in England. If you choose to drink tea as the British do, then you will have your tea with milk and sugar.

Just as in other European countries, it is not typical to have ice included in cold beverages.

Unusual foods: British food is rarely seasoned strongly and can be described as rather plain. Meals are typically served in courses, as they are in the United States.

Throughout London, you will find restaurants serving various ethnic specialties that include Asian, Middle Eastern, and Italian cuisine, among others.

To find what you might consider traditional British fare, look for fish and chips, scones, and biscuits (cookies), all of which you will find in abundance.

Conversation

After you have established rapport with the British, you can be sure that your conversations with them will address a variety of subjects. The British are a well-read group and appreciate that trait in others. You will find that they enjoy sharing their viewpoints on current events and will also want to get your perspective on a particular topic of conversation.

Remember that the British are not very animated nor are they an excitable group. For that reason, you will do well to follow suit by speaking in a low rather than loud voice and keeping overly emotional reactions in check.

As already mentioned, British English contains many terms that have definitions different from their U.S. meanings. One way to keep the lines of communication open is to make a point of avoiding American slang terms that could confuse your British contact.

Suitable topics of conversation include the country's history, culture, and sports. You will also be safe to share your experiences in England. When initiating a conversation, stick with subjects that involve your immediate surroundings.

You will find the British to be a private people. Rather than attempting to get too "chummy," respect their privacy and keep your distance unless you are invited into more intimate topics of conversation. In particular, you should not ask questions about your British contact's personal life, nor should you inquire about the person's family, what he or she does for a living, and any questions related to social class.

It won't take long for you to discover that the British as a rule are sensitive to the position and power England once had. For that reason, avoid any conversations that may sound like you are criticizing their country. Also avoid discussing politics, religion, Scotland, or Northern Ireland.

Gestures and Public Manners

In keeping with their need for privacy, the British people tend to be discreet in their public behavior. Voices are never raised above a moderate volume, shouting is unheard of, and drawing any sort of attention to oneself is deemed a disgrace and causes immense embarrassment.

Hand gestures and body language are not a part of English conversation. People usually keep their hands at their sides, never in their pockets. Do not make large gestures or rely on nonverbal communication to express your message.

Physical contact is taboo. Do not touch others, pat people on the back, or stand very close to someone else. Personal space is maintained at a greater distance in England than America.

Eye contact should be kept light and vague. The British are uncomfortable with intense, continuous looks. By no means should you ever stare at someone.

Queuing: Put your patience hat on in England, especially in the larger cities, because waiting is the name of the game. British people are accustomed to and obedient about joining the end of the longest lines and waiting to be served. Lines are one of the few places you can acceptably strike up conversation with the strangers around you.

Gift-giving Etiquette

Exchanging gifts among business associates (such as upon the successful completion of a negotiation) is not a typical practice in England. Christmas is one of the only times that a gift should be given to a British colleague with whom you are working.

If you are presented with a gift, it is acceptable to reciprocate. Appropriate gifts would include desk accessories, pens, and books. Do not go overboard with an expensive present.

Greetings and Introductions

Although the British enjoy meeting new people and are usually very interested in meeting those from abroad, they are very reserved, private people for the most part. Do not mistake their reserve for rudeness or indifference towards meeting you, which is unlikely to be the case.

Handshakes are the accepted form of formal greeting in England. The proper term to use while shaking hands is "How do you do?" Rather than giving what may be thought of as a "pumper," keep your handshake brief and less firm than you would with individuals from the United States or Germany. While eye contact should be made during the handshake and greeting, it should be broken as you release your hand. Just as in most other countries, a handshake should also take place upon departure.

Proper forms of address: Once again, formality presides in England. Business etiquette dictates that individuals be addressed by their last names unless you have been invited to do otherwise.

While it is appropriate to use professional titles when meeting individuals from Germany and certain other European countries, this is not the case when greeting the British, who rarely use their academic and professional titles. "Doctor" is reserved only for those who are medical doctors (not dentists, eye doctors, and so on) or those who have earned doctorate degrees.

Men who have been knighted by the Queen are addressed as "Sir," followed by their first names. For example, Sir Andrew Lloyd Webber should be addressed as "Sir Andrew."

How Decisions are Made

A very important aspect of the British values system is being accepted by others. Contrary to many other countries where decisions are made autocratically, emphasis in this country is placed on teamwork. Typically, a consensus is obtained before taking the final decision to the person highest in power. Because of this, decision-making can be a long process. It is therefore important to exercise patience in your business negotiations.

Meeting Manners

British businesspeople are terrific planners. For that reason, be sure to make your own arrangements well in advance. In addition to scheduling and confirming the date of the meeting, be sure to confirm your agenda and any other specifications a few weeks prior to that date.

Rather than arriving too early or too late, it would be best if you arrive right on time, in keeping with British business etiquette. However, avoid making a comment if you have been kept waiting yourself.

Be sure to project a degree of professionalism in both your demeanor and your manner of speaking and responding. The British will not hesitate to ask questions, so use documentation to support your presentation and also to provide clarification.

It won't take long to see that the British have a natural disdain for being told what to do and for following orders. Thus, rather than telling them what to do, offer suggestions and recommendations.

Punctuality

There's punctuality and then there's punctuality. As already noted, British business etiquette dictates that you arrive at meetings and appointments on time. Once again, if your British contacts are running a bit late, prepare to wait without insinuating that your time could have been better spent doing something else.

Social engagements, however, follow an entirely different form of promptness. It is considered more proper to show up no earlier than a quarter of an hour after the time you were given and no later than 30 minutes after the appointed hour. The only time that you should be on time during a social function is when the engagement is at a restaurant where reservations have been made.

Seating Etiquette

Seating etiquette dictates that the host and hostess take seats at opposite ends of the table, facing one another. In turn, the most senior male guest of honor will be seated to the right of the hostess while the most senior female guest of honor will be placed to the right of the host.

Taxi Etiquette

You will have little trouble hailing cabs on major streets. You can also call ahead to set up a specific pickup time. Be sure to inform the driver of your destination prior to getting in the cab. You should also exit the cab before paying your fare. Keep in mind that cab rates increase dramatically after midnight.

Major cities also have what are called "minicabs." These are small versions of taxis, which are normally quite popular in England. Minicabs are less expensive and easier to maneuver in London traffic. If you are alone with little baggage, consider taking one of these.

Tipping Tips

In taxis, you should tip 10 to 15 percent of your fare.

Restaurant bills usually include gratuities of 10 to 15 percent. Leave some change if the tip is included. If it appears that a tip has not been included, 10 to 15 percent of the total bill should be left.

Hotel porters should be tipped about 25p for each bag. Chambermaids should be given £1 for each day of your stay.

Toasting Etiquette

There are two times during a meal when toasts will and should be proposed. The first is the "pre-drink" toast that is initiated by the host. Guest etiquette encourages you to wait until the host or hostess has initiated this toast before you take the first sip of your drink. The second toast, which is dedicated "to the Queen," will be proposed by the host or hostess after the meal has come to an end.

Toilet Etiquette

You will be pleased with the quality and abundance of the public restroom facilities in England. Look for doors marked "W.C.," "lavatory," and "toilet." The British often call the bathroom the "loo." Train stations, hotels, restaurants, gas stations, and department stores all provide facilities. They are even located on busy streets. You may be charged a small fee for using the loo.

When You Are Invited to an English Home

Unlike many other Europeans, the British enjoy entertaining in their homes. Once again, avoid insulting your host and don't show up until at least a quarter of an hour after the time of the invitation.

Be sure to go with a small token in hand, but nothing extravagant. A box of chocolates, wine, or flowers (other than white ones, which are equated with mourning) make good gifts.

The chances are excellent that your meal will be good, the conversation invigorating, and the company even better. Take your cue from your host by preparing to leave shortly after coffee has been served.

Women in Business

Despite the fact that women make up almost half of England's work force, they still encounter many obstacles in their climb up that slippery ladder of success. Although you may sense that British men maintain traditional attitudes about women and their roles outside the workplace, do your best to put your professional self forward, and know that this attitude is being dispelled slowly but surely, thus opening more equal opportunities for women in British business.

Whatever You Do...

- Don't assume a defensive attitude if you are a woman and are addressed by men with terms of endearment. Phrases such as "deary," "love," and "darling" are common and accepted expressions men use when addressing women.
- Don't forget to stand when you hear England's national anthem. "God Save the Queen" is often played in public and at theater and sporting events.
- Don't schedule business meetings for the summer months. These are the popular months during which the British go on holiday.
- Don't invite a businessman to dinner if you are a woman. It is much more acceptable for women to take men to lunch, if they invite them anywhere. If you must extend an evening invitation to a male business associate, be sure to invite his spouse.
- Don't forget your "p's and q's." The British are sticklers for proper protocol. You should always follow local customs and use the utmost courtesies.
- Don't display much emotion. The British tend not to reveal what they are feeling in dramatic terms. Keep your excitement or disappointment under wraps.
- Don't make any jokes about the British people's love of the Royal family. The monarchy is sacred and an important focal point of the culture in England.

Chapter 7

Finland

The Republic of Finland is an archipelago in the northern European region of Scandinavia. The country borders Sweden on the east and Russia on the right, and shares a border on the north with Norway; its southernmost points are surrounded by the Gulf of Bothnia, the Gulf of Finland, and the Baltic Sea. More than a fourth of its land lies north of the Arctic Circle. Despite this location, Finland's climate can be surprisingly mild, especially in the southern sections of the country. Its latitude also makes for long summer days and winter nights. In the northernmost portion of the country, especially, there can be as many as 70 days in the summer that pass without night, while the prolonged winter night can last almost six months. It is a spectacular night, however, with the snow, moonlight, and Northern Lights creating a special glow over the land.

While more than 65 percent of Finland is filled with forest and wilderness, it is primarily known for its lakes (187,888 of them) and islands. In fact, with 179,584 islands to its credit (45 percent in the Baltic Sea alone), Finland has more than any other country in the world, which also makes it the densest archipelago. Overall, the country is highly developed, with all the most modern conveniences and a strong and stable economy. The main sources of income come from manufacturing, finance, and services. Major industries include lumbering, fishing, and mineral mining. Agriculture forms only a very small part of the Finnish economy. Despite being the 7th largest country in area in Europe, Finland's population numbers only 5 million, of which 62 percent lives in urban areas and the remainder in rural sections. The capital, Helsinki, lies on the Gulf of Finland in the southernmost section of the country.

Among Finland's many contributions to the world's culture are the invention of the sauna and numerous achievements in the arts and architecture. Its most famous native son is composer Jean Sibelius.

Established as an independent republic in 1917, Finland had previously been under the control of Sweden for more than 600 years, and then Russia for another 100 years. Both countries have left their traces in the land and its people, who are tough, determined, and resilient. The government is a democracy headed by a president, who is elected to a six-year term and who appoints the prime minister and cabinet members. The system is largely social in nature and includes a solid heath care system, social security, free and compulsory education, and subsidized housing for low-income families. The government has a controlling interest in most of the country's industries.

Statistics and Information

Air Travel

When flying into Finland, you will arrive at the capital's international airport, which is called Helsinki-Vantaa. To get to downtown Helsinki, both buses and taxis are available.

Country Code

Finland's country code is 358.

Helsinki's city code is 9.

Currency

The currency of this country is the *mark* (Fmk). One *mark* is equivalent to 100 *pennies*. *Marks* are available in denominations of

Fmk 1,000, 500, 100, 50, and 10. Besides the 1 *mark* in coin form, you will also see coins of 50, 20, 10, and 5 *pennies*.

Credit cards are accepted throughout the country, even in many taxis. You may cash traveler's checks only in banks. You may also purchase "cash cards" (called the Avant card), which can be used in a variety of locations, including pay phones, vending machines, and fast food restaurants.

Dates

Be sure to follow the European standard when writing dates. List the day, followed by the month, and then the year. For example, March 30, 2000, should be written 30/3/00.

Ethnic Makeup

While the vast majority of the population is comprised of Finns, approximately 6 percent consists of Swedes and Lapps.

Holidays and Religious Celebrations

The following is a list of Finland's celebrated holidays. Because these are national holidays, it is best to avoid scheduling meetings on these days.

January 1	New Year's Day
January 6	Feast of the Epiphany
March/April	Good Friday through Easter Monday
May 1	Labour Day
May/June (49 to 50 days following Easter)	Whitsunday and Whitmonday
The first Saturday of November	All Saints' Day
December 6	Independence Day

December 25	Christmas Day
December 26	Boxing Day

Language

The official languages of Finland are Finnish and Swedish. English is also commonly spoken.

Religion

Nearly 90 percent of Finland's population is Evangelical Lutheran. A very small percentage belongs to the Greek Orthodox Church of Finland.

Time Zone Differences

Finland is:

- Two hours ahead of Greenwich Mean Time.
- Seven hours ahead of U.S. Eastern Standard Time.

Weather

One of the most important things to remember when traveling to Finland is to take clothes that you can wear in layers, because while generally moderate, the climate can vary from one region of the country to the next. For instance, in northern Finland, the temperature can have as much as a 60-degree variance from the southern section.

Etiquette

Business Attire

Finns dress conservatively, but they are very conscientious about high fashion. With this in mind, men should wear suits with ties. Sport coats will do in less-formal occasions, while just shirts and ties are acceptable only when the temperature is very hot.

Likewise, businesswomen will be dressed properly in chic suits or conservative, yet fashionable dress. Slacks for women are acceptable in casual settings outside of the business environment, as are jeans for both men and women.

Business-card Etiquette

Be sure to take plenty of business cards with you. However, because many Finns speak, understand, and read English, it is not necessary to have your cards translated into Finnish on the reverse side. As in other countries, the business cards you receive should be treated with respect.

Business Entertaining/Dining

One of the most unique aspects of doing business in Finland is that it will be common for you to relax in a sauna either before or after lunching in a restaurant. In addition to relaxing and meditating, it is common for business to be discussed while you are in the sauna.

Most meals will take place in a Finnish restaurant, rather than at a home.

As in the United States, business dinners tend to be more social events than working meals. For that reason, allow your host to set the tone of the conversation.

You will find that food is an important part of Finnish hospitality. Like Greeks and Arabs, Finns will encourage you to eat several servings of foods.

Lunch is typically soup and a sandwich with vegetables in the form of a salad. Believe it or not, milk is a common beverage taken with lunch.

The heavier or bulkier foods, such as meat (most commonly fish, pork, veal, or chicken) and potatoes, are served at dinner. This meal also includes a salad, which is usually considered to be a vegetable.

Unlike in the United States, what may look like "finger food" to you should be eaten with utensils. If you are unsure, play it safe by taking your cue from the person hosting the meal.

Prepare for people to smoke at meals. It is common for people to light up when they are taking a "breather" or are waiting for the next course to be served to them.

Alcoholic beverages (such as whiskey or vodka) may be served at a social gathering that precedes dinner. If wine or beer is served, it will be with the meal itself.

Dinner may consist of as many as four courses, and is likely to include a fish appetizer, a meat, and bread and butter. Cheese is commonly served with dessert, which will probably be something sweet.

Coffee is considered to be an after-dinner beverage. In fact, it may be offered quite a while after the dinner has been completed. You may also be offered coffee with your breakfast and again with cookies and other pastries during the afternoon if you are in a living room-like setting.

Conversation

When conversing with Finns, safe topics of conversation include sports (skiing, hockey, soccer, rowing, and so on), the city you are visiting and its history, as well as Finland's national history.

Finns are very private people. Therefore, avoid asking questions about their personal lives unless they bring up the topic first. You should also avoid asking what they do for a living.

Gestures and Public Manners

Try to maintain a distance of two arms' length when talking to Finns, as this is considered appropriate. The only bodily contact should take place when shaking hands.

Avoid crossing your arms, because this is considered to be a haughty gesture in Finland.

Finns are private people. They prefer to keep to themselves rather than make small talk when they are in line, on public transportation, and so on. It is important to follow suit and not try to initiate conversations with people you don't know, as well as to avoid getting too personal.

Eye contact is considered important in Finland. While in other countries you should break off any sustained eye contact, in this country it should always be maintained when talking to others.

Gift-giving Etiquette

When planning your trip to Finland, be sure to pack a few gifts. It is best to be prepared if, upon completing a business deal, you are invited to a home.

Appropriate gifts would be books about your homeland, a CD, or liquor of some sort. Other items that make especially good business gifts include a crystal vase or an office item with your organization's logo engraved on it.

Greetings and Introductions

A handshake is always in order when meeting another person for the first time and when taking your leave of that person.

Because many Finnish women are in very high-ranking positions, it is unnecessary for men to wait for a woman to initiate a handshake. Either sex may take the initiative.

Do not address Finns by their first names unless you are given permission to do so. Always use last names until you are asked to do otherwise.

If someone has earned the title of doctor, engineer, or professor, that person's title should be used rather than *Herra* (Mr.), *Rowva* (Mrs.), or *Neiti* (Miss).

Hierarchy Is Important

Because the managing director of an organization is the person who is considered to be the highest-ranking individual, defer to that person before the more junior people.

How Decisions Are Made

The Finns are planners and they appreciate this trait in others. Therefore, never pay an unexpected visit to a Finnish company. Rather, be sure to request a meeting in advance.

Although others may be involved in your meetings, the person who has the final say is the managing director, who is the equivalent of a U.S. operating officer.

When everything else is equal, business decisions will most often be based on the personal rapport that has been established between two sides. For that reason alone, it is important to remember that you can't get in trouble being nice. It just may pay off.

Meeting Manners

Be sure to respect punctuality and don't be late when attending meetings. This is a very important trait to Finns.

Wait to be offered a seat at any meeting you attend, to ensure that you will abide by Finnish seating protocol.

You will find that time is money to the Finns. Therefore, don't expect to engage in much small talk, as the Finn spearheading the meeting will likely want to get right down to business.

When attending a business meeting, bear in mind that the individuals in attendance may be the messengers rather than the actual decision-makers.

In Finland, silence is golden—at least for a few minutes. For that reason alone, if you ask someone a question, allow that person a few minutes before answering it.

Punctuality

Finns respect time and will expect you to do so, too. Unlike the Greeks, if you arrive for a meeting a few minutes earlier than the appointed time, the Finns will appreciate it.

Seating Etiquette

Seating etiquette in Finland is similar to that in the United States, with the host and hostess seated at opposite ends of a rectangular table. The difference is that guests sit on opposite sides, by gender, rather than rotating man-woman-man-woman around the table.

Tipping Tips

As in many European countries, a service charge will be included on your restaurant bill. These charges are unique in Finland, in that a higher amount (for example, 1 to 2 percent higher) will be posted on your bill on Sundays as opposed to other days of the week.

When a porter assists you with luggage or a coatroom clerk assists you with your coat, it is in order to tip 5 Fmk. Chambermaids should also be given 5 Fmk. When you are traveling by taxi, it is not necessary to tip the driver, but it is appropriate to round out the fare to the next highest Fmk. Unlike in many other European countries, it is not necessary to tip a theater usher for handing you a program and/or showing you to your seat.

Of course, one of the greatest ways to show that you have been pleased with the service you have received is by expressing your gratitude verbally.

Toasting Etiquette

A common Finnish toast is "*Kippis*," which means "Cheers."

If you are interacting with Swedes in Finland, you will want to be sure to toast in Swedish by saying, "*Skäl*."

Guests should propose a toast only after the host or hostess has initiated one.

When You Are Invited to a Finnish Home

If you are fortunate enough to be invited to a home, be sure to go with something in hand. Appropriate items include good quality chocolates, a bouquet of flowers (in odd numbers, and avoid yellow or white blossoms), or liquor.

Don't be surprised if you are invited to relax in the home sauna while you are there. While it is par to go in nude, you may wrap a towel around yourself or wear a bathing suit if you have one with you. This experience is very much part of Finnish hospitality.

Women in Business

Finnish women are some of the most liberated in the world, in both their personal and professional lives. In fact, more than three quarters of Finnish women work outside the home. Women traveling from abroad will find it very easy to do business in Finland.

Whatever You Do...

- Don't give yellow or white flowers as gifts. These colors are reserved for funerals.
- Don't give an odd number of flowers to a Finn, because odd numbers are considered offensive.
- Don't try to converse with a Finn when you are standing in line. Finns are very reserved people and prefer not to kibitz with strangers.
- Don't be boisterous in public settings. Talking loudly is considered offensive.
- Don't invite a Finn to breakfast, because this meal is usually reserved for family members prior to the start of the workday.
- Don't put more food on your plate than you expect to eat, for two reasons: The first is that it is considered wasteful to leave something on your plate. The second is that Finnish hospitality will encourage you to have two and three helpings.

Chapter 8

France

Officially called the French Republic, France is a nation in western Europe lying between the Atlantic Ocean and English Channel on the west and northwest and the Mediterranean Sea on the south. The country is bordered on the south and west by Spain and Andorra, on the east by Italy, Switzerland, and Germany, and on the northeast by Luxembourg and Belgium. The island of Corsica in the Mediterranean Sea is also a part of France. Paris, the capital, lies in the northern part of the country along the Seine River. Other notable French cities include Lyon, Marseilles, Nice, Grenoble, Nantes, and Chartres.

Nearly three-fifths of the land in France is arable, with soil conditions being especially suitable for growing the grapes that provide the source of this nation's best-known industry, wine-making. France also produces wheat, corn, barley, and oats in abundance. In addition, it is among the world's leaders in the production of iron ore. A highly industrialized nation and major economic power, it is known for its beautiful countryside and a rich and varied history that has seen it endure through both triumphs and tragedies over the centuries.

France has also long been a cultural leader in Europe and throughout the world. Its development as such has been influenced by the ancient Celtic tribes that first invaded its shores around 1,000 B.C., followed by Germanic and Roman invaders in later centuries.

The country became united under the rule of King Charlemagne in the early 800s, but continued to fight with other countries, including England, over land claims. France's current borders were established by King Louis XIV through both battle and purchase. However, the extravagant expenditures and high living style of the Sun King and his successors eventually brought about a revolt against royalty and the eruption of the French Revolution in 1789. With the monarchy destroyed, the dictatorship of Napoleon Bonaparte followed, then several attempts at establishing a democratic republic. The fourth republic was proclaimed in 1946, following World War II, and with help from the Marshall Plan and the leadership of Charles de Gaulle (who established a new constitution and the fifth republic in the late 1950s), France eventually rebuilt itself into the world power that it is today. At one time highly socialist in its government, in recent years the country has seen a trend towards more conservative policies. France is also one of the leaders behind the creation of the European Community.

The people of France are famous for their outspoken opinions, great national pride, finely honed fashion sense, outstanding cuisine, and devotion to the arts. They are known for their formality, yet they are also warm and friendly, with a tremendous tolerance for other cultures. Great French authors, painters, scientists, and philosophers have influenced thinkers and doers throughout the ages, making this one of the world's most predominant cultures.

Statistics and Information

Air Travel

The major airport of France is the Charles de Gaulle International Airport. It is located 27 km north of Paris. Shuttles, taxis, and buses are available from the airport to the city.

Country Code

France's country code is 33.

City codes include:

City codes include:

- 556 for Bordeaux.
- 491 for Marseilles.
- 1 for Paris.
- 388 for Strasborg.

Currency

This country's monetary unit is the *French franc* (FF). One *franc* equals 100 *centimes.* Notes come in denominations of FF100, 50, and 20. Coins come in FF10, 5, 2, and 1, and as well as 50, 20, 10, and 5 *centimes.*

The lowest rates for exchanging your money can be obtained at banks and ATM machines.

Dates

Dates are written according to the European standard—that is, the day is written before the month, followed by the year. For instance, January 30, 1999, would be written as 30/1/99.

Ethnic Makeup

The vast majority of the population is of native French descent. You will also find individuals of North African, Spanish, and Portuguese heritage living in France.

Holidays and Religious Celebrations

Below is a list of France's celebrated holidays. Because they are national holidays, it is wise not to schedule meetings for these days.

January 1	New Year's Day
January 6	Epiphany
Late March/ April	Easter
May 1	Labour Day (also called May Day)

May 8	Fete de la Victoire 1945 (WW II Victory Day)
July 14	Bastille Day
August 15	The Assumption
November 1	All Saints' Day
November 11	Armistice Day
December 25	Christmas Day
December 26	2nd Day of Christmas (In Alsace-Lorraine only)

Language

The official language is French. Regional dialects are gradually dying out. English is the most popularly spoken second language; French students study it for a minimum of four years.

Religion

More than 90 percent of the French are Roman Catholics. Less than 2 percent of the population practices Protestantism, while Jewish and Muslim followers each make up 1 percent. Approximately 6 percent of the population does not practice a religion of any kind.

Time Zone Differences

France is:

- One hour ahead of Greenwich Mean Time.
- Six hours ahead of U.S. Eastern Standard Time.

Weather

The temperature and weather conditions are rather consistent throughout France, based on the seasons. Most of France experiences warm summers and cold winters. Temperatures range upwards from the low 70s in the summer. The winter temperature is typically in the mid 30s. Southern France, however, experiences higher temperatures and more rain.

Etiquette

Business Attire

The majority of the world's fashion sense comes from the designers and runways of France. The French reflect this sense of fashion in their everyday appearance. Clothes are made of the best fabrics and fit the figure to a "T." Thus, when doing business with the French, you should be sure to dress the part. The French will interpret the image you present as an indication of the level of status you've attained and the measure of your business success. Clothes and accessories of high quality will therefore count for a lot.

Men should choose dark suits, white or striped oxfords, and complementary ties. Women should select modestly cut suits or dresses and elegant accessories. It is important to note that unlike many countries, women still dress in a feminine manner and want to be seen as feminine. Soft colors, delicate jewelry, updated hairstyles, and makeup creating an overall chic look are all essential.

Beware of invitations that suggest "casual" or "informal" dress. The French idea of "casual" is more formal than what might be interpreted as such by Americans. When you are unsure about what should be worn, play it safe by dressing simply yet elegantly.

Business-card Etiquette

Cards should be exchanged with new business acquaintances following your initial handshake and greeting. Be sure to present your card to the most senior person first as a gesture of respect.

You may find that the typical French business card is larger than the standard American card. Be sure to acknowledge any card you receive with a word of thanks before placing it in your wallet or portfolio.

Business Entertaining/Dining

Lunch is the main meal of the day in France, and therefore the best one to which you may invite your French contacts. While they are less common than lunches, "power breakfasts" are now on the rise in France.

It is important to remember that the French prefer not to mix their private and professional lives. For that reason, when a meal invitation is extended to you, the event will probably be at a restaurant rather than in the person's home. If your spouse has accompanied you to France, only include him or her at the meal if your French client has made reference to bringing his or her spouse (or clearly includes your spouse in the invitation).

When hosting a meal, be sure to make your reservations in advance. Remember that the French use military time, so this is the method you should use in speaking with both the restaurant personnel and your guest (for example, when making a 7 p.m. reservation, refer to the hour as 1900).

If you are the guest, make a point of asking your host to make the food recommendations. Besides being assured of excellent cuisine, this will also help you learn an appropriate price range for occasions when you are the host.

The French follow the continental-style of dining—that is, after cutting your food, the knife remains in the right hand, while the fork in the left hand transports the food to the mouth, tines down.

Like the Italians, it is common for the French to place bread directly on the table, because bread plates are uncommon. French etiquette also allows you to enjoy sauces with a piece of bread (unlike what you may have been taught to do).

As in most European countries, your hands should be visible at all times. That means rather than laying one hand on your lap, your wrists should be placed on the table.

Although you may enjoy adding extra salt and pepper to your food, be sure to refrain from doing this in France. If you add additional seasoning to food, the chef may interpret this as meaning that the food was less than desirable for your palate.

It won't take you long to learn that the French live to eat, rather than eat to live. Therefore, be sure to appreciate and compliment whatever you are served. Otherwise, it may be thought that you did not enjoy the meal that had been prepared for you.

When you have completed your meal, place your fork and knife in a 10 o'clock-5 o'clock position, with the fork tines facing upward.

Beverage etiquette: Wine can be considered the official drink of France; it is offered with both lunch and dinner. Sip from your glass only after everyone has been served and the host has offered a toast. Note that your beverage will continue to be replenished as the meal progresses. If you prefer not to have anymore, the appropriate cue is to leave your goblet about one quarter full.

One of the best parts about doing business in France is its exquisite and large variety of cheeses, fresh breads, and savory sauces. You will also find that each region of France has distinctly different specialties. You will enjoy just about all your dining experiences!

Conversation

When doing business in France, little will suit your French contact more than if you are ready to debate. The French dearly love a good—and even a heated—discussion. While this manner may appear argumentative to some Americans, it should be recognized and accepted as the way your hosts like it.

When first meeting a French person, you will do best to stay on general topics. "Small talk" topics can include sports, art, music, and the like. You also will fare well in conversation by boning up on French history, politics, and art.

Be sure to remain well-informed about what is going on in your own country, especially the political scene, because you are likely to be asked about it.

When conversing with the French, stay away from any topic that is deemed personal, especially in regards to their private lives or your own.

Gestures and Public Manners

The French are very conscious of their own physical presence and are also quite observant about the presence that others project. Therefore, good posture is a must. Be aware of sitting, standing, and walking in an erect manner, rather than slouching. The French interpret these attributes as a reflection of your breeding. For these reasons, your gestures and public manners should never be overly casual.

Maintaining any sort of distance is not as much of an issue to be concerned about when interacting with the French, because this nationality does not place as much emphasis on "personal space" as North Americans do (except Mexicans). The French are quite comfortable standing close, as well as touching.

Be wary of how much eye contact you use with others. While it is important to have eye contact, you should avoid holding another person's gaze for too long.

When pointing at someone or something, do it with the entire hand rather than just the index finger.

The "okay" sign that is so common in the United States can be considered an offensive gesture in other countries. In France, it means that someone or something is "useless" or "good for nothing." The best way to indicate to a French person that all is well is by putting your thumbs up.

Do not snap your fingers. While this is an acceptable gesture in some countries, it is considered offensive in France.

You may consider smiling to be a good nonverbal indication of happiness or friendliness. However, this is not the case in France. Smiling is neither expected nor accepted as a nonverbal form of communication when passing others on the street or as an acknowledgement.

The French (especially Parisians) are unfairly notorious for having an "attitude" towards foreigners, particularly Americans. In fact, they will warm up to you quickly if you simple make an attempt to speak even a few words of their language and to learn something about their culture. Try to do as the French do, and you will find yourself being accepted quickly!

Compliments should be used to express an opinion instead of saying something about how good someone looks or applauding the person's success. While the French believe that a compliment can and should be acknowledged, it should be done in a very low-key manner and need not be reciprocated with a verbal "thank you."

Gift-giving Etiquette

Rather than presenting a gift at your first meeting, wait until a business relationship has developed to give a gift to your French contact. The present itself should be representative of your organization.

The French love literature, art, and music, so books or CDs make great presents. Gourmet food items are also ideal, as are flowers (which should be presented in even numbers). Rather than placing any emphasis on the cost, consider the other person's interests (if known) when selecting a gift.

If you are giving a flower arrangement, avoid chrysanthemums, because they are associated with mourning. In addition, be sure not to give carnations, as they are thought to bring bad luck, and a French person may interpret this gift as an intentional jinx on your part. Finally, save red roses to give to someone with whom you are romantically involved.

Greetings and Introductions

Contrary to what many Americans believe, the French enjoy having individuals from other countries visit their homeland. What they may find offensive, however, are certain mannerisms that are considered acceptable and even expected in the United States. For instance, when meeting your French contact, shake hands with a lighter grip than you would give to a person in the United States, and do not hold onto the other person's hand for too long.

Do not feel obliged to offer an "air kiss" (as popularized by the media). This gesture is reserved for close friends. You should also avoid smiling at others as a gesture of friendliness (see "Gestures and Public Manners").

Proper forms of address: The French are very formal in how they address strangers and acquaintances. Even using last names is considered to be too up-front. Instead, you should address people as *Monsieur, Madame,* or *Mademoiselle.* Never use a first name until you have been invited to do so.

How Decisions Are Made

When negotiating with the French, prepare for the probability that it will take a long time for decisions to be reached. One reason for the delay is that the French are interested in examining every detail before drawing any conclusions.

You will also find that decisions are made by the highest person in authority, rather than by group consensus. This is important to remember in terms of hierarchy, especially when you are in a meeting. The middle management team with whom you are dealing may simply be the messengers, rather than the final decision-makers.

Meeting Manners

Business meetings tend to be formal and adhere to a rigid protocol. Do not expect much small talk or any emphasis on getting to know one another. Also refrain from rattling off personal or company accomplishments, as the French detest boasting and draw conclusions based on what they see you do, rather than what they hear you say.

The French businessperson may want to maintain an air of superiority, and therefore, may not make you feel very welcome, at least initially. In addition, they will probably not react to your proposal as you'd first hoped. Meetings are seen more as vehicles for discussion, as opposed to a forum for decision-making. The French are slow to change and enjoy arguing an issue. Stand firm and know your stuff. You can win them over with persistence and knowledge.

Be sure to involve everyone in your meeting. The French are a people who love to ask many questions, so you may find them often putting the carriage before the horse. Rather than allowing this to frustrate you, make a point of explaining every detail in your presentation. Your patience and understanding of how the French process works will prepare you for successful negotiations in France.

Punctuality

The French prefer to avoid the pressure of worrying about time, and thus are much more relaxed about it than U.S. businesspeople are. In fact, the rigid American view of time and scheduling is high on the list of subjects for French jokes. Bear this in mind, so you will be less surprised when meetings begin late, without explanation, or may be canceled without notice.

In the same regard, be prepared for the possibility that a meeting that is in progress may be interrupted by incoming phone calls or drop-in visitors.

Seating Etiquette

Never assume a seat until you have been invited to do so by the host or hostess. The most common arrangement places the host and hostess in the center of the table facing one another, while the guest of honor of the opposite sex sits to the right of each. Other guests are seated in descending order of importance to the right and left.

Taxi Etiquette

When selecting a taxi, look for one with a sign on the roof. Also, be sure that the taxi you choose has a meter so that you are charged fairly. Prepare to pay an additional fee based on the pieces of luggage you have.

Tipping Tips

Plan on tipping those individuals who render a service for you. Some guiding rules:

- At restaurants, 10 to 15 percent will be included in your bill. If the service was outstanding, make a point of leaving an extra 15 to 20 *francs*.

- Tip hotel and airport porters 5 *francs* for each bag they handle.
- Taxi drivers should be tipped 10 percent of the cab fare.
- Give coatroom attendants 2 *francs*.
- Washroom attendants should be tipped 1 *franc*.

Toilet Etiquette

Once notorious for its antiquated plumbing facilities, France has, by and large, updated most of its public restrooms. While you may encounter a squat toilet once in a while, new toilets labeled "W.C." are most common in the metro, cafes, and train stations. However, prepare yourself by carrying a small amount of tissue with you—just in case.

Toasting Etiquette

Toasting etiquette dictates that guests wait for the host to initiate the first toast, but should then offer a toast in return at some point during the meal as a form of gratitude to the host(s).

When You Are Invited to a French Home

Because the French place a strong separation between work and family, an invitation to an associate's home will be a rare occurrence. If such an invitation is extended to you, take it as a compliment and an indication of the esteem in which you are held.

Arrive no later than a quarter of an hour later than the requested time. Be sure to go with something in hand (such as flowers, a good box of chocolates, or toys for the children).

Following initial introductions, you will be offered a cocktail and appetizer. After-dinner drinks may also be served. If you smoke, your time to do so is after the meal has concluded.

Besides expressing your appreciation when you leave, be sure to send a thank-you note to your host(s) the following day.

Women in Business

While French women continue to conduct themselves in a conservative and feminine manner, there is equality between the sexes on a business level. However, the French are very open in their belief about the inherent differences between the sexes.

Be prepared for French men to act in a flirtatious manner with women. This behavior is considered acceptable. In addition, French men may comment on a woman's appearance.

Rather than approaching this country with the liberated "I am woman" instinct, women from abroad will have an easier time in France if they conduct themselves in a more low-key manner.

Whatever You Do...

- Don't ask a French person about his or her profession. This question is regarded as intrusive.
- Don't wear anything less than the best-quality clothing. The French look "chic" in even their most casual wear.
- Don't chew gum in public. This action is considered very gauche.
- Don't be surprised if you walk into a W.C. and learn that it is co-ed.
- Don't schedule a meeting between noon and 2 p.m. This is the time that most French like to take their lunch.
- Don't plan your trip for the month of August. Many French businesses close and people go on holiday during this time.

Chapter 9

Germany

The Federal Republic of Germany, once known as East Germany and West Germany, is located in central Europe. Historically and geographically one of the key European countries, it borders the Netherlands, Belgium, and Luxembourg on the west, France on the southwest, Switzerland and Austria on the south and southeast, Poland and the Czech Republic on the east, and Denmark on the north. The country also meets the North Sea and the Baltic Sea on the north.

Prior to its current unified state, Germany had a long history of divisiveness within its borders related to land and power disputes. Once a land of distinct states and duchies that formed a part of the Holy Roman Empire and subsequently the German Confederation, it did not become a whole country until 1871, when a statesman from Prussia, Otto von Bismarck, overcame considerable cultural and political obstacles to bring about unification. Wars and land disputes with its neighbors over the years continually affected Germany's boundaries, to the point where the country today is nearly 40 percent smaller than it was in Bismarck's time. Germany's defeat in World War I and its subsequent humiliation by other world powers led to a nationalistic fervor that gave rise to Adolph Hitler's dictatorship in the 1930s, which in turn led to World War II. After the country's defeat in that war, Allied superpowers sought to suppress Germany's militaristic tendencies by dividing the country into a western half, to be controlled by the United States and its allies, and an eastern half, to be controlled by the Soviet Union. Over the years, West Germany was built into a solid democracy with a strong economy, while East Germany became a socialist stronghold in central Europe. However, with the fall of Communism in the Soviet Union and elsewhere, a rising movement to unify the country reached its apex in the late 1980s, and on October 3, 1990, a single nation known as the Federal Republic of Germany was formally established. Politically, it has retained West Germany's parliamentary system of government. Transition of the national capital from Bonn to Berlin has taken place over several years and will be completed in 1999.

Germany is a beautiful country of mountains, rivers, and valleys—a varied landscape that is home to a population of more than 82 million, from the Bavarian Alps to the Rhine valley. Its people are known for their great pride and dedicated work ethics. Those in the eastern portion of the country are still struggling to catch up to the standard of living long enjoyed by their neighbors in the west. Reunification has been an expensive process for the entire country, and the result has been higher prices and a higher rate of unemployment than other European countries. However, as its hardy, hard-working citizens make the adjustment to a unified, democratic way of life, Germany has once again established itself as an economic power and a nation to be reckoned with.

Statistics and Information

Air Travel

Germany is home to five major airports, located in Frankfurt, Düsseldorf, Cologne, Munich, and Berlin. All of these airports provide transportation services to their respective cities.

Country Code

Germany's country code is 49.

City codes include:

- 30 for Berlin.
- 228 for Bonn.
- 221 for Cologne.
- 89 for Munich.

Currency

German currency is the *Deutsche mark* (abbreviated DM). One *Deutsche mark* is equal to 100 *pfennig*. Bills come in denominations of DM1,000, 500, 200, 100, 50, 20, and 10. The *Deutsche mark* is also obtained in coin form in DM10, 5, 2, and 1. The *pfennig* comes in coins of 50, 10, 5, 2, and 1.

You will find the best rates at German *Wechselstubens*. These are exchange houses found in airports, train stations, banks, and post offices.

Dates

Dates are written in the European standard form—that is, when writing the date in numeric form, the day should precede the month, followed by the year. For example, January 30, 2001, would be written as 30/1/01.

Ethnic Makeup

More than 90 percent of the population is native German. There are also small percentages of Turks, Italians, Greeks, and Poles.

Holidays and Religious Celebrations

The following is a list of Germany's celebrated holidays. Because many of the dates are national holidays, offices, shops, and other places of business will be closed.

January 1	New Year's Day
Late March/ April	Good Friday, Easter
May 1	Labour Day
Five weeks after Easter	Ascension Day
Eight weeks after Easter	Whitmonday
October 3	German Unity Day
After November 8	Repentance Day
December 25/26	Christmas
December 31	New Year's Eve (Government offices are closed and shops are closed in the afternoon)

Language

Germany's official language is German, which is spoken by the entire population, with minor exceptions. You will encounter a variety of dialects throughout the country. You will find many people who speak English.

Religion

Although religion is not a focus of public life for Germans, nearly 40 percent of the population is Protestant, while more than one third is Roman Catholic. The remaining part of the population is a mixture of various religions, including Muslim.

Time Zone Differences

Germany is:

- One hour ahead of Greenwich Mean Time.
- Six hours ahead of U.S. Eastern Standard Time.

Weather

Germany's climate is generally moderate throughout the year and tends to be cloudy and wet. Temperatures in the winter are around freezing (32 degrees Fahrenheit), while summer temperatures usually reach only into the mid-60s.

Etiquette

Business Attire

Unlike many other Europeans, Germans dress in a very conservative manner. Attire during the workday is business professional. Men should wear a complete suit, even in the summer, with a modest tie and starched white shirt. Once in a while, men will wear a sweater and tie in place of a jacket. Germany is one of the few places where it is actually considered appropriate for men to wear white socks with suits if they so choose.

Women should choose modestly cut suits that mean business. Pants are not the custom for women in Germany. Colors such as dark blue, black, gray, or burgundy are good choices until one becomes familiar with an organization's culture. At that point, a brighter color may be acceptable if it doesn't seem like it would be out of place.

Both men and women should be conservative when choosing accessories. Avoid wearing gaudy-looking jewelry. This is especially important if you are conducting business in the former East Germany. Poverty still prevails and showy jewels may be seen as an attempt to outdo your German counterparts.

Business-card Etiquette

Take plenty of cards and exchange them with your German counterparts upon your initial meeting. It is advisable to have your cards translated into German on the reverse side, because it will demonstrate the attention you pay to detail.

Titles are important in Germany, so make sure that yours is noticeable on your card. In addition, if you have earned a graduate degree or represent an organization that has been in business for many years, it is helpful to include these points on your business card. Germans are most impressed with organizations that are well-established.

Business Entertaining/Dining

While you may not get this impression initially, under the staunch German exterior is a fun-loving person who is ready to have a good time. Entertaining is an important part of business in Germany and many companies have a decent budget allotted just for this. Much entertaining is done at night, beginning around 8 p.m. Spouses should be included and business should not be discussed, unless it is brought up by your German associates.

Arrive on time for your social engagements. Although cocktails are served before sitting down to dinner, this is only for a short time. Meals usually begin soon after the scheduled time.

Germany is famous for its beer. Ask your host for a suggestion about what beer to order. He or she will be flattered to share expertise on this country's most beloved beverage. In more formal settings, alcoholic beverages such as vermouth, sherry, or wine will most likely be offered. Wine is usually served with the meal. Do not feel compelled to drink it, but if you accept a glass of wine, it would be rude not to at least sip it. Wait until the host has offered a toast to the party before drinking.

Depending on the formality level of your meal, you may receive a plate with food presented to you. In a less-formal restaurant setting, however, "family-style" may be the case, in which everyone will serve themselves from platters.

Germans eat heartily and simply. The food itself is rather heavy and filling. You will also find that Germans tend to eat a lot of meat. In fact, the pig is the most popular source of meat. (Note: Germans hold the European record for eating the most pork per year.) Wurst or sausage, of which there are countless varieties, are additional German favorites.

Utensil etiquette dictates that knives be used only to cut foods that are not soft enough to be cut with the side of a fork. Otherwise,

Germans may misinterpret this action as their food not being tender enough for you.

"Finger foods" are practically nonexistent in Germany. Many foods customarily eaten with the fingers in the United States, such as sandwiches, are eaten with utensils in Germany. When unsure of what you should do, play it safe by following the lead of your German host or the guests at your table.

This is the country that encourages you to belong to the "clean plate club." Make a point to eat everything served to you. If you typically eat only small portions, be sure that only a little is put on your plate.

As in other European countries, Germans eat continental-style. The way to demonstrate that you have completed your main course is to place your fork next to your knife on the center of your plate.

After dinner, drinks will be served with coffee. Most likely, the drink will be a choice of brandies.

Conversation

"Small talk" is not a concept readily understood in Germany. Germans tend to converse about topics of substance, rather than mere form. For instance, if you ask a German the commonly asked American question of "How are you?" rather than responding with "Fine," a German will tell you exactly how he or she feels in a very direct way.

A typical first impression you may form of Germans is one of indifference—that is, they are disinterested in getting involved in conversations with strangers. One reason for this is that Germans do not respond to questions from strangers or even acquaintances that they perceive to be improper to too "personal," nor do they believe in being spontaneous. Thus, they tend to remain at arms' length distance from individuals they hardly know and will be standoffish until they get to know others better.

Once you are engaged in a conversation with a German, take care to stick to safe topics. In Germany, these would include world politics, travel, and sports.

There is a firm line in Germany between public matters of business and private or casual matters. Thus, be wary of introducing topics that may cross this line. These include marital status, family life, and income. In addition, World War II and the Holocaust are topics that may cause emotions to flare and are best left untouched.

Avoid complimenting a German, because you may embarrass him or her. On the other side of the coin, you can interpret a "no comment" from a German as a compliment. Words of praise are hard to come by in Germany. Individuals of this nationality are much more likely to point out your shortcomings than your strengths, so if they say nothing at all, that is a form of approval. You will also learn that people of this nationality have no problem telling it like they see it, because being blunt is considered acceptable.

Gestures and Public Manners

The correct way to get another person's attention from a distance is by extending your index finger with your hand raised and your palm facing outward.

Because Germans do not like calling attention to themselves in public, your emotions should be kept in check and your voice kept at an "indoor" tone.

Be sure to avoid making the "okay" sign used by North Americans. Forming a circle with the index finger and middle finger is an obscene mannerism in Germany.

Keep your hands out of your pockets at all times; it will be interpreted as a rude gesture.

You would think that a society as conservative and private about personal lives as Germany's would consider sex a taboo topic. However, this is not the case. Although they would be offended if you asked about their spouses, Germans think nothing of bringing up the topic of sex in public. One reason for this may be that prostitution is legal in Germany. What many cultures may consider pornographic publications are in plain view on German newsstands. Although it is not considered acceptable to blatantly stare at these publications, discussing them with friends in public is permissible.

Queuing: As orderly as Germans are with presentations, this is not the case when standing in line. Get ready for some pushing and shoving, both when you're in a line and when you're walking down the street. If someone does bump into you, don't expect an apology.

Smiling: Germans are thought to be very serious people, and animated looks are not the norm. For that reason, if you are given a stern look when you are talking with someone, don't misinterpret it as being anything other than typically German.

If you see a German knocking on a table, that person is *not* playing "knock-knock, who's there?" with you. Instead, this may be a form of greeting if you are not close enough to shake hands. Or he or she might be applauding you for a job well-done.

Greetings and Introductions

When possible, wait to be introduced to another person by a third party. If this is not possible, you may go ahead and initiate the introduction. In either case, you should be standing when you are shaking hands.

German etiquette dictates that you shake hands both when meeting and leaving another person. Be sure to use a firm grip; your handshake should convey confidence.

When opposite sexes are meeting, men should always wait for women to initiate a handshake.

Proper forms of address: German names follow the American format, with first or given names followed by surnames. Just as in most countries, a person's last name should always be used until you have been invited to use the first name. Because formality prevails in Germany, being invited to address another person by his or her first name could actually take years. (In fact, many people working together do not even know each other's first names, because last names are the norm.)

If the person you are addressing has a professional title, such as engineer, doctor, lawyer, or president, use that title and the person's last name (for example, "Dr. Schmidt"). If there is no work-related title, use the appropriate courtesy title:

- *Herr*: Mr.
- *Fräu*: Mrs./Ms.

For single, professional women, *Fräu* is more commonly used than *Fräulein*, just as Americans use Ms. rather than Miss when addressing a woman in her 20s or 30s.

There are two forms for saying "you" in German: the formal and the informal. If you are making an attempt to speak German, be sure to make a point of using the more formal form of "you," which is "*Sie*." The "*Du*" form is used with close friends, family, and anyone who gives you permission to use this informal mode of address. Wait until someone has addressed you in the more casual form before doing the same.

Gift-giving Etiquette

The gift exchange is not a common occurrence in Germany. If you choose to bestow a token of appreciation on your German counterpart, keep it simple. If you attempt to present a gift that may be perceived as too extravagant to the Germans, it could be misinterpreted as a bribe, and therefore, considered to be an insult. Thus, play it safe by giving gifts only when there is a legitimate reason to do so (for example, after signing a contract or on a holiday).

Gifts should be moderate and unassuming. Quality pens, office products, such as notebooks or coasters with your company's logo, or an imported liquor make good gifts. If you are fortunate enough to be invited to a German's home, be sure to go with something in hand. An unwrapped bouquet of flowers in an odd number is considered a good gift for the hostess. However, avoid giving red roses, which imply a romantic interest, as well as lilies, which are flowers for mourning.

How Decisions Are Made

Prepare to be patient when forming agreements with the Germans. They make a point of paying attention to detail, seeing to it that every "i" is dotted and every "t" is crossed before moving forward.

While many individuals may be involved in preliminary meetings, only top management will make the ultimate decision. In fact, sometimes the final decision will not even be discussed by individuals who participated in the initial meeting. Germans are very private people, and they frequently see no need to update others who are no longer responsible.

Germans consider the signing of contracts to be a very serious matter. Once pen has been put to paper, you can expect that anything that has been agreed to in writing is an absolute guarantee. In return, your German partners will expect you to execute what you have agreed to in writing without deviation.

Meeting Manners

German meeting manners dictate that you arrive at the exact appointed time. You will know that a meeting is about to begin when the doors of the room are closed. If you are hosting a meeting, be sure to see to it that the doors are closed before you begin the meeting. If you don't, Germans may see it as an invasion of privacy.

A typical meeting with Germans will be formal in its approach. You will not find any kibitzing taking place.

After beverages are served, the person spearheading the meeting will get right down to business. Even though the Germans present may have a command of English, it will be in your best interest to have your presentation material translated into German.

The German temperament is something that you will want to understand in order to make your business relationship move smoothly. For instance, it will be important to remember that Germans value structure, and they will expect it from you in both your verbal and written presentations to them. In addition, this nationality is cautious by nature and not very risk-oriented, so you will find it in your best interest to lay the facts on the table in a very methodical manner in order for them to give your proposal serious consideration.

Whatever you do, avoid giving your German colleagues information in a "by-the-way" manner. Besides making them uncomfortable with this lackadaisical approach, you may lose your chance to develop a long-term relationship with them.

You can count on your German associates to be thorough in their approach to conducting business and their attention to detail. As a result, their finished products (Mercedes or BMW automobiles, for example) are noted for being of the highest quality. In turn, they expect the highest performance from you.

For clarification's sake, make sure that whatever you present includes documentation in German. This not only demonstrates consideration for your German associates, but it is also wise because the individuals in attendance may share your information with the managing director of the organization who will have the final decision-making authority.

Finally, recognize that Germans move slowly yet surely. For that reason, expect a business relationship with a German to take time.

Punctuality

Once again, part of structure and order is respecting time. One of the many ways that Germans adhere to this "order" is by respecting others' time and also by abiding by time schedules. Punctuality is therefore a must.

Seating Etiquette

German seating etiquette dictates that the center seat at the table furthest from the door be reserved for the most senior guest. That person's counterpart should then sit across from him or her. The next most senior German should sit to the immediate right of the most senior German executive. Finally, the third most senior German should sit to the immediate left of the most senior executive.

When in business entertaining mode, the male guest of honor will be seated to the right of the hostess and the female guest of honor will be seated to the right of the host.

Don't be surprised if you are sitting in a casual restaurant and you are approached by a German who asks if he or she may join you at the table. This is a very common occurrence. Once the person joins you, you need not feel obliged to make conversation. You have only to wish the person a hearty appetite when the food arrives and to bid him or her farewell at the end.

Tipping Tips

Tipping at restaurants is left up to you. The law requires restaurants to include a gratuity in your bill. This will be about 10 to 15 percent. However, most Germans and visitors leave a bit more if they have received satisfactory service. Be sure to give a tip to the server, rather than merely leaving it on the table, as you prepare to exit the restaurant.

Hotel porters should be given DM2 per bag and maids DM2 per day. When traveling by taxi, add a 10 to 15 percent tip to your fare.

Toasting Etiquette

Two German toasts that you will want to know are "*Prost*" and "*Zum Wohl.*" The first toast is considered to be less formal and may be heard in a more casual environment or among friends.

As in most countries, the host typically initiates the toast to the guest of honor and also to those at the table. During the course of the meal, the most senior individuals are responsible for proposing a toast in return. Just as in other situations, eye contact should be made with those at the table as toasts are being made.

When You Are Invited to a German Home

Germans do not customarily entertain in their homes. If you are invited to attend a dinner at a business associate's home, you should feel honored and do all you can to be an excellent guest. Here are four rules to guide you:

1. Arrive on time. Avoid being a few minutes early or fashionably late. Precision is an important part of the German culture.

2. Be sure to go with a gift in hand. While it is not necessary, it certainly will be appreciated. If there are children in the home you are visiting, include a gift for them.
3. Prepare to sit down to dinner within a few minutes after you arrive. There is rarely any time put aside for chitchat before the meal's appointed hour.
4. Eat what is put on your plate. Whatever you do, avoid looking wasteful by not finishing your meal.

Women in Business

Women traveling from abroad will be treated with great respect by German men and in a continental manner. For instance, men will wait until a woman initiates a handshake, stand when meeting her, and walk with her on the outside of a sidewalk, closest to the curb.

One way for women to be sure they are taken seriously as businesspeople is to dress and behave conservatively and professionally, and to have a strong, knowledgeable command of the information being presented. Women should also either do what they can to master the German language or arrange for an interpreter to represent them. By going that extra mile, they will be seen as intelligent and able businesspeople.

Whatever You Do...

- Don't think of being late for an appointment. Germans are some of the world's most punctual people and few excuses will hold water. Plan ahead and arrive early.
- Don't expect to be given any praise for a job well-done. Rather, be prepared to hear only criticism for what you have forgotten to do. Germans are direct in their comments, and you are not likely to hear any euphemisms.
- Don't wait to be seated at a restaurant. Most restaurants do not have a hostess to seat you, so go ahead and find a table. Only in the finer restaurants should you need to wait to be seated.

- Don't feel ostracized by the lack of outward hospitality. Germans tend to keep to themselves and value their privacy. Doors to offices are always kept shut and people rarely engage in conversation with strangers. Once your associates have gotten to know you, they will begin to be more outgoing.
- Don't schedule business meetings in the months of July, August, and December. These are the months when many Germans schedule lengthy vacations.
- Don't fail to be thoroughly prepared for your presentation. Few people are more meticulous and inquisitive than the Germans. They will exhaust you with questions and attention to detail. Failure to "know your stuff" will hurt your attempts to make a deal.
- Don't be surprised by the prominence of the sex industry. Prostitution is legal in Germany and news racks display seamy magazines in plain view. Germans may be hard, reserved people, but they are very open and comfortable with their sexuality.

Advice From the Experts

"Never call Germans by their first names until they tell you that you can. Use formal titles where there is one (for example, Dr., if that person has earned a doctorate)."

—Paul Allaer, Partner, Thompson, Hine & Flory Law Firm, Honorary Consul of Belgium

Chapter 10

Greece

Officially called the Hellenic Republic, Greece occupies the southernmost point of the Balkan Peninsula, jutting out into the Mediterranean Sea, with the Ionian Sea on the southwest side of the country and the Aegean Sea on its eastern border, separating it from Turkey. Greece's long northern border abuts the countries of Albania, Macedonia, Bulgaria, and Turkey. With the exception of a small interior section, there is no part of the country that is more than 50 miles from the sea. There are also more than 1,400 islands belonging to Greece, the largest and best known of which is Crete, in the Aegean Islands. Corfu is the best known of the Ionian Islands. Thirty percent of the population of more than three million lives in or around the capital, Athens, while only 10 percent occupies the islands.

The vast majority of the country is mountainous, with only occasional fertile stretches of lowland, mostly along the coasts and in mountain basins. About one-fifth of the land is forested. Its Mediterranean location gives Greece a very temperate climate, and it is especially known for its hot summers. This beautiful nation attracts millions of tourists each year, accounting for a major source of income in addition to its fishing industry. Greece is a primary exporter of magnesite, and produces iron ore, lead, and zinc, as well as petroleum. Manufacturing accounts for one-fifth of the country's gross national product. Among its other exports are food (especially olive oil), tobacco, textiles, and petroleum products.

Once the home of conquerors such as Alexander the Great, Greece was eventually conquered itself, and was under the domination of the Ottoman Empire as recently as 1821, finally achieving independence in 1830, when a monarchy was established under Otto I. The monarchy was eradicated in 1924, restored in 1935, then abolished for the last time in 1973, six years after a military coup d'etat. Greece is now a democratic republic with a parliamentary system of government. The parliament is unicameral and headed by a prime minister who is the majority party leader. This group also elects a president, whose role is largely ceremonial. Socialist factions predominate in Greek politics.

The Greek heritage is evident throughout the country in its famous ruins dating back to the world's earliest civilizations. Greece has long played an important role in the development of art and philosophy, and has influenced other nations' cultures far more than it has been influenced itself. This is the birthplace of music, poetry, architecture, medicine, law, and politics, the home of Socrates and Plato, and the place where you will find a warm, generous, and open-hearted people.

Statistics and Information

Air Travel

Greece has many airports. Athens's major international airport is the Ellinikon Airport, situated about 30 minutes outside the city.

Taxis are one of the most efficient ways to travel between the airport and the city, and can be found outside each terminal. Once you arrive in Greece, however, you may prefer to travel by bus for shorter trips and passenger ships for longer ventures to the islands.

Country Code

Greece's country code is 30.

Athens's city code is 1.

Currency

Greek currency is the *drachma* (Dr). 100 *lepta* is equivalent to 1 *drachma. Drachmas* come in denominations of Dr5,000, 1,000, 500, 100, and 50. You will also find them in coins of 50, 20, 10, 5, and 2.

Banks will provide you with the best rates for exchanging your currency.

Dates

Dates are written the same way they are throughout Europe, with the day preceding the month, followed by the year (for example, March 10, 1999, should be written 10/3/99).

Ethnic Makeup

Greece is an ethnically homogeneous society. All but a small percentage of the population is of Greek descent, with the remainder being of Albanian, Armenian, Bulgarian, Macedonian, and Turkish origin.

Holidays and Religious Celebrations

Greece celebrates many national holidays and religious observances. These days should be avoided when scheduling meetings.

January 1	New Year's Day (also the Feast of St. Basil)
January 6	The Epiphany
March 25	Greek Independence Day
May 1	Labor Day
August 15	Feast of the Virgin Mary
October 28	National Day
December 25	Christmas Day
December 26	Second Day of Christmas

Language

Greek is the official language of Greece and is spoken by the vast majority of the population. French and English are also spoken.

Religion

The majority of the population practices Greek Orthodox. The remainder practices Judaism, Islam, or Roman Catholicism.

Time Zone Differences

Greece is:

- Two hours ahead of Greenwich Mean Time.
- Seven hours ahead of U.S. Eastern Standard Time.

Weather

Greece has a Mediterranean climate, with hot and dry summers. Winters in this country are mild, with temperatures in the 40s.

Etiquette

Business Attire

When in Greece, be sure to dress in a professional yet understated manner. Men should wear a dark suit in the winter months. During the warmer months, casual dress is an open-collared shirt and sport coat. While you may see Greek men wearing shoes without socks, you'd be better off not mimicking this look.

For women, a suit or dress with pumps is acceptable for a professional environment. While slacks may be worn during casual situations, they should be avoided when visiting a church or monastery.

Being well-groomed is of utmost importance when doing business in Greece. That includes maintaining good hygiene, being clean-shaven, and so forth.

Business-card Etiquette

The business card exchange is a common practice in Greece. For that reason, be sure to take plenty of cards with you and prepare to present them to anybody you meet on a business occasion.

While it may not be necessary, it certainly will be appreciated if you have the reverse side of your card translated into Greek.

Business Entertaining/Dining

When you are interacting with Greeks, you will quickly learn that they love to celebrate life and work to live, rather than live to work. You also will find that they are extremely hospitable and that food is an important part of the Greek culture.

While breakfast meetings are not very common, you may be involved in a get-together during lunch or dinner. Lunch usually takes place in the early afternoon (for example, 1 to 3 p.m.). Dinner may begin as late as 9 to 10 p.m. Between eating, drinking, and conversation, a dinner can continue into the morning's wee hours, so be prepared to stay up late.

Breakfast is usually taken at home and is simple. It commonly consists of a piece of bread with jelly, and coffee as the beverage.

When you are invited out to eat, you will find that it is as much a social occasion as it is for satisfying the appetite, if not more so. It is common for menus not to have prices listed. For that reason alone, allow the person hosting the meal to set the tone by asking the wait person, "What do you recommend?"

Most Greek meals begin with "finger foods" as appetizers. Rather than ordering these foods as individual servings, several appetizers will be placed in the center of the table for everyone to enjoy.

Beer, wine, and water are typically enjoyed as beverages during both lunch and dinner.

As in most countries, hands should be showing at all times. For that reason, be sure to keep yours at table level, rather than on your lap.

When you are served bread, you will not be offered a bread and butter plate. Thus, feel free to put the bread on the table by your plate, just as your host will do.

Note that Greeks take pride in eating healthy foods that are prepared from fresh ingredients, rather than canned or frozen items. Also, olive oil is a common ingredient with most Greek meals. It helps to be prepared for this and to appreciate it when you are eating.

Conversation

Greeks enjoy lively discussions. With that in mind, prepare to hear what may sound like an argument among friends, family, and co-workers. Bantering and debating are very much part of the national personality.

It won't take you long to find out that Greeks have the gift of gab. This is one reason that dinners will last for hours.

When making "small talk" with a Greek, stick to safe topics, including sports, your home country, art, music, Greek history, and so forth. Avoid talking about Cyprus or any topic relating to Turkey. These are rather touchy subjects because of the cultural, political, historical, and religious tensions that have existed between Greece and Turkey for centuries. Also do not talk about the Greek government. Although Greeks may be heard complaining about how the government handles certain situations, it will be in your best interest to listen, rather than take part in this conversation.

Having "the last word": If you know what's good for you, you should employ your skills of reverse psychology when debating with a Greek—that is, you should allow the person to end the conversation feeling as though he or she has had the last word. Greeks are a very proud people and do better if they feel they have come out ahead.

While Greeks are by nature very private, they may ask you questions that could have you feeling as though your own privacy is being invaded. Nevertheless, if you are asked questions about your salary, your family life, why you're not married, don't have children, and so on, answer them, even if you have to be evasive. These questions may be atypical of what you are accustomed to asking or being asked, but they are part of the Greek culture.

Gestures and Public Manners

Whatever you do, avoid being critical of a Greek in public. They are very proud people and are likely to be offended if you contradict or disagree with them, even if they are wrong.

Patience is not necessarily a virtue that Greeks possess. For that reason, when you are standing in line, don't be surprised if you are pushed or shoved. In turn, you will want to get pushy yourself, especially if you intend to accomplish your goals when you are in Greece.

Although the Greeks are a very proud people, they are likely to behave in a humble manner when receiving compliments. Thus, instead of receiving a "thank you" for your kind words, you may see the person pucker the lips and blow air out of the mouth, a gesture intended to ward off evil spirits. Greeks believe that if they acknowledge the compliment, they may jinx the good implications of your compliment.

When Greeks speak, they use their hands and facial expressions to communicate their message. One way to get on their wavelength is to be animated when speaking.

Be careful! What you may interpret as being a "yes" may really be a "no." In other words, if you see a Greek give an upward nod, it typically will mean "no." On the other hand, if the person moves his or her head from one side to the other, it may mean "yes."

Obscene gestures: When in Greece, be sure to do as the Greeks do—but watch out for certain gestures! In particular, if you want to stay out of trouble, avoid doing the following:

- Making what Westerners interpret as the "okay" sign. The proper Greek way for indicating that things are going well is by putting your thumbs up.
- Waving your hand in greeting as you would in the United States. Like the "okay" sign, this gesture is most offensive in Greece. The way to motion "goodbye" to a Greek is by lifting your index finger as the hand itself remains closed.

Gift-giving Etiquette

When doing business with Greeks, keep in mind that they are a very hospitable nationality. For that reason, in preparation for the possibility that you will be given a gift, be sure to bring a small gift with you to reciprocate. Appropriate presents would be a good bottle of wine or liquor, something from your homeland, or an item for the person's office.

Greetings and Introductions

When first meeting and greeting Greeks, you will receive a handshake. However, after you have had a few meetings with them, don't be surprised if you receive a hug or and even a kiss on each cheek. This nationality is known for its personal warmth.

Be sure to address a Greek person by his or her last name, unless you are requested to do otherwise. This rule especially applies with individuals who are one or more generations older than you, as well as heads of organizations.

When addressing Greek individuals, the terms below should precede a person's last name:

- *Kyrios*: Mr.
- *Kyria*: Mrs.
- *Despinís*: Miss

When addressing a married woman, bear in mind that she may have a different last name than her husband. The reason is that a married woman may opt to keep her family name, rather than assume her husband's name when she marries.

How Decisions Are Made

You will find that a very important part of developing business relationships with the Greeks is becoming acquainted on a personal basis and building rapport. In this respect, it is very common for Greeks to go into business with family members and close friends, based on the trust level they have with each other. Therefore, if you and your contact have a mutual associate, this will certainly help in your negotiations.

Rather than attempting to control the decision-making process, you should allow your Greek partner to set the negotiating tone. Also, recognize that the actual decision will be made on his or her terms—or at least, it should appear that way.

Although the top person has the final say about decisions, remember that it is a group process. Therefore, the relationship you establish with the group as a whole will be an important factor.

Meeting Manners

If you are going to be part of a business meeting with Greeks for the first time, be prepared for a gathering with plenty of lively discussions, many options, and perhaps even heated debates. In other words, it could be a free-for-all!

When you first arrive, be sure to extend a handshake to everyone you meet, and always offer your business card as you greet them. You will probably be offered a beverage after you are asked to sit. Rather than getting down to business right away, there may be a certain amount of small talk, during which topics such as current events may be discussed. You should wait for your Greek contact to initiate the business discussion, so take your cue from him or her.

Prepare to meet several times before a decision is reached. In fact, you may think of the first meeting as laying the foundation, the second as building trust and respect, and the third meeting as the one in which the negotiating process may begin. Keep in mind that driving a hard bargain is part of the normal Greek business relationship.

Once again, allow your Greek contact to save face—or feel as though he or she has had the last word. Besides making the person feel good, you just may win the business.

Punctuality

When doing business in Greece, you will often find yourself waiting for people, even during scheduled meetings. In fact, some may arrive as much as a half hour late. However, whatever you do, do not mention it, as this would be offensive to the proud Greeks.

Double standard or not, be sure that *you* arrive on time. Simply take plenty of reading material so that you can use wisely what might otherwise be considered "down time."

Seating Etiquette

The best way to determine where you should sit is to take your cue from your host, who will gesture where you and the other guests should sit. Typically, your Greek host will invite a female guest to sit to his right, while a male guest will be invited to sit to the Greek hostess's right.

Tipping Tips

While service charges are usually built into the bills at restaurants, in hotels, and in taxi fares, it is appropriate to tip over and above the 10- to 15-percent service charge if you have made a special request or if someone did a favor that was above and beyond the call of duty.

When you are in theaters and have been shown to your seat by an usher, an appropriate tip would be Dr50. If a washroom attendant gives you tissue or a towel for washing your hands, it's appropriate to tip the person Dr100. When a hotel bellman assists you with luggage, tip the person Dr200 per piece of baggage handled. A coatroom clerk should be tipped about Dr200.

Toasting Etiquette

Toasting etiquette dictates that the person initiating the invitation propose the first toast. When a toast is proposed, lift your goblet and join in.

If you are not the last of the big drinkers, simply accept a beer, wine, or *ouzo* (a popular Greek drink), then either avoid drinking it or sip it—it's your choice. If you don't drink it, it will not be replenished. If you prefer to decline the drink, you may "save face" by citing health or religious reasons.

When You Are Invited to a Greek Home

Greeks tend not to plan far in advance, so if an invitation is extended to you to visit someone at home, don't be alarmed by the short notice. Impromptu gatherings with only a few hours notice are very much the norm.

It is appropriate to show up at your host's home at least 15 minutes after the time given in the invitation. If you arrive early or even on time, your host may not be prepared for you.

When you are invited to the home of a Greek, expect to be the beneficiary of the utmost hospitality. However, if you notice an item in the home that you consider lovely or charming, avoid complimenting it, because your host may perceive your sincere compliment as an insinuation that you would like the item, and would then feel obliged to give it to you.

Be sure to go with a modest gift in hand. Just as in many countries, a high quality box of chocolates or flowers are acceptable. If children are part of the family, be sure to acknowledge them by taking a toy.

Rather than overextending your stay, remain only an hour or so after the meal has neared an end, unless you are encouraged to do otherwise.

Women in Business

Unlike in other countries, many Greek women are in high-ranking professional positions. Women traveling to Greece will be given the utmost respect. However, much of it will be earned based on their professional demeanor and dress.

Women should prepare to hear compliments from Greek men that may border on harassment in the United States. It is important to remember that whistling and gawking at women are very much part of the Greek culture. One way for women to discourage such behavior is to simply not acknowledge it.

Whatever You Do...

- Don't follow a Greek's lackadaisical attitude about time. Although you may be kept waiting, two wrongs don't make a right, and you should always be prompt yourself.
- Don't bring up Turkey in your conversation. Many Greeks are bitter over Turkey's occupation of Greece and the casualties that resulted over the years.
- Don't schedule a meeting between 1 and 3 p.m. These are the hours when lunch is usually taken.
- Don't be shocked if you see a Greek customer walking out of the kitchen of a casual restaurant. It is very common for Greeks to actually go into the kitchen to make their food specialty selection.
- Don't be surprised if you are invited to a dinner that begins as late as 9 to 10 p.m.
- Don't be alarmed if sex is discussed in public. Sexual humor is most common.
- Don't think that a riot is going to break out if you hear two or more Greeks talking in loud, excited voices. Greeks are very passionate people and openly express their emotions.
- Don't be surprised if a married woman is addressed by a different last name than the one her husband carries. Greek law dictates that a woman is free to keep her family name, and many do.
- Don't be surprised if you are offered second and third helpings at a meal. Food is an important part of Greek hospitality.

Chapter 11

Hungary

The Republic of Hungary, also known as the Hungarian Republic, is one of several countries in Central Europe formerly under Communist control that is now making a successful transition to a democratic, capitalistic society. A landlocked country, it is bordered by Slovakia on the north, the Ukraine on the northeast, Romania on the east, Serbia on the south, Croatia on the southwest, and Slovenia and Austria on the west. The capital is Budapest, a cultural center in Europe that is divided by the renowned Danube river. Hungary's population consists of approximately 10.3 million inhabitants (nearly 2 million of whom live in Budapest).

More than half the country consists of arable land, making agriculture one of Hungary's primary industries, and also allowing this nation to be self-sufficient in food production. Other major industries include mining. Hungary is one of the world's major producers of bauxite, and also has reserves of coal, iron, and copper. This country also manufactures and exports numerous products, including cement, steel, fertilizers, textiles, electrical products, and motor vehicles, among others. At one time a centralized, socialist economy, in recent years Hungary has adopted increasingly capitalistic plans to improve its status as a viable market economy. This has been due in large part to changes in its governing structure since 1989, which came about as a result of the Soviet Union's weakening political strength and ultimate downfall.

Hungary had long been dominated by other countries, from the Magyars who first settled the region to the Mongols to the Ottoman Turks to the Austrian Habsburgs. In 1867, Austria-Hungary was formed and remained a nation until after World War I, when it was dismembered and divided among numerous other central European countries. The Hungary that remained was comprised of the dominant Magyars. In the hopes of retrieving lost territory, Hungary cooperated with Germany during World War II, and as a result, was placed under Soviet control immediately after the war. Eventually a Communist government led by János Kádár was put into place and would remain in power for 40 years. In 1956, an armed uprising against Stalinism was crushed by Soviet troops. However, by 1990, the Hungarian constitution had been amended and a democratic parliamentary system of government had been established. The country's president is elected by the National Assembly, while the majority party leader is appointed as premier. Despite these advances towards a democratic society, Hungary still has socialist leanings, which are reflected in such programs as their social welfare system.

Hungarians have long been major contributors in the arts and sciences. Among some of the country's better-known native sons are scientists Edward Teller and John von Neumann, and musicians Béla Bartók, Franz Liszt, and Zoltan Kodály. The Hungarians have a deep love for music, which you will hear everywhere, even as you enjoy the spicy foods and fine wines for which Hungary has become famous.

Statistics and Information

Air Travel

When traveling to Hungary's capital, Budapest, you will fly into the Ferigehy Airport. An airport minibus or standard bus are available sources of transportation from the airport into the city.

Country Code

Hungary's country code is 36.

Budapest's city code is 1.

Currency

Hungary's currency is called the *forint* (abbreviated Ft). 100 *fillér* is equivalent to 1 *forint*. Bills are available in denominations of Ft5,000, 1,000, 500, 100, and 50. Coins are in denominations of 50, 20, and 10 *fillér,* as well as Ft200, 100, 50, 20, and 10.

You will receive the best exchange rates at ATM machines located throughout Hungary's cities. Be sure to exchange only what you know you will be using, because changing your Hungarian currency back into U.S. currency may be a challenge. If you do need to exchange Hungarian money, it will be very important to keep the receipts you were given when you exchanged your U.S. dollars or traveler's checks into Hungarian currency. You may also only be able to exchange a maximum of $100 into U.S. currency.

Dates

Hungarians use the European standard format when writing dates, listing the day first, followed by the month, and then the year. For instance, January 31, 2000, would be written as 31/1/00.

Ethnic Makeup

The vast majority of Hungary's population is Magyar. Individuals of German, Slovak, Jewish, and Gypsy descent make up approximately 10 percent of individuals living in Hungary.

Holidays

January 1	New Year's Day
April 4	Liberation Day
May 1	Labour Day
August 20	Constitution Day

October 23	Remembrance Day (Remembrance of the 1956 Revolution and the 1989 establishing of the Republic)
December 25	Christmas Day
December 26	Boxing Day

Language

The official language is Hungarian, spoken by 97 percent of the population. However, most Hungarians are fluent in at least one other language, which is usually German. Travelers will find that English is commonly seen on signs and menus.

Religion

With the end of Communism, the Hungarian government has become supportive of religious freedom. More than 60 percent of Hungarians practice Roman Catholicism, with just under one quarter of the population following the Protestant religion.

Time Zone Differences

Hungary is:

- One hour ahead of Greenwich Mean Time.
- Six hours ahead of U.S. Eastern Standard Time.

Weather

Hungary's climate tends to be moderate and dry. Temperatures are only as high as 73 degrees Fahrenheit in the summer and as low as 25 degrees Fahrenheit in the winter. Rain is most common in the late spring and autumn, with the Transdanubia region receiving the greatest amount.

Etiquette

Business Attire

Business dress in Hungary follows the standard Western professional attire. Men should wear suits with white pressed shirts and ties. Women should wear conservatively cut suits and dresses. The same holds true if you are attending an evening social event or are invited to dinner in a restaurant or home.

Business-card Etiquette

The business card exchange is an important part of Hungarian initial meetings and greetings. For this reason, bring a good supply of cards along to present to those individuals you meet.

It will be appreciated if you have your card translated into Hungarian on the reverse side. Be sure to have your last name printed first, followed by your first name, which is how Hungarians write their names. Doing this will also demonstrate that you've done your homework.

Business Entertaining/Dining

Hungarian dining is rather formal in nature. The continental-style of holding utensils is the norm, with the fork in the left hand and knife in the right.

The meal will officially begin after the host wishes each of his or her guests a hearty appetite. Each course should not begin until the host has given this cue, inviting one and all to eat and/or beginning him- or herself.

More often than not, soup will be the first course served, followed by the main course. It won't take long to find out that Hungarian food is very spicy, rich, and heavy. Paprika is the most common spice, giving Hungarian food a reddish tint and much more flavor than the food in many other Eastern European countries. Soups, stews, meats, and vegetables are fixed a variety of ways and served at most dinners.

You will probably be offered second and third portions. For that reason, take only a small amount of food the first time around, because your Hungarian hosts will consider wasting food to be offensive.

When you have finished eating, place your utensils to the side of your plate.

Conversation

Hungarians are very hospitable people. They welcome visitors from abroad and enjoy conversing with them.

Because family is a major focus of Hungarian life, the people you meet will enjoy talking about their families and hearing about yours. Other topics that will encourage conversation include your travels, the Hungarian food and beverages you have enjoyed, and your experiences while in Hungary. Topics to avoid include politics and religion.

Hungarians have been taught to play down compliments. For that reason, don't be surprised if the compliment you offer is not accepted very graciously.

When making conversation, be sure that you say what you mean and mean what you say. Frequently, Westerners extend invitations as part of small talk that Hungarians take as gospel. For that reason, if you say, "Let's get together sometime," be sure to follow through by calling to schedule a time to do just that.

Gestures and Public Manners

It is considered good manners to have your feet facing the ground, rather than to have the soles of your shoes showing.

While the peace or victory sign is not commonly used, when it is used, be sure your index and middle finger are out with your palm facing outward. It is considered an obscene gesture if your palm is facing toward you.

If you want to indicate that something is going well, do not make the "okay" sign as you would in the United States, because this is also considered an obscene gesture in Hungary.

Gift-giving Etiquette

While gift-giving is not a common ritual during initial meetings in some countries, it *is* part of the Hungarian way, both in the business and social arenas. It is wise to also have a gift in hand after business deals have been agreed upon, as a way of showing your appreciation for the confidence your Hungarian contacts have in you and the product or service you represent.

Recommended gifts include items brought with you from your homeland. Other suggested items are cigarettes, liquor, and/or a desk accessory.

Greetings and Introductions

Handshakes are the most common way of greeting and meeting others for the first time. Once you have established rapport with Hungarians, men may add a kiss on the cheek to other men along with the handshake. After women have established rapport with each other, they greet each other by embracing and bestowing a kiss on each cheek.

When meeting women, men should wait for them to initiate a handshake, rather than first extending their hands.

Titles are considered an important part of a Hungarian greeting. For that reason, rather than being addressed by his or her last name, anyone who has a professional title, such as doctor, teacher, engineer, architect, president, and so on, should be addressed by the professional title followed by *úr*, which is the equivalent of Mr., or *kisasszony*, which is the Hungarian term used for both Mrs. and Ms. It is important to note that lawyers are also referred to as doctors.

Do not address a Hungarian by his or her first name alone until you have been given permission to do so.

Hierarchy Is Important

Unlike in many other countries, you will find that there is not much emphasis placed on rank in Hungary. However, hierarchy will play different roles in different Hungarian companies, which means you will need to do some judgment work. Often, employees of lesser rank will have some impact on your success, because many executives will rely on the opinions of their subordinates when deciding whether to develop a relationship with you and the organization you represent. For that reason, it is important to cultivate relationships with everyone you meet.

How Decisions Are Made

While decisions may be made by the person(s) with whom you will be meeting, these individuals may also get input from others within their company. For that reason, decision-making may be a long process and will require patience on your part.

When a decision is made, be sure to get the specifics in writing.

Meeting Manners

One of the first things you will want to do is to arrange for a good interpreter to be part of your meeting. It will be especially helpful to hire one that has a working knowledge of the type of industry you represent. A hotel business center may be able to assist you in locating the person who can best represent you.

Hungarian meetings usually begin with an offer of beverages, followed by small talk. Once it is time to get down to business, you will be expected to present your information in a clear and concise manner. Charts, graphs, and other written material will be helpful to the individuals present. Because the majority of people present may not have a working knowledge of English, be sure to have your material translated into Hungarian.

Punctuality

Arrive on time for all business meetings. If you are invited to a social engagement in your Hungarian contact's home, however, it is acceptable to arrive within 30 minutes from the time you are given.

Seating Etiquette

Traditional seating will place the host and the hostess at opposite ends of the table. The male guest of honor will be seated to the right of the hostess and the female guest of honor to the right of the host.

Tipping Tips

Servers should be tipped a minimum of 10 percent of the bill. Porters should receive 10 *forint* for each bag handled. Taxi drivers should be tipped 10 to 15 percent of the fare. Bathroom attendants should be given a few *forints* for their assistance.

Toasting Etiquette

Many Hungarians begin social meals with schnapps or wine. Wine is a commonly consumed beverage in Hungary. *Pálinka* is another favorite Hungarian beverage. It is a strong, distilled brandy made from a combination of fruits.

It is the responsibility of the guest of honor to propose the toast. One appropriate toast salutes the health of the individuals present. Another expresses appreciation to the host and hostess for the hospitality they have offered.

When You Are Invited to a Hungarian Home

Hungarian families often live in small flats. Because space is limited and it is common for a few generations to live together, dinner invitations may be the exception rather than the rule.

No matter how poorly maintained the outside of a building may be, Hungarians compensate for it with their personal belongings (furniture, carpets, artwork, and so on). Be sure to acknowledge their good taste in decor.

When you are invited to a Hungarian's home, you should take something to the hostess. Flowers (other than chrysanthemums, which are associated with funerals) make a suitable gift. If you are going to be staying with the family for awhile, be sure to bring other gifts (for example, liquor for men, perfume for women, and toys for children).

Women in Business

Businesswomen from abroad will feel both comfortable and safe conducting business in Hungary. Hungarian women are commonly seen in certain industries, such as retail and tourism.

It will be important for Western women who initiate a meal invitation to understand that Hungarian men will want to pick up the check.

Whatever You Do...

- Don't schedule your business trip during the months of July or August, as well as December and January. These are popular months for Hungarians to go on holiday.
- Don't expect business transactions to move quickly. The Hungarian government and the country's businesses are slow to develop relationships.
- Don't leave your passport with hotel clerks. Allow them to write down the necessary information they need in your presence instead, and make sure your passport is returned to you.
- Don't point at others, because it is considered rude.
- Don't use your left hand for eating. This hand is considered taboo.
- Don't order food at restaurants without seeing a menu with the cost of the item(s).
- Don't expect Hungarians to stand in an orderly line while waiting for a train or bus. Pushing and shoving will be the order of the day.

Chapter 12

Ireland

The Republic of Ireland constitutes five-sixths of the island lying in the Atlantic Ocean to the west of the larger island of Great Britain. The remainder, occupying the northeast section of the island, is Northern Ireland, which is part of the United Kingdom. Between Ireland and Great Britain lies the Irish Sea and St. George's Channel. The country's population consists of more than 3.5 million inhabitants, one-third of whom live in Dublin, the nation's capital.

Slightly more than half the size of New York State, the "Emerald Isle" is a land of mountains, low hills, lakes, and beautiful countryside dotted with the ruins of ancient Irish civilizations and through which the River Shannon flows freely. Only about an eighth of Ireland's land is arable, but what there is is quite fertile. There are also many meadows and pastures—grasslands that support the raising of livestock. Agriculture, chemical industries, and services form the greatest part of Ireland's economy. Among its biggest exports are livestock and livestock products, potatoes, cereals, poultry, and sugar beets. Despite Ireland's location, fishing is not a major industry. The country depends greatly on tourism as a source of income, with most tourists coming from the United Kingdom, the United States, and western Europe. The government is also encouraging industrial development from other countries in an effort to ease unemployment.

Ireland's government is a parliamentary democracy headed by a prime minister. The head of state is an elected president who serves for a term of seven years. Ireland's history is pockmarked by the tension and strife caused by Great Britain's claims on the lands and the imposition of the Anglican religion on a predominantly Catholic population. Irish Protestants eventually took control and began agitating to be released from the English dominion and allowed home rule. This agitating continued over centuries, through open revolts and the devastating famine of 1846 to 1851, and into the 20th century. In 1920, the British government divided Ireland into northern and southern sections, and official independence was granted on December 6, 1921. In 1937, a new constitution ratified the creation of Eire, or the Republic of Southern Ireland. Meanwhile, the "Troubles" caused by religious differences and resistance to English rule have continued to wreak havoc in Northern Ireland.

A nation of storytellers, Ireland has a rich literary heritage, although its authors have achieved their fame chiefly in the English language, rather than the native Gaelic. Among this nation's best-known favorite sons are George Bernard Shaw, Oscar Wilde, James Joyce, Jonathan Swift, William Butler Yeats, Samuel Beckett, and most recently, Frank McCourt. Ireland was also the first in the world to see a performance of Handel's *Messiah*.

Statistics and Information

Air Travel

The Dublin airport is less than 7 miles from the center of the city. A cost-efficient way to travel to Dublin from the airport is on the express bus. It leaves every hour on the half hour and the ride can take as long as 30 minutes.

Country Code

Ireland's country code is 353.

Dublin's city code is 1.

Currency

While the currency of Ireland is called the *punt*, it is most widely known as the Irish *pound* (£). One *pound* is equivalent to 100 *pence* (p). Bills are in denominations of £ 50, 20, 10, 5, and 1. Coins come in denominations of 50, 20, 10, and 5 *pence*.

Banks and the bureaux de change are the best places to exchange your currency.

Dates

Dates are written in the European style, with the day preceding the month, followed by the year. For instance, December 22, 2010, would be written as 22/12/10.

Ethnic Makeup

Ireland is the home of the Irish. While nearly the entire population is of Celtic descent, less than 2 percent is of English and Welsh heritage.

Holidays and National Celebrations

The following is a list of Ireland's religious holidays and national celebrations. Because these are official holidays, it is wise not to schedule meetings for these days.

January 1	New Year's Day
March 17	St. Patrick's Day
Late March/ April	Good Friday, Easter
First Monday of June	June Bank Holiday
First Monday of August	August Bank Holiday
October 31	Halloween
December 25	Christmas Day
December 26	St. Stephen's Day

Language

Gaelic, which is most commonly known as "Irish," is the country's official language, although it is mainly spoken in areas along the western seaboard and rural areas. English is the most frequently spoken language elsewhere in the country, especially in the urban areas, which makes communication easy for Americans doing business in Ireland.

Religion

Religion is a very important part of the Irish culture. The vast majority of the population is Roman Catholic, while less than 5 percent of Ireland's population is either Presbyterian or Anglican.

Time Zone Differences

Ireland is:

- On the same time as Greenwich Mean Time (and Great Britain).
- Five hours ahead of U.S. Eastern Standard Time.

Weather

Ireland's climate is predictable and constant. While it drizzles nearly every day, the country's temperatures stay the same, in a generally mild range. Temperatures in the summer are typically in the 60s and usually drop no lower than the mid-40s in the winter.

Etiquette

Business Attire

While the Irish take pride in the way they dress, they do not place the same emphasis on attire as many other Europeans do. For instance, clothes with designer labels, ornate jewelry, and other ostentatious garb are not an integral part of the Irish culture. In fact, anything that flaunts wealth is considered a turnoff to the Irish.

Business attire should be modest and comprised of conservative colors rather than bold ones. Both men and women from abroad will do well wearing clothes made of wool and tweed. Businessmen should wear suits with starched white shirts and ties. Women will be taken more seriously by wearing suits or blazers with conservative blouses and skirts. While slacks may be fine for more casual environments, they should not be worn in business settings.

In addition to the above garb, a raincoat and umbrella will come in handy.

Business-card Etiquette

Although a specific business-card etiquette does not exist in Ireland, it is still wise to take several with you and exchange them when it seems appropriate. The majority of Irish speak English, so there is no need to translate them into Gaelic.

Business Entertaining/Dining

Entertaining during lunch is a common way of socializing. Getting together during a meal at a restaurant is one of the most popular ways of breaking bread with clients. If business is to be discussed, lunch rather than dinner is the time to do so.

On the other hand, dinners are social gatherings at which spouses may be included. If you would like to invite your spouse, be sure to also extend the invitation to your Irish contact's spouse.

You will find that potatoes are a very important starch for the Irish. You also will find that meat and fish are commonly eaten proteins. Frequently, fresh vegetables will round out the meal.

Contrary to many other European countries, there is much less formality during meals in Ireland. Utensils are handled the continental way, by retaining the fork in the left hand and the knife in the right hand at all times. (In other words, use the fork in your left hand to transport the food to your mouth, rather than putting your utensils down after cutting and transferring the fork to your right hand.)

One thing that is unique to an Irish table setting is that bread is not served at any time during the meal. There will be what looks like a bread and butter plate on the table—but don't think of it as such! Instead, this plate is for boiled potato skins, which are not to be eaten.

It is best to adopt the "clean plate club" school of thought to avoid being considered wasteful. Thus, only place on your plate what you are able to eat.

Beverage etiquette: Just as wine is a commonly enjoyed beverage in France, beer is the favored drink in Ireland. One of the most commonly consumed beers is Guinness Stout, which could almost be considered Ireland's national beverage. Because enjoying a drink is very much part of the Irish culture, not partaking in the ritual could offend your Irish contact. If you prefer not to drink, however, it will be accepted if your explanation focuses on health or religious reasons.

Conversation

You can rest assured that almost any Irish individual you meet will be very friendly. Because the Irish are "people people" by nature, you can also be sure that they will ask you a lot of questions about yourself.

Recommended topics of conversation include the parts of Ireland you've visited and Irish sports.

Topics that you want to avoid include religion, Irish politics, and any controversial social issue in Ireland.

Gestures and Public Manners

The Irish are rather low-contact people who value their personal space and will expect the same of you. If you speak in an animated manner, tone down your hand gestures as a way of mirroring their body language.

As in Russia, the peace sign, or "V" made by extending the index and middle finger with the palm facing out, is an obscene gesture in Ireland and should not be used.

Queuing: Lines are the name of the game in Ireland. As in the United States, people are willing to stand in line patiently, rather than pushing and shoving in front of others. Lines can even be a social occasion, so when you find yourself in one, take advantage of it by making small talk with those in front of you and behind you.

You may be surprised to receive a compliment about your conservative appearance and actions. Any behavior that plays down attention to yourself will be considered proper in the eyes of the Irish. By maintaining a low-keyed manner in both your personal and your professional presentations, you will be on your way to thinking and acting the way the Irish expect you to be.

Gift-giving Etiquette

Although the gift exchange is not a common ritual when first meeting the Irish, it is an accepted and appreciated part of establishing relations once a business deal has been firmed up. Gifts should be practical items that are conservative in price. Suggested items include quality pens, items for a desk, and books about your homeland.

When you are presented with a gift, be sure to thank the giver and proceed to open it in front of him or her.

Greetings and Introductions

When meeting the Irish, the proper greeting is to shake hands and extend a warm greeting as you maintain eye contact. Handshakes should also be exchanged upon departure.

When meeting a woman, men should wait for her to extend her hand before initiating a handshake.

Proper forms of address: Irish names follow the same order as those in the United States—using a person's last name with the proper courtesy title of Mr., Mrs., or Miss. If the person has a professional or educational title such as vice president or professor, it is proper to address him or her as such. You will find that the Irish are not big on formalities and that many people address one another by their first names. Although you will likely be doing this yourself within a short period of time, wait to be invited before addressing anyone by his or her first name.

How Decisions are Made

When you are waiting for a business decision to be made, prepare to be patient. When it comes to making business decisions, it is common for the Irish to plan for the short haul. Frequently, decisions are even made on a day-to-day basis. The Irish are also very practical. For that reason, be sure the information you provide is of a realistic nature.

As in most countries, there is a respected hierarchy in Ireland. The person who has been given the title of managing director will have the final say on a decision.

Meeting Manners

When it comes to the work ethic, you will find that the Irish are at the top of the list. Besides being hard workers, they are very good businesspeople. On occasion they may appear to be remiss about meeting deadlines. When this happens, keep in mind that it may be part of their overall style.

If you are invited out for a round of golf, know that you will be doing more than engaging in the sport—you will also be laying the foundation for a long-term business relationship. Golf is a favorite pastime, so it is commonly part of rapport-building with the Irish.

Punctuality

Although individuals of other nationalities may make remarks about an Irishman's concept of time, be sure to avoid doing so yourself. You will find the Irish to be more casual and relaxed than Germans or other Western Europeans. As an individual from abroad, however, you should always arrive on time for your business appointments. If you are kept waiting for even 30 minutes, don't acknowledge it with any remarks at all.

Seating Etiquette

Because there are no strict rules governing seating etiquette, be sure to take the cue from the person(s) hosting the meal regarding where you should sit.

Tipping Tips

Restaurants usually include a service charge in the bill, so you will not be expected to leave an additional tip. When one has not been included, leave a tip of 10 to 15 percent. Note that you will not be expected to leave a tip for service people at pubs.

Tipping etiquette encourages you to give hotel porters approximately 25 *pence* per bag. While chambermaids may be left a *punt* or so, if you have made special requests, such as asking for extra towels, be sure to leave a bit more. When riding in a taxi, a proper tip for a short distance is 50p. If your ride takes a quarter of an hour to half an hour, be sure to tip £1.

Toasting Etiquette

When beer is enjoyed, you can be sure that a toast will follow. Allow your Irish host to initiate the first toast, upon which you may propose one in return. A common Irish toast that may be said as your glass is being lifted is the word *"Slainte."*

Toilet Etiquette

Unlike some other European countries, public toilets are available in Ireland. Men should keep their eyes open for a door labeled "*Fir*" which is the "Men's Room," while women should look for one with the word "*Mna*" or "Women's Room" on the door.

When You Are Invited to an Irish Home

The Irish enjoy entertaining in their homes and will make you feel welcome, like part of the family. Besides family members, you may also enjoy the company of priests in the homes to which you have been invited.

Be sure to go with a small gift in hand—flowers, wine, or chocolate for the hostess are best. If children will be part of the gathering, be sure to remember them with a gift, as well.

Following dinner, your Irish contact may offer you coffee and perhaps even an after-dinner drink. Rather than leaving within an hour or so following dinner, which is considered acceptable in many European countries, recognize that the evening may just be beginning and you are likely to stay into the wee hours. With chatting, singing, and even telling stories to each other, the evening will be very enjoyable.

Women in Business

Although Irish women are climbing the business ladder slowly yet surely, few women are a part of the higher ranks in this country where male chauvinism still predominates. (Note, however, that a woman, Mrs. McAleese, is currently Ireland's president.)

One way businesswomen from abroad can be assured of being taken seriously is by adopting a professional appearance and demeanor at all times.

When hosting a business meal, women should make a point of ordering juice or a soda. If they prefer to drink beer, however, a smaller quantity should be requested than the full pint ordered by their male counterparts.

Whatever You Do...

- Don't schedule meetings for the months of July or August. These months are a favorite time of the year for the Irish to go on holiday.
- Don't ask someone for a "ride." Instead, the proper term to use is "lift."
- Don't dress in an ostentatious manner, but wear clothes that are more conservative in color and style.
- Don't assume that a "maybe" answer means "yes." The Irish, like many Asians, do not like to tell anyone "no." You will find they will say a myriad of pleasantries, rather than coming straight out and refusing something.

- Don't lump Ireland or Irish culture in with Great Britain or the English. The Irish are adamant about their independence from English rule. Any generalizations will severely hurt your business relationships.
- Don't be surprised if you have only cold water in your shower. Many hotels save money and energy by turning off the hot water during the day. Check with your hotel's concierge and plan your showers accordingly.
- Don't turn your nose up at Irish beer. Ireland is known for its outstanding breweries. Flatter your host and ask for a recommendation as to what pubs are the best and what beer you should sample.

Chapter 13

Italy

The boot shape of the European peninsula known as the Republic of Italy is one of the most familiar sights in the world. A renowned center of art, fashion, food, and wine, most of this country is surrounded by the various waters of the Mediterranean Sea—the Adriatic Sea on the east coast, the Ionian Sea on the southeast, and the Tyrrhenian Sea on the west. Nearby, at the toe of Italy's boot and in the Mediterranean Sea to the west, are found the Italian islands of Sicily and Sardinia. The Campione, located in Switzerland, and the states of San Marino and the Vatican City are also considered to be part of Italy, whose northernmost boundaries adjoin France, Switzerland, Austria, and Slovenia (known as the Alpine Arc). Its peninsula lies across from Croatia and the Adriatic Sea and almost touches the coast of Africa.

Italy is a country that is rich in history, tradition, and culture—so much so that its vast contributions to Western civilization are impossible to describe in full. It is the birthplace of countless artists, authors, musicians, explorers, politicians, philosophers, scientists, filmmakers, and other great thinkers whose influence has been felt throughout the world. This is the home of Da Vinci, Michelangelo, Dante, Donatello, Rossini, Verdi, Fellini, and hundreds of other great names in the arts and sciences. Italy's language has affected numerous other languages, and its people are renowned for their passion for life, as well as for their devotion to the Catholic faith.

Italy has frequently fallen on hard times since the days the Roman Empire ruled much of the world. Subject to frequent invasions and occupations, the country was often divided and subdivided, and it did not achieve unification until 1870. Allied with Germany for most of World War II, in 1943 the Italians deposed their Fascist leader, Benito Mussolini, and joined the fight against the Nazis. A republic was proclaimed in 1946. Since then, the country has experienced much political and social unrest, going through numerous coalition governments and waging an ongoing battle against terrorism. However, in recent years, Italy has enjoyed more political stability and solid industrial growth that made it the world's fifth biggest economic power. Fishing, forestry, agriculture, manufacturing, and tourism are among its biggest industries.

The Italian government owns and operates a large portion of the businesses in this country, although there are also many privately owned companies. The government itself is a republic, with multiple political parties and a bicameral parliament. The country's president, who is elected by an electoral college, appoints the prime minister, who directs the country's affairs with the assistance of a Council of Ministers. There have been numerous coalition governments over the years, often dominated by the Communist Party, which has lost a great deal of power in more recent years. Italy is also a member of NATO.

Statistics and Information

Air Travel

Italy has two major international airports that serve the majority of visitors from abroad. The Leonardo Da Vinci International Airport is located about 30 km from Rome's center. Trains are available directly from the terminals to the main station in the city. Milan's Malpensa Airport is located 50 km from the city. It provides shuttles to the main train station in Milan.

Country Code

Italy's country code is 39.

City codes include:

- 81 for Capri.
- 31 for Como.
- 55 for Florence.
- 6 for Rome.
- 184 for San Remo.
- 942 for Taormina.
- 40 for Trieste.
- 11 for Turin.
- 41 for Venice.

Currency

Italian currency is called the *lira* (L). Notes come in L100,000, 50,000, 20,000, 10,000, 5,000, 2,000, and 1,000. Coins come in denominations of L500, 200, 100, and 50.

You will find the best exchange rates at the electronic exchange machines located in the airport, train stations, and banks.

Dates

Dates are written in the standard European manner, with the day written before the month, followed by the year. For example, January 30, 1999, should be written as 30/1/99.

Ethnic Makeup

The majority of Italy's population is Italian by descent. Very small percentages of Sloven-Italians, French, and Germans live in the northern part of Italy, while small percentages of Albanians and Greek Italians reside in southern Italy.

Holidays and National Celebrations

The following is a list of Italy's celebrated holidays. Because many of them are national holidays, you should avoid scheduling meetings for these days.

January 1	New Year's Day
January 6	Epiphany
March 8	Women's Pride Day
March/April	Easter
April 25	Liberation Day
May 1	Labor Day
August 15	Assumption
November 1	All Saints' Day
December 8	Immaculate Conception
December 25	Christmas Day
December 26	Boxing Day/St. Stephen's Day

Note: The month of August is an especially popular time of year for Italians to go on holiday. Therefore, you should avoid scheduling meetings during this month.

Language

Although Italian is the official language of Italy, it is important to note that Italians speak many dialects, based on the part of the country where they live. English is also a commonly spoken second language. You may even hear a minority of Italians who are fluent in French or German, especially if their business dealings are with individuals from France or Germany. There is a small German-speaking minority located in the north.

Religion

The vast majority of Italians—more than 90 percent—practices Roman Catholicism. The remainder is either Jewish or Protestant.

You won't have to be in Italy long to determine that religion is a very important part of everyday life in this country.

Time Zone Differences

Italy is:

- One hour ahead of Greenwich Mean Time.
- Six hours ahead of U.S. Eastern Standard Time.

Weather

The majority of the country experiences Mediterranean temperatures year round, with hot summers and rainy winters. However, the weather in the north near the Alpine arc can be more variable, making for colder, wetter winters. The southern regions are extremely dry, and Sicily and Sardinia tend to be even milder and dryer.

Etiquette

Business Attire

The key to dressing appropriately in Italy is to make sure that what you wear consists of excellent quality fabrics, such as lightweight wools and silks. Italians love to dress in the best, and they will notice what you wear. Italy is home to many top designers who have created internationally recognized fashions (such as Ferragamo, Versace, and Valentino).

What you know will be important, but the way you dress will be considered even more important in Italy. This includes the accessories you wear: high-quality silk scarves, jewelry, shoes, and so on. Designer clothing and elegant jewelry are worn by most people in business, regardless of their positions.

While men should dress in dark suits, especially during the winter months, an elegant suit or dress is appropriate attire for women.

Note: Shorts are not permitted in churches, and women will be expected to have their arms and heads covered.

Business-card Etiquette

While exchanging business cards is important, in Italy this ritual is slightly different from other European countries. For instance, a business card should be given to others only in business environments. Avoid handing out your card in a social environment. As an alternative, you may use a calling card, which includes your name, where you live, and your personal telephone number.

Business cards are seen as a way of developing a rapport with others, rather than as marketing tools. For that reason, present only one card to each person during the initial meeting, rather than during subsequent get-togethers.

Although many Italians understand English, it is recommended that you get your business card translated into Italian on the reverse side.

Business Entertaining/Dining

You can be sure that you will eat very well when you are in Italy. Because these meals are such a feast in themselves, Italians tend to focus on the food, rather than the business at hand. For that reason, you should keep business-related conversation out of the restaurants.

Italian lunches are the main meal of the day. Italians are very family-oriented and frequently go home for two-hour stretches to spend this meal with their families. They are equally generous with their time on business lunches. Thus, if you are invited to a business lunch, prepare to be there for a minimum of two hours.

Delicious bread is certain to be part of every meal. However, bread plates are not the norm, so prepare to put yours on the table. In addition, bread is typically not served with butter, but rather with olive oil that is made available for dipping.

In Italy, food may be served "family-style," where guests serve themselves from community platters that are set on the table. When this is the case, observe how platters are passed around to others, and act accordingly.

You will undoubtedly be offered a second helping. However, don't appear too anxious by accepting "seconds" the first time it is offered. If the host insists, then it is safe to accept more.

As with other Europeans, Italians follow the continental-style when using utensils—that is, the fork should be held in your left hand and the knife in the right. Unlike the "American" style, keep both utensils in these hands, with the fork tines down and the serrated edge of the knife facing the plate when taking food to your mouth.

Contrary to what most people raised in the United States have been taught, your hands should be visible above the table and should not be placed below it. In fact, it is considered rude for hands not to be showing at the table.

Another difference between eating in the United States and Italy is that utensils are commonly used when eating cheeses and fruits (except for those that are on a branch or stem, such as grapes or cherries). These are common desserts in Italy.

Pasta p's and q's: Always twirl pasta, rather than cutting it. If you are offered a pasta spoon (which will be more common in southern Italy), use this second utensil to assist in securing strands on the fork.

Beverage etiquette: Wine is an integral part of both lunch and dinner in Italy. Although Italians savor wine and are known for producing some of the best in the world, they also are very conscientious drinkers. Be sure to gauge your intake so that you control the wine, rather than letting it control you.

If you are not a big drinker, don't refuse the wine that is offered to you, because you will need it for any toasts that may be proposed during the course of the meal. If you prefer to limit your wine intake, simply sip it, rather than drinking it. This way, it will not be replenished.

Conversation

Italians love to engage in lively, expressive conversations. Good small talk openers include acknowledging the beautiful landscape, the delicious cuisine, or the hospitality you have received in the particular region you are visiting. The subjects of travel, art, and wine are also good conversation starters. However, it is important to be diplomatic when expressing your views.

While inquiring about a person's job may be perfectly acceptable in some countries, this is not the case in Italy. Other topics to avoid include religion, Italian politics, taxes, and the Mafia.

When both listening and talking, be sure to maintain eye contact. If you don't, Italians may perceive you as disinterested.

Gestures and Public Manners

Italian hands "talk" as much as the mouth. You should mirror this and use expressive body language to emphasize what you are saying. However, you will want to be aware of certain gestures that are considered offensive in Italy. For instance:

- Extending the index and little finger at someone means you wish them bad luck.
- Placing your hand on your stomach means you dislike someone.
- Two obscene hand gestures you should avoid are slapping your raised arm above the elbow and thumbing your nose.

Italians are a very animated people. Besides using their hands when they talk, they embrace people whom they know as a form of greeting. It is also common to see individuals walking together holding hands or walking arm in arm. This includes men with women, men with men, and women with women. These people may be taking part in the evening ritual known as the *passeggiata*, a time when friends and family make a point of dressing up to stroll around visiting, conversing, taking coffee, and relaxing.

Queuing: A little push or a harmless shove is what you will probably receive from Italians when you are standing in line. Because this culture operates more in an emotional vein, queuing is far from commonplace.

Gift-giving Etiquette

Gift-giving is an important part of business relationships in Italy. Although gifts are not commonly exchanged during preliminary meetings, it is always a good idea to have small gifts with you in case you are presented with one.

Italians are very generous in their giving. Your gifts should be of fine quality and wrapped elegantly. Gifts should be opened as soon as they have been given, rather than doing so in private.

Choose high-quality gifts. Bottles of fine liquors, books, and desk accessories are safe bets.

What to avoid:

- Never give anything that appears inexpensive.
- Sharp items are a sign of negative feelings.
- If you are giving flowers, give an odd number and leave chrysanthemums out of the arrangement, because they are reminiscent of funerals.
- The color purple is synonymous with bad luck.
- Finally, gift wrapping with black and gold should not be used, because these colors are equated with mourning.

Greetings and Introductions

Italians are, by nature, high-contact people—that is, physical contact is important to them, beginning with the greeting. While the traditional handshake is common, you may see an "air kiss" or a "brush" on each cheek exchanged between friends and perhaps even acquaintances. Be prepared to receive and respond to whichever comes your way.

Women should initiate a handshake with men and expect to get either a handshake or a kiss on the hand in return. Handshakes or some form of contact occur not only when you meet someone, but also when you are departing, no matter what length of time you have spent with the person.

When introducing others, the pecking order should be followed. Introduce the higher-ranking or more senior person first, followed by the more junior individuals. As in most countries, you should stand up when you shake hands.

Proper forms of address: Follow the formal rule of addressing others by their last names until you've been asked to do otherwise. If the person holds an engineering, doctorate, or other degree, be sure to address the person using his or her professional title, followed by the last name. Otherwise, the equivalent of Mr., Mrs., or Ms. should be used, as follows:

- *Signor:* Mr.
- *Signora:* Mrs.
- *Signorina:* Mrs.

Hierarchy Is Important

Although many people will be involved in business meetings, there will be a chain of command that is observed. You may see this based on where people are seated and the respect that is shown to the head honcho, who may be the managing director or company director. It will be important to understand this chain of command, both when meeting and greeting and when paying your respects to the most senior person first.

You will also learn that you are who your family is. For that reason alone, individuals who come from a well-respected family are more likely to have risen to decision-making roles.

How Decisions Are Made

The basis of a business relationship depends on whether your Italian contact likes and trusts you. Thus, decisions in Italy are much more commonly made on intuition, rather than logic. Italians are also very attracted to people who are inventive and imaginative.

Note that from the moment you first meet an individual representing an Italian organization until negotiations come to a close, several months, if not a year or more, may pass. For that reason, be patient, rather than attempting to rush the process. In addition, do not attempt to "close" a deal while you are meeting with Italians face-to-face, because most decisions are made behind closed doors by several people, rather than by just the head person.

Meeting Manners

Do not expect any conclusions to be drawn or final decisions to be made at the meetings you attend in Italy. While there will be plenty of active discussion, this is the time to lay the facts and figures on the table that the Italians can then take and discuss among themselves.

Be punctual in your arrival time, and be sure to acknowledge each person with a greeting—for example, "*Buon giorno*" ("Good morning") or "*Buona sera*" ("Good afternoon" or "Good evening"). Use the proper form of address (see Greetings and Introductions) and offer a handshake.

Italian meetings usually begin with small talk, which is an important part of conversing in Italy. Be sure to stay abreast of Italy's current events, because this topic is often one of interest.

If you are talking, don't be offended if you are interrupted more than once. This is the Italian way—they consider it perfectly acceptable to jump into a conversation before another person has finished speaking.

If you are even slightly fluent in Italian, try to use the words you know as much as possible. This will show your contacts that you are making an effort to speak their language, which they will appreciate.

Your Italian associates may be fluent in English. However, consider the degree of fluency. If you are presenting important information that merits an interpreter, it will be well worth the investment.

Prepare well for your presentation and have all your charts and supporting materials ready. Because Italians are animated by nature, be sure to include facial expressions, hand gestures, and voice inflections in the delivery of your presentation. This will not only help you to be a better speaker, it will also create a higher interest level for those viewing your presentation.

Punctuality

Italian businesspeople see time as money. For that reason, it is important to always be punctual and to start meetings on time. However, keep in mind that two wrongs don't make a right. If you're kept waiting a few minutes, be patient and don't complain. It is far less acceptable to keep your Italian hosts waiting than for you to be kept waiting yourself.

Seating Etiquette

Seating etiquette in Italy follows an arrangement that differs from many other European countries. Rather than sitting at either end of the table, the individuals hosting the meal sit in the middle, across from each other. The most senior female guest sits to the immediate left of the person hosting the meal, while the most senior male guest is seated to the immediate left of the host's spouse.

Taxi Etiquette

Before getting into a taxi, let the driver know your destination and then ask what the fare will be. By checking the facts beforehand, you will know what to expect. It will also prevent a driver from overcharging you.

Check with your hotel bellman to ensure that you are paying the appropriate taxi fare and not being overcharged.

Tipping Tips

Tipping is very much the norm in Italy, in recognition of those individuals who render a service for you.

Restaurants usually include a 15-percent gratuity as part of the bill. However, if your service happens to be particularly outstanding, leave an additional 5 to 10 percent for your wait person.

Hotel attendants should be tipped an additional amount over and above the gratuity already included in the hotel bill. For instance, give bellhops 1,200 to 1,500 *lire* per bag. Chambermaids, doormen, and theater ushers should be given L1,000. Washroom attendants should be given about L100, while coatroom clerks should be given triple that amount. Although a tip will be built into the taxi fare, it is still appropriate to tip an additional 10 percent.

Toasting Etiquette

Italian toasting etiquette dictates that the equivalent of "To your health" be said as wine goblets are raised for a toast. The most common term you may hear for this toast is "*Salute*."

Toilet Etiquette

When nature calls, you will want to find a door marked "W.C." While you may not find them in restaurants, they will be more available in cafés and hotels.

Bathrooms designated for men will have "*Uomini*" or "*Signori*" on the doors. Women's restrooms will be labeled as "*Donne*" or "*Signore*." Because tissue may not be provided, it is best to be prepared and bring some along with you.

When You Are Invited to an Italian Home

Most business entertaining will be done in restaurants. However, an occasional invitation to the home of an Italian associate may be extended to you. If you receive such an invitation, you should arrive at least a quarter of an hour later than the time you were asked to be there. By doing so, you will be on Italian social time.

Be sure to show your appreciation for the invitation by taking a small gift, such as candy or a bouquet of flowers (in an uneven number). While the hostess will appreciate almost any variety of flowers, stay away from chrysanthemums, which are equated with mourning.

The evening will begin with small talk over white wine and appetizers. Follow your hostess's cues as to when it is appropriate to seat yourself and begin eating.

Women in Business

In the past, it was not the norm for Italian women to have jobs outside the home. Rather, a woman's main responsibility was to focus on caring for her family. Today more than a third of Italy's women do the balancing act of work and home. Some find this to be rather challenging and resort to doing one or the other so that they can do it well.

Although the Italian business arena consists primarily of men, you will find a few women in high positions. This will be especially true for those who are part of family-owned businesses. There are several very powerful Italian women who are terrific role models for females in the fashion industry.

When addressing Italian women on a last-name basis, it is important to know that they commonly use their birth name in the business arena and their married name in their personal lives. If you are unsure of the proper way to address a person, listen for cues from others who are on the same level as you are with this person.

Although women from abroad will be treated with respect, they should recognize that Italian men are charmers and may be slightly flirtatious, and they should accept this as the Italian way. One way to encourage proper respect is by looking and acting professional at all times.

Whatever You Do...

- Don't take your hotel room key with you when you leave the property. Just as in many European countries, Italian protocol dictates that you to stop at the front desk and leave your key there before departing the hotel.
- Don't drink too much. Although wine is consumed with gusto by Italians, they drink for pleasure, without letting the wine get the best of them, and they will expect you to do the same.
- Don't ignore "X" signs you see posted. This means that photos should not be taken in that location.

- Don't say "Hello" when answering a phone in Italy. Instead, use the appropriate Italian greeting of "*Pronto*."
- Don't be surprised if you are served salad following the entrée, rather than before it.
- Don't ask people what they do for a living. This is seen as an intrusion into Italians' private lives. Wait until this information is offered to you.
- Don't address anyone by his or her last name if the person holds a title such as doctor, lawyer, engineer, or so on. Instead, use *Signor*, *Signora*, or *Signorina,* followed by the person's title.

Advice From the Experts

"No casual dressing. Also, be ready for conversation about politics, soccer, food, and wines."

—Enzo Ferraris, Manager, International Trade Relations, The Procter & Gamble Company

"Do not look for bread plates. Italians break rolls and loaves and leave them next to the plate. Also, do not cut salad or bread."

—Barbara G. Toms, Traffic Manager, Goettsch International, Inc.

Chapter 14

Luxembourg

The Grand Duchy of Luxembourg is a small, autonomous nation located in the heart of western Europe. A constitutional monarchy, it shares borders with Germany on the east, Belgium on the north and west, and France on the south. The country is 51 miles long and 32 miles wide. Despite its size, Luxembourg has two distinct geographic regions: A forested and mountainous area in the Ardennes region, comprising the northern third of the country; and the "good country" of farmlands, meadows, and woods that comprise the remainder. It is also filled with rivers, the best known of which are the Moselle, the Sûre, the Our, and the Alzette. Its capital is the city of Luxembourg, which is located on the Lorraine Plateau in the southern region of the country. Most of its population of more than 418,000 lives in this southern region.

Once under the control of numerous nations, including the Holy Roman Empire, Spain, Austria, France, the Netherlands, Prussia, and finally Belgium, the duchy of Luxembourg was often the center of disputes among these nations until the Treaty of London, signed in 1867, affirming its territorial integrity and political autonomy. Subsequently, Germany invaded and occupied the country during both world wars, experiences that made the nation determined to enter into a spirit of cooperation with all its European neighbors. Soon after

World War I had ended, the country's citizens began agitating for a republican form of government and an economic alliance with France. Instead, the Belgium-Luxembourg Economic Union was formed in 1921. As the duchy grew in economic stature, it began to assume increasing political importance in Europe. In 1948, the duchy formed an alliance with Belgium and the Netherlands, and the Benelux Economic Union was created. In 1949, Luxembourg was made a member of NATO, and it subsequently became one of the driving forces behind the creation of the European Economic Community.

Luxembourg's hereditary Grand Duke is the country's chief of state and retains executive power, assisted by a cabinet of 12 ministers called the Council of Government. There is also an elected parliament called the Chamber of Deputies. The two leading political parties in Luxembourg are the Christian Socialists and the Socialists. A constitution that has been in effect since 1868 puts ultimate sovereign power in the hands of the people.

The economy is largely dependent on imports and exports. The production of iron and steel comprises its biggest industry, while manufacturing, commerce, and tourism are also heavy contributors to the GNP. Luxembourg's healthy economy and participation in the European Common Market have ensured a high standard of living for its citizens.

Statistics and Information

Air Travel

Luxembourg's major airport is the Findel Airport, located approximately 4 miles from the heart of the city. While taxis are available, there is also access to an airport bus. A bus ride to the city costs approximately LF40.

Country Code

Luxembourg's country code is 352.

Currency

Luxembourg's currency is the *franc* (abbreviated LF). One LF is equal to 100 *centimes*. Notes are available in units of LF5,000, 1,000, and 100. Coins come in units of LF50, 20, 10, 5, and 1, as well as 50 and 25 *centimes*.

The best exchange rate is found at banks.

Dates

Luxembourgers follow the European standard format when writing dates, with the number representing the day, followed by the number of the month, followed by the year. April 1, 2015, would be written as 01/4/15 or 1 April 2015.

Ethnic Makeup

Luxembourg's checkered history has created a population that is made up of several European nationalities. However, Germans and French comprise more than three-quarters of this country's population.

Holidays and Religious Celebrations

As in many countries across the globe, national holidays and religious celebrations are an important part of Luxembourg's culture. For that reason, the following dates should be avoided when scheduling meetings:

January 1	New Year's Day
February	Shrove Tuesday (Day before Ash Wednesday)
Late March/ Early April	Easter
May 1	Labor Day
June 23	National Day
August 15	Assumption
September	Fair Monday (1st Monday)

November 1	All Saints' Day
November 11	All Souls' Day
December 24-26	Christmas

Language

There are two commonly spoken languages in this country: German and French. However, the official language is Luxembourgish (also called *Letzeburgisch*), which is a combination of both German and French. Luxembourgish is typically spoken in the home settings. It is also used in writing. English is also commonly used, especially in the business area.

Religion

The vast majority of the population is Roman Catholic, while a very small percentage of the population is Jewish or Protestant.

Time Zone Differences

Luxembourg is:

- One hour ahead of Greenwich Mean Time.
- Six hours ahead of U.S. Eastern Standard Time.

Weather

Luxembourg's climate is moderate. Fall and spring are often wet and mild. Winters can get chilly, yet rarely have freezing conditions.

Etiquette

Business Attire

As in Belgium, Luxembourgers take great pride in their sense of style and how they present themselves. They do so by wearing finely tailored clothing when interacting with others, both socially and in business.

Men typically wear dark-colored suits with starched shirts and compatible ties. Women wear classic-looking suits or business dresses.

Business-card Etiquette

When doing business in Luxembourg, business cards are a must. Be sure to take plenty with you, and print either a German or a French translation on the reverse side of your card. If you have earned an academic title, be sure it is in a large print size, along with the position you hold within your organization.

Business Entertaining/Dining

Socializing over meals is more often conducted in Luxembourg's restaurants than in private homes. Lunch is the main meal of the day, while dinner will consist of three courses, including soup, an entrée, and salad. Business should be discussed at dinner only if your Luxembourger contacts bring up the topic. Spouses are sometimes part of business-social functions.

Meals are usually served "family-style," which means that community platters are placed on the table and then offered to each person. On these occasions, it is appropriate to help yourself, rather than waiting to be served. Bread will also be offered and should be placed on the side of your plate.

The way to indicate that you are resting, rather than finished with your meal, is to place your utensils in a criss-cross position, with your fork placed diagonally over your knife. Once you have completed your entrée or salad, your utensils should be placed in a 10 o'clock-4 o'clock position to indicate to that you have completed your meal.

It is polite to eat everything on your plate. Therefore, take only what you know you can complete. Be sure to demonstrate your satisfaction with the meal by extending compliments to your host(s).

Conversation

Appropriate topics of conversation include world affairs and other current events, sports, and your travels. Avoid talking about politics or religion.

Gestures and Public Manners

Keep your hands out of your pockets and visible at all times. It is considered good manners to always have your hands showing, rather than hidden.

Behavior tends to be reserved in this country, so you should follow suit. Keep your voice low, play down hand gestures, and don't chew gum or eat while you're walking.

If you have to blow your nose, find a private place to do it. Luxembourgers consider it rude to blow your nose in public.

Gift-giving Etiquette

While gift-giving is appreciated by Luxembourgers, it is not a necessary practice during initial meetings. However, be prepared to give something after a deal has been solidified or during a holiday. Possible good gifts would include books about the city you represent, a CD or orchestral music recorded by your homeland's symphony, desk accessories, or a good bottle of liquor.

When you are presented with a gift, be sure to open it in front of the giver only if you are encouraged to do so.

Greetings and Introductions

Luxembourg greetings are very proper and formal. Meetings begin and end with a handshake, which should be extended to all persons you meet in a business environment.

Do not grip a Luxembourger's hand too firmly. Give a sincere handshake that is lighter in strength than what you would give to an individual from the United States.

As in other European countries, use last names only, unless your Luxembourg contact has requested you do otherwise.

Hierarchy Is Important

In the past, there was greater focus on the pecking order within Luxembourg companies. While a hierarchical order still exists in some organizations, there is now more focus on teams. Each organization will be different, so try to investigate how the one with which you will be interacting is set up.

How Decisions Are Made

Luxembourgers are private people, so it follows that they prefer to make their decisions in private. For that reason, don't expect them to give you any answers at a meeting. They will most likely reserve time to meet amongst themselves to decide how they would like to proceed.

Meeting Manners

You will find that Luxembourgers tend to cut to the chase quickly, rather than taking time at the beginning of the meeting to make small talk. These people are also very efficient in matters of time management and tend not to let meetings linger too long.

When asking questions and making comments, be sure to use tact and diplomacy, rather than taking a direct approach that your hosts might find too blunt.

Punctuality

With a large Germanic population in Luxembourg, it's no wonder that punctuality is such a valued characteristic. Thus, you can be certain that you will not be kept waiting for a scheduled meeting—and the same promptness will be expected of you.

Seating Etiquette

In a business meeting, the most senior seat will be the one in the center, furthest away from the door. Each participant should sit opposite his or her counterpart in the other organization who is closest in rank.

During social situations where food is involved, the most senior seats are at the head of the table and are reserved for the hosts. The most senior female guest is seated to the immediate right of the host, while the most senior male guest is seated to the immediate right of the hostess.

Tipping Tips

Restaurants commonly include a 15-percent gratuity charge as part of the bill. When this is not the case, leave a tip of 12 to 15 per cent. Tip taxi drivers 15 to 20 percent of the total fare. Hotel porters should be tipped between LF50 and LF150, depending on the number of bags they carry for you.

Toasting Etiquette

Wine is the most common beverage served with meals. You may find that your place setting has three glasses. One is for water and the other two for white and red wines. Wait for the host to propose a toast of "*Prost*" (meaning "Cheers") before lifting your goblet.

When You Are Invited to a Luxembourger Home

Be sure to go with a gift in hand when you have been invited to a Luxembourger home. A bouquet of flowers is a good idea (although avoid chrysanthemums, because they are associated with mourning), or you may bring a box of fine chocolates. If there are children in the family, be sure to remember them with either candy or a toy.

Part of the dinner ritual is enjoying coffee in another room after the meal. Thus, you should not depart too soon after the dinner's completion, but instead stay on to participate in this ritual.

Women in Business

Although the Luxembourg business scene is still male-dominated, the political scene has had a female presence. Women are also entering the business environment, slowly yet surely.

Luxembourg men will be most comfortable interacting with businesswomen from abroad. When hosting a male guest, try to have transportation and meal costs arranged ahead of time as a courtesy. (This is a chivalrous country, and some men may feel awkward about a woman's paying bills in public.)

Whatever You Do...

- Don't make light of the similarities between Luxembourg and other European countries, especially Belgium. Luxembourgers are very sensitive about maintaining their own identity.
- Don't schedule your business trips during the months of July and August or in late December. These are typical times for Luxembourgers to go on holiday.
- Don't take your hotel key with you when leave the premises. Instead, drop it off at the front desk.
- Don't underestimate the power that learning a few words in Luxembourgish can have on your business relationships.
- Don't initiate an afternoon meeting before 2:30 p.m. Many Luxem-bourgers may still be having lunch at this time.
- Don't be overly animated with your gestures. This nationality is a rather reserved group of people and they act in a low-key manner.

Advice From the Experts

"When you are in a café and are drinking a bottled beverage, be sure to use a glass. If you drink from the bottle, it is considered a major *faux pas*."

—William R. Spinnenweber, Management Major, Miami University

Chapter 15

The Netherlands

The Kingdom of the Netherlands, also known as Holland, is a constitutional monarchy located in northwestern Europe. Its northern and western boundaries lie on the North Sea. It is bordered by Germany on the east and by Belgium on the south. The Netherlands Antilles, a group of islands in the Caribbean, and Aruba (which is self-governing) are also part of this country.

For centuries, the people of the Netherlands have claimed a good deal of their land from the sea, through drainage and water management projects (that is, dikes, dams, and canals). Most of its coastal areas lie below sea level, and the country itself can be considered Europe's delta, with the Rhine and Maas rivers flowing through the country and emptying into the North Sea. The majority of the population lives in the large southeastern section, where the lands are, for the most part, low and flat. There is very little forest, and many of the country's resources are given over to agriculture. The Netherlands is one of the largest exporters of farm produce in Europe. Nevertheless, this accounts for less than 5 percent of the GDP. The Netherlands' economy is largely dependent on industry and trade, as well as financial services. Shipping, fishing, and banking have been centerpieces of the Dutch economy for centuries. It is also, of course, known for the beauty of its tulips, which it grows and exports in abundance.

This is one of the most densely populated countries in the world, with more than 15.4 million inhabitants. The people of the Netherlands are referred to as the Dutch, and are probably of Germanic origin. At one time under Spanish dominion, the country achieved independence in the late 1600s. It became a French protectorate known as the Batavian Republic from 1795 to 1806, after which William of Orange established a kingdom that included the Netherlands, Belgium, and Luxembourg. By 1848, these had become separate countries. The Netherlands maintained neutral status during World War I and was occupied by Germany during World War II. It subsequently became a member of NATO.

The capital of the Netherlands is Amsterdam, but the seat of government is the Hague. Other major cities include Rotterdam and Utrecht. The country's constitution dates back to 1814, and allows for a bicameral parliament led by a prime minister advised by an appointed cabinet. There have been numerous coalition governments over the years, with the predominant political organizations being the Labour and Catholic parties.

At one time, the Dutch culture revolved around a system of "pillars," with every institutional facet of life dependent on Protestant, Catholic, or nondenominational viewpoints. In recent years, many institutions have pulled away from this system, and viewpoints have become more liberal and independent. The people are highly cultured, and the country has been home to many great artists and thinkers, several of whom were not born here but chose to live here. Holland is especially known for artists such as Vincent van Gogh, Piet Mondrian, and Karel Appel.

Statistics and Information

Air Travel

The major international airport is Schiphol, located 11 miles from Amsterdam. Trains leave the airport for the city every quarter hour. They are much less expensive than taking taxis to the city.

Country Code

The Netherlands' country code is 31.

City codes include:

- 20 for Amsterdam.
- 70 for the Hague.
- 10 for Rotterdam.

Currency

The currency is the *Netherlands Dutch Guilder* (NDG). One *guilder* is equal to 100 *cents*. Coins come in units of NDG5, 2, and 1, as well as 25, 10, and 5 *cents*. Bills come in denominations of NDG1,000, 250, 100, 25, and 10.

Banks provide the best rates for exchanging your money.

Dates

Dates are written in the standard European format, with the day preceding the month, followed by the year. For example, January 30, 1999, would be written as 30/1/99.

Ethnic Makeup

The majority of the population is native Dutch. Turks and Moroccans make up about 5 percent of the population.

Holidays and National Celebrations

January 1	New Year's Day
April 30	The Queen's Birthday
May 5	Liberation Day
December 5	Feast of St. Nicholas
December 25/26	Christmas

Language

The official language in the Netherlands is Dutch. You also will hear individuals speaking French, German, and English. A very small percentage of the population is also fluent in Frisian, Turkish, and Arabic. Most Dutch people are at least bilingual and many are multilingual.

Religion

The three predominant beliefs in the Netherlands are Roman Catholicism, Protestantism, and Calvinism. More than a third of the population is reported to be atheist.

Time Zone Differences

The Netherlands is:

- One hour ahead of Greenwich Mean Time.
- Six hours ahead of U.S. Eastern Standard Time.

Weather

The climate is generally temperate in the Netherlands. Winters tend to be chilly, with temperatures dropping into the low 30s Fahrenheit. Summers are warm and balmy, with temperatures ranging into the upper-60s or low-70s. Most days are cloudy here.

Etiquette

Business Attire

The Dutch place very little emphasis on personal appearance. Rather than dressing formally, the Dutch prefer comfort and dress accordingly. However, in business situations, traditional business dress is more appropriate. For men, that means wearing suits or sports coats with shirts and ties. For women, proper dress means classic suits, business dresses, or tailored slacks.

Business-card Etiquette

Although most Dutch speak English, it may be a good idea to plan ahead. Prior to your trip, determine the number of people you will be meeting who may or may not have a command of the English language. If you find that the individuals with whom you will be meeting do not know English very well, have your cards translated into Dutch, German, or French.

Business Entertaining/Dining

You will find that the Dutch love to wine and dine. Although lunch is a common meal for business discussions, dinner is a very popular time to integrate business with social engagements. In most instances, this entertainment will take place at restaurants.

While you will be served hearty foods in the Netherlands, most Dutch meals consist of meat, vegetables, and potatoes. You will also find many ethnic restaurants, from Indian to Argentine.

As in other countries, hands should be showing at all times, which means keeping them above the table, rather than beneath it.

Although it may be a bit unusual for Westerners, salad is not considered a separate course in the Netherlands. Instead, it is enjoyed with the entrée and is served on the main course plate.

Because a second serving will be offered, be sure to make your first serving a small portion so that you can graciously accept seconds.

Most foods require utensils. It is important for individuals from the United States to take the cue from those around them. Even some foods that are typically considered "finger foods" in the United States (for example, fruit or cheese) are taken to the mouth using utensils.

As in other European countries, the continental-style of holding utensils is used, with the fork remaining in the left hand and the knife in the right. Similarly, use the cues that show when you are "resting" (cross your utensils on your plate with the fork over the knife in the form of an X) and when you are finished eating (place your knife and fork in a 10 o'clock-4 o'clock position on your plate, with the fork tines facing up).

Conversation

Before going to the Netherlands, be sure to brush up on world affairs, because this country's people are well-informed about current events. Other appropriate topics of discussion include travel and sports.

The Dutch frequently comment on Americans' obsession about money. Rather than adding fuel to the fire, make a point of not discussing any topic that relates to money.

Prepare for the Dutch to be rather direct with their comments and to be reserved with any kind words. They are unlikely to hide anything and will say what's on their mind straight out.

Avoid praising or complimenting your Dutch contacts. At the same time, if you are paid a compliment yourself, consider it quite an honor, because flattering comments are usually reserved for individuals with whom they have established rapport.

Gestures and Public Manners

The Dutch tend to be reserved, and are not very expressive with their nonverbal communications. It will be in your best interests to emulate this behavior as much as possible.

It is highly unlikely that you will see people hugging or touching in public. Thus, rather than patting or back-slapping your Dutch contacts, be sure to stand an arms' length from them, to give them the distance they prefer.

Like many Americans, you may misinterpret some gestures used by the Dutch. For example, if a Dutchman moves his index finger in a circle next to his ear, an American may believe that he's saying that he's crazy. However, in the Netherlands, this nonverbal signal means that the person has a telephone call. Thus, take care in how you interpret the gestures that you see.

Greetings and Introductions

There is an air of formality when meeting and greeting in the Netherlands. Wait for your Dutch contact to introduce you to others.

If this is not done, you may take the initiative by introducing yourself by name to those present and extending your hand. It is also appropriate to shake hands as you are leaving.

Just as in other countries, the last name should always be used unless you are asked to do differently. One difference in this routine in the Netherlands is that a man from abroad may initiate a handshake with a woman, rather than waiting for her to extend her hand.

Proper forms of address: Always address your Dutch colleagues by their last names and appropriate titles, until you have been invited to call them by their first names. Titles include either a professional or academic degree that has been earned.

- *Mijnheer*: Mr.
- *Mevrouw:* Mrs.
- *Juffrouw:* Miss
- *Mejuffrouw:* Ms.

Gift-giving Etiquette

Rather than going with a gift in hand during a first meeting, wait until after you have developed a relationship with your Dutch contacts. Good gifts include books about your homeland or other practical items, such as desk accessories.

How Decisions Are Made

Although making a decision may take more time than you may want, the good news is that the Dutch tend to be people of their word and can be trusted to stick to the bargain once a deal has been put together and contracts have been signed.

In many countries, the most senior person within the organization will have the final say. It is becoming more common, however, for decisions to be made by a group of people, and this is becoming the case in the Netherlands. The best approach to take is to become acquainted with the company you will be visiting to learn how their organization is structured and who will be making the decisions.

Meeting Manners

The Dutch are keen on punctuality; therefore, you should always be prompt for meetings.

The person spearheading the meeting will set the tone and make the transition from the small talk that will start the meeting to the agenda itself.

While it may not be necessary to translate your presentation material into Dutch, be sure the material is clear and concise. Also, visuals and documentation will allow your Dutch contacts to follow along with you during your presentation. Be sure to define the topics you want to deliver in your presentation material.

Punctuality

You will score high marks with your Dutch contacts if you are punctual for all appointments and meetings. If you find you are going to be delayed, be sure to phone ahead with the reason.

Seating Etiquette

The host and hostess will sit on opposite ends of the table, facing one another. The male guest of honor is placed to the left of the hostess and the female guest of honor is seated to the left of the host.

Tipping Tips

Restaurants automatically include a 15-percent gratuity in your bill. However, if you were pleased with the service you received, you should round the bill up when paying to give an extra tip. When traveling by taxi, round out to the closest *guilder*. Chambermaids should be left 1 to 2 *guilder* per day. When you are given a hand towel by a washroom attendant, be sure to tip the person 25 Dutch *cents*.

Toasting Etiquette

Wine is a common beverage enjoyed with meals. Allow the host to propose a toast with the term "*Prost*," which means "Cheers." You will find that the toast will be repeated after taking the first sip.

When You Are Invited to a Dutch Home

The Dutch welcome people to their homes with much pride and warmth. It is quite common for businesspeople to invite associates to their homes.

Always arrive on time and bring a wrapped gift to the hostess. Appropriate gifts include a box of fine chocolates or a book. If there are children, candy or a toy will be appreciated.

Because food is not always the focal point of a visit, do not count on the invitation to mean that you will be eating a meal. If there will be a meal, this will probably be mentioned when the invitation is extended to you.

Women in Business

Women currently make up no more than a third of the Dutch work force. This is one of the lowest percentages in all of Europe. Despite so few women working outside the home, Dutchmen will treat businesswomen from abroad with the utmost respect.

Whatever You Do...

- Don't expect a cheerful greeting when placing a telephone call. The Dutch commonly answer their phones by stating their last names.
- Don't enjoy "finger foods" with your fingers. The Dutch use utensils for everything, including sandwiches and pizza.
- Don't chew gum in public. It is considered rude.
- Don't plan a trip to the Netherlands in the summer. This is the most popular time for people to go on holiday.
- Don't be shocked to see people smoking and selling marijuana. Believe it or not, it is legal to do so in this country.
- Don't be surprised if you see a sign advertising sexual services. Prostitution is legal in the Netherlands.

Chapter 16

Norway

The Kingdom of Norway is located in Europe's Scandinavian peninsula. The fifth largest country in Europe, its coastline lies along the Barents Sea in the north, the Norwegian Sea in the west, the North Sea in the southwest, and the Skagerrak Strait in the south. Its eastern border abuts Sweden, Finland, and a small piece of Russia. In addition to its extensive coastline, Norway is a mountainous country consisting of some of the oldest rocks found on earth, as well as large tracts of forest land and beautiful fjords. It also has numerous natural resources, including offshore petroleum and natural gas fields, titanium ore, and magnesium metal. Only about 5 percent of the land is arable. The country is vast, but it is home to just 4.3 million people, allowing for plenty of open living space.

Norway is known as the Land of the Midnight Sun, because of its high altitude. From the middle of May to the end of July, the sun does not set in northern Norway, and from the end of November to the end of January, the sun does not rise above the horizon. If you want to see impressive displays of the Northern Lights, this is the place to come to! The country's natural beauty has attracted tourists and sportsmen. It has twice played host to the Winter Olympics.

Shipbuilding, fishing, and ocean trade have all been a vital part of the Norwegian lifestyle for centuries. Viking ships sailed to other lands long before other Europeans and were the first to land in North America. Norway dominated northern Europe, Iceland, Greenland, and the Orkney Islands until the mid-1300s, when the Black Death wiped out more than half the population. Shortly after that, Norway entered into a union with Denmark that lasted until 1814, when an independent Norwegian constitution was established and a new union was entered into with Sweden. This lasted until 1905, at which time Norway chose a king and created its current constitutional monarchy. The government is led by a prime minister, with the assistance of 18 ministers. There is also a national assembly called the Storting, with representatives elected every four years. Economically, the country is still dependent on its maritime industries, but even more so now on the large fields of offshore oil and gas that were discovered in the late 1960s. In addition to copper, Norway is also one of the world's major producers of aluminum.

Once the land of Vikings, Norway is now the home of the Nobel Peace Prize, awarded in its capital, Oslo, every December. Among its more famous native sons are author Henrik Ibsen, composer Edvard Grieg, and artist Edvard Munch, as well as explorers Roald Amundsen and Thor Heyerdahl.

Statistics and Information

Air Travel

Believe it or not, Norway has 58 airports. The most widely frequented international airports are the Fornelou and the Gardermoen Airports, both located in Oslo. Limos, buses, shuttles, and taxis are available from the airports to most destinations.

Country Code

Norway's country code is 47.

If you are calling Oslo, Narvik, Bodo, Trondheim, Bergen, or Stavanger, you will not need to dial what used to be a city code. Instead, telephone numbers in Norway now consist of eight, rather than six, digits. For that reason, what used to be the city code has now become the first two digits of the eight-digit telephone number.

Currency

Norway's currency is the *Norwegian krone* (abbreviated NOK). One *krone* is equal to 100 *øre*. Notes are available in denominations of NOK1,000, 500, 100, and 50, as well as in coin form in NOK10, 5, and 1. A coin is also available in 50 *øre*.

Banks and ATM machines provide the best rates for exchanging your money.

Dates

Norwegians write dates following the European standard format, with the day of the month listed first, followed by the month, and then the year. For example, January 30, 1999, would be written as 30/1/99.

Ethnic Makeup

Norwegians are originally of Germanic descent, including Nordic, Alpine, and Baltic Germans. You also will find a small population of native Norwegians, originally called Lapps and now called the Sami, who live in the northernmost parts of the country. The Sami originated in the northern regions of Norway, Sweden, Finland, and Russia, and have been a nomadic people.

Holidays and Religious Celebrations

The following is a list of Norway's holidays. As these are national holidays, it is wise not to schedule meetings for these days.

January 1	New Year's Day
March/April	Maundy Thursday, Good Friday, Easter Sunday and Monday
May 1	Labor Day
April/May	Ascension Day

May 17	Constitution Day
April/May	Whitsunday, Whitmonday
June 23	Midsummer Feast
December 25	Christmas Day
December 26	Boxing Day

Language

The country's official language is Norwegian. Norwegian has two deviations, a written form, called *Bokmål* (standard Norwegian), and a spoken form, called *Nynorsk* (new Norwegian). English is the most common second language and is understood by most businesspeople.

Religion

Most Norwegians practice Evangelical Lutheranism. Many of these individuals practice in the Church of Norway.

Time Zone Differences

Norway time is one hour ahead of Greenwich Mean Time and six hours ahead of U.S. Eastern Standard Time.

Weather

The temperatures in Norway are influenced by the Gulf Stream, which gives it a more temperate climate than most northern countries. Winter temperatures can fall as low as 20 degrees. Summers, however, are rather pleasant, with temperatures in the 70s. Precipitation is greater in the western part of the country.

Etiquette

Business Attire

Norwegians believe in practical rather than ostentatious clothes. Their sensible taste includes the basic garb in conservative colors.

Norwegians do not wear a lot of ornate jewelry and other accessories. Instead, individuals of this culture present a clean-cut, streamlined appearance.

It is considered appropriate for men to wear either suits or sport coats and ties. Women should wear suits, business dresses, or tailored slacks in a professional environment.

While jeans may be worn in more casual atmospheres, they should be clean and pressed.

Business-card Etiquette

Norwegians are not known to have a defined form regarding the business card exchange. However, cards should be taken and offered when first meeting a Norwegian contact. Because most Norwegians have a command of the English language, it is not necessary to translate your card into Norwegian on the reverse side.

Business Entertaining/Dining

You will most likely be invited to both lunch and dinner. However, you will find that lunches will be the more likely setting in which business will be discussed over food. If you are dining with your Norwegian client in the evening, allow him or her to set the tone of the conversation as a safety measure.

In normal cases, sandwiches are commonly served at the lunch hour. Because they will be open-faced, be sure to use utensils, rather than lifting them with your hands.

If you have been invited to dinner, plan to be there for a few hours, because you will be served several courses.

You will enjoy quite a variety of food in Norway, including various meats, cheeses, and fish. Your Norwegian dining experience may also be a first for eating goose and reindeer. At the end of a dinner, cheese will be served, followed by fruit and perhaps a pastry. The entrée itself will be accompanied by a vegetable, then followed by salad.

As in all European countries, hands should be kept in view above the table. If they are not, you will be seen as impolite.

Even if it is your custom to use the American-style of holding utensils, be prepared to use the continental style in Norway. This method entails holding your fork in the left hand (tines down) with your knife in the right hand, both when you cut your food and when you take it to your mouth.

It is common to be served "family-style" in casual restaurants, where food is placed on platters in the center of the table and passed around. However, in more formal dining environments, you will be served, rather than expected to pass around platters.

When eating "family-style," make a point of putting only a little on your plate, especially if you are not sure that you will eat it. Norwegians are very conscientious about not being wasteful of food.

Conversation

You will find that Norwegians keep their voices low, and they are rarely, if ever, boisterous. Therefore, when you are talking, be sure to use an "indoor" voice, whether you are inside or outside.

Norwegians keep their noses to the grindstone at work, and use their time wisely by making a point of focusing on business-related issues, rather than their personal lives. For that reason, in any professional setting, be sure your conversation is related to work topics.

Whatever you do, avoid bringing up information about your personal life or asking questions about their personal lives. Norwegians are very private people and tend to compartmentalize their personal and professional lives.

Safe topics of interest include cross-country skiing or any other outdoor sport, as well as Norway's topography. Other appropriate subjects to bring up are your positive impressions of Norway and your travels to other countries.

Gestures and Public Manners

Because Norwegians make a point of acting in a low-key manner, try to mimic them. This includes not calling attention to yourself through animated body language and a loud tone of voice.

When interacting with Norwegians, maintain a distance of two arms' length, in order to avoid invading their space. You should also avoid touching other people, even to the point of patting them on the arms.

Do not use the "okay" sign made by joining the thumb and index finger in a circle. While this is a popular gesture in the United States, it is considered to be obscene in Norway.

Gift-giving Etiquette

While giving gifts in a business setting is a ritual in many countries, this custom is not commonplace in Norway. On the contrary, gifts may make your Norwegian contact leery. In a social setting, however, it is a different story. In this case, wine, liquor (such as scotch or whiskey), flowers, or sweets are acceptable.

When you are given a gift, it is appropriate for you to open it in front of the giver, rather than in private.

Greetings and Introductions

When meeting someone for the first time, be sure to stand as you offer your hand. Your handshake should be brief, but firm and confident. Handshakes should also be exchanged upon departure.

The Norwegians are curious people by nature and enjoy meeting people from abroad. One way to establish rapport is by greeting the other person with the expression "*Morn.*" Norwegians will appreciate this effort.

Proper forms of address: When you first meet a Norwegian, be sure to greet the person in a formal manner, using *Herr*, *Fru*, or *Froken*, followed by the person's last name. If you are addressing a woman, be sure to note the last name that others are using to address her. Norwegian woman frequently use their birth names, even when they are married.

Once you have established a relationship with a Norwegian, you may be asked to address the person using only his or her last name, without a title.

Norway is a society that takes pride in treating people equally, and they make a point of doing things in a very low-key manner. Thus, they rarely, if ever, use their academic or professional titles and do not encourage others to address them by those titles.

Hierarchy Is Important

While there is a hierarchy in Norwegian companies, the managing director usually delegates decisions to his or her management team. The team is a vital part of the organization. Individuals in business organizations may be given titles, but they aren't flaunted during an introduction any more than academic or professional titles are.

How Decisions Are Made

Unlike many cultures, Norwegians will rarely haggle over price. Typically, the amount that Norwegians first tell you they are willing to spend is the amount they intend to spend. One reason for this is that this culture tends to be very down-to-earth, trustworthy, and practical in nature, and expect the same of the individuals with whom they are developing a business relationship. You should, therefore, avoid any attempts to negotiate at length with them, otherwise you will risk losing their business altogether.

Because decisions are most often based on consensus, it sometimes takes time for Norwegians to arrive at a decision. Rather than attempting to rush the process along, the best thing to do is to prepare a clear and concise presentation, provide as much detail as possible, and practice patience. When the final decision has finally been made by management, the head person will give the final stamp of approval by signing the necessary documents.

Meeting Manners

When scheduling meetings, be sure to avoid the midsummer months. This is a very popular time for families to go on holiday.

Norwegians are punctual by nature and will want to begin meetings on time. Small talk may take place initially, but it will be brief and business will follow soon afterwards.

Most Norwegians see things as black and white, rather than allowing for a lot of leeway. Therefore, present your topic in a clear and concise manner. Rather than adding a lot of bells and whistles to your presentation, provide straight facts and figures, on which Norwegians will base their decisions. Your visual presentation should be very detailed and prepared well enough that it can be presented in the time allotted. Because most Norwegians are fluent in English, it usually isn't necessary to arrange for your presentation to be translated.

Finally, prepare to support the facts and figures in your presentation if questions are asked. Norwegians are a very inquisitive people and will not hesitate to ask questions of you, even if their questions may cause you an embarrassing moment.

Punctuality

Whether you are meeting someone for business or social reasons, you will be expected to be on time in Norway. Conversely, Norwegians will be respectful of your time by being punctual. If there is even the slightest chance that you will be a few minutes late, make sure to call ahead. Making excuses should be the exception rather than the rule, however.

Seating Etiquette

Seating is very much the same in Norway as it is in the majority of European countries. The host and hostess will take seats at both heads of the table. The most senior woman guest will be seated to the host's left, and the most senior male guest will be invited to sit on the hostess's left.

If you are hosting and more than six people are involved in a gathering, it is advisable to arrange for name cards to be placed on the table as a cue to tell guests where you would like them to sit.

Taxi Etiquette

Taxis are a popular way of getting around in Norway, and they are especially in demand for people before the start of the work day and between 4 and 5 p.m.

If you are under a time crunch, rather than attempting to hail a taxi on a street corner, call ahead to reserve one.

Tipping Tips

Typically, restaurants will include a 15-percent gratuity in your bill. Many patrons, however, round out the bill as a way of saying that the service met or exceeded their expectations. Although the tip for a taxi is automatically built into the fare, just as in restaurants, it is appropriate to round your fare up rather than requesting change.

When hotel porters have been of assistance to you, give them 3 to 5 *kroners* for each bag handled. It is not necessary to leave a tip for chambermaids or doormen.

Toasting Etiquette

Toasting etiquette dictates that the host initiate a toast at the beginning of the meal. Guests should wait until this ritual has taken place before lifting their beverages.

The most common toast that you will hear in Norway is "*Skål.*" A very important part of toasting etiquette in Norway is to make eye contact with the person being toasted, sip your beverage, and then look at the person you have toasted once again before placing your goblet on the right side of your place setting.

It is appropriate for the person who has been toasted to offer a toast to the meal's host as a way of expressing gratitude.

It is common to toast with beverages such as wine or champagne. Sherry and scotch are also common beverages of Norway. Because hard liquor is costly for Norwegians, it also makes a great gift. Note: You may be offered *aquavit*, which is a hard liquor made from potato spirits.

When You Are Invited to a Norwegian Home

Once you have established a social relationship with your Norwegian contact, invitations to have dinner in his or her home may be few and far between. One reason is that Norwegians take pride in having a very meticulously tended house and would not think of inviting you over if it were anything except immaculate.

When you are extended an invitation to someone's home, be sure to go with something in hand. Flowers other than lilies or carnations will be appreciated by the hostess. Hard liquor may be given to the host and/or chocolates may be given to the entire family.

Rather than kibitzing before being invited to the dinner table, you will find that the meal will be served within minutes after you arrive.

Although Norwegians will extend the greatest of hospitality to you, you will also find that they are not night owls. For that reason, prepare to depart by 11 p.m. at the latest.

Women in Business

Norwegian women have already made huge advances in the corporate world. In fact, their presence is visible in virtually every profession. Many of them also have climbed that slippery ladder to success in upper level management.

Because Norwegian businessmen are used to interacting with Norwegian businesswomen as colleagues, they will treat women from abroad with the respect that is due to them. They also will feel comfortable with women from abroad inviting them to a meal and allowing them to take care of the check.

Whatever You Do...

- Don't address a Norwegian woman by her husband's last name. Many married Norwegian women keep their birth names.
- Don't give white flowers or carnations as gifts. These items are equated with signs of mourning.
- Don't refer to Norwegians as Swedes or Danes. Although these three countries are "Scandinavian," each of their cultures is unique.

- Don't do anything that may be interpreted as bringing harm to the environment. Norwegians are environmentalists and will expect you to respect their earth as they do.
- Don't forget to pack warm clothes for your trip. You will especially need them if you are traveling to Norway in the winter.
- Don't waste food. This gesture will insult your Norwegian contacts.
- Don't say anything that may be misinterpreted as bragging. Norwegians are much more interested in becoming acquainted with you than they are in your achievements.

Advice From the Experts

"The exchange of business gifts is not a common practice. However, gifts from your own country or native town are well-received. Recognize that Norwegians are especially uncomfortable about the number 13."

—Barbara G. Toms, Traffic Manager, Goettsch International Inc.

Chapter 17

Poland

A onetime-Communist country now making the transition to a free-market economy, the Republic of Poland is located in central Europe. It is bordered on the west by Germany, on the southwest by the Czech Republic, on the southeast by the Ukraine, on the east by Belarus, and on the northeast by Russia and Lithuania. Its northern border lies along the Baltic Sea. Poland has a population of approximately 38.6 million people, more than 1.6 million of whom live in the nation's capital, Warsaw.

More than three quarters of Poland's geography consists of lowlands, with some mountains located in the southern region of the country, and forests taking up more than a quarter of the total land area. (The Bialowieza forest is the last virgin forest on the European mainland, providing a home to the biggest herd of European bison on the continent.) Approximately one half of the land is arable, and agriculture provides a major source of income, as does the production of softwood. There are numerous mineral resources, especially coal, sulfur, and zinc, all of which Poland exports in large quantities. Fishing and manufacturing are also large contributors to the GDP.

Poland's proximity to Russia and Germany has made it subject to invasion from those countries (in Germany's case, the Prussian nation), and its borders have often been affected by quarrels over and divisions of its land. In the late 1700s, it was partitioned into Russian, Prussian, and Austrian sectors. The Kingdom of Poland was established in the Russian sector in 1815, although the Polish people chafed against tsarist rule and there were several revolts over the years. An independent Poland was finally formed from all three sectors and officially recognized by the Allies following World War I, and the country coexisted between Germany and Russia until 1939, when the Nazis invaded its borders and occupied two-thirds of the country. During the second World War, the country was devastated by the Nazi program of eradicating the Jewish population. Subsequently, the Soviet Union took control and a Communist government was set up in Poland. In the years that followed, workers revolted against Communist oppression time and again. The 1980s marked a time of growing unrest, as the Solidarity union led by Lech Walesa organized numerous uprisings against Communist rule, finally leading to major reforms in Poland's political system. A coalition between Solidarity and the Communists was formed in 1989, and since then Poland has become a democratic, free-market society with a parliamentary form of government.

Poland has made numerous contributions to the arts and sciences, and many of its composers and writers have achieved international renown. These include Frederic Chopin, Jan Paderewski, Artur Rubinstein, Wladyslaw Reymont, and Czeslaw Milosz.

Statistics and Information

Air Travel

Individuals traveling to Poland usually fly into either Warsaw's Okecie Airport or Krakow's Balice Airport. In Warsaw, the 4-mile trip to the city's center is best done on the Airport City Bus, which costs only 5zl. A taxi ride will run more than 50zl. In Krakow, take Bus D from the airport for a 30-minute trip into the city at a cost of only 1.50zl.

Country Code

Poland's country code is 48.

City codes include:

- 32 for Katowice.
- 22 for Warsaw.

Currency

Poland's currency is the *zloty* (zl). One *zloty* is equal to 100 *grosz* (gr). Notes come in units of zl200, 100, 50, 20, 10, and 1. Coins are available in units of gr50, 20, 10, 5, and 2, and zl5, 2, and 1.

The best place to exchange your money is at a *kantor*, which is Poland's private exchange office. These are readily located throughout Poland's cities.

Dates

The Polish follow the European standard format when writing dates, with the number representing the day listed first, followed by the month, and then the year. For instance, February 4, 2010, would be written as 04/2/10.

Ethnic Makeup

Approximately 98 percent of Poland's population is of Polish descent. Other ethnic groups represented include Germans, Ukrainians, and Belarussians.

Holidays and National Celebrations

January 1	New Year's Day
January 6	Epiphany
April	Easter/Easter Monday
May 1	Labor Day
May 3	National Day
May 21	Ascension Day

August 15	Assumption Day
November 1	All Saints' Day
November 11	Independence Day
December 25	Christmas Day

Language

Polish is the official language, and the majority of the population speak it exclusively. German is also spoken by some, as is English.

Religion

By and large, the Poles are a very religious people. More than 95 percent of the population follows the Roman Catholic faith. A very small percentage is Eastern Orthodox, and there are also some Protestants.

Time Zone Differences

Poland is:

- One hour ahead of Greenwich Mean Time.
- Six hours ahead of U.S. Eastern Standard Time.

Weather

Poland's weather is influenced by the country's location next to the Baltic. For that reason, summer climates tend to be quite hot, while the winters are cold and snowy. During the autumn months, it rains frequently.

Etiquette

Business Attire

Poles tend to characterize people on the basis of first impressions. For that reason, be sure to follow the conservative dress rule. Men should wear business suits with pressed white shirts and ties. Note:

It is typical for Poles to wear lighter-colored suits during the day and darker ones during the evening.

Women should also dress in a professional manner by wearing tailored suits or dresses that command a business presence, with heels.

Business-card Etiquette

Be sure to go to Poland with plenty of business cards in hand, because you will be exchanging them with virtually everyone you meet.

You will make a lasting impression on your Polish contacts by having the reverse side of your business card translated into Polish. The Poles also place value on titles, so make a point of having the name of your position enlarged on the Polish side of your business card. If you have earned any academic degrees, these should also be printed on your card.

Business Entertaining/Dining

Most Poles entertain in restaurants. However, you may want to acclimate yourself to eating both lunch and dinner later than you would normally do on the Western front. For example, lunch (which is called *obiad*) is taken between 2 and 5 p.m. If you are invited to dinner, it will most likely start anywhere from 9 p.m. or later.

As in the United States, you will be wined and dined by someone who is your equal in professional rank. In return, be sure to extend a reciprocal lunch or dinner invitation only to the individuals who invited you to eat. You need not feel obliged to invite individuals who may have been part of your meetings.

One way to decide if you should extend an invitation to spouses is if the dinner will be business or strictly social. If the latter is the case, and your Polish contact indicates that his or her spouse will be joining the party, then be sure that your spouse is included.

The continental-style of dining is observed in Poland, with the fork held in the left hand and the knife in the right. In addition, food is typically served "family-style"—that is, platters from which you can serve yourself will be placed on the table. Wait until after your host has given the cue before you begin.

As in many other European countries, eating is an important part of Polish hospitality. Therefore, serve yourself only a small portion so that you can accept a second and perhaps even a third portion of food.

It is likely that a consommé will be presented to you in a soup bowl with side handles. When this happens, you may drink directly from the bowl rather than using a spoon. When in doubt, take the cue from your host or hostess.

Polish food is rich and quite heavy. A typical course begins with a soup followed by meat and potatoes. Bread is a staple at every meal.

Conversation

You will find Poles to be extremely inquisitive about life in the United States. They are also likely to ask questions that you may consider personal and would never think of asking (for example, how old you are, your income, if you're married, or the number of children you have). Be prepared for such questions so you'll know how to handle them when they come up.

Topics of conversation that would be pleasing to Poles are life in the United States, your travels in Poland, what you've seen and enjoyed in the country, and family. Topics to avoid include politics, the Communist regime, and religion. Although this is a universal travel rule, avoid using slang terms, acronyms, and even humor with the Poles, as this leaves you open to miscommunications that may be embarrassing or cause rancor.

Gestures and Public Manners

When in Poland, be sure to act reserved in public through your actions and tone of voice.

As in many countries, it is considered rude to chew gum in public.

Gift-giving Etiquette

You should give a gift to your Polish contact the first time you meet. Desk accessories, liquor (except for vodka), cigarettes, and even coffee are gifts that would be appreciated.

Flowers (except for chrysanthemums) make nice gifts for a hostess. Be sure to give an even number of flowers. As in many other European countries, giving an odd number is considered bad luck.

Greetings and Introductions

The handshake is the most common Polish greeting, both when meeting and departing. Men traveling from abroad should allow a Polish woman to initiate the handshake.

While it is inappropriate for Western men to do so, Polish men may greet a woman by kissing her hand.

Always address Poles by their last name and courtesy title. *Pan* is the appropriate courtesy title for a man, while *Pani* is used for a woman. If a person has earned an academic or other title, it should be used as part of the address, rather than *Pan* or *Pani.*

As in other countries, Poles should be addressed by their last names unless they ask you to do otherwise.

Hierarchy Is Important

The pecking order is an important part of the Polish management structure. For that reason, be sure to recognize the hierarchical order and to acknowledge individuals by title, when possible.

How Decisions Are Made

The highest-ranking person in an organization is authorized to make the final decision. However, in order to reach that person, you may have to give presentations to those in control under him or her.

Meeting Manners

Prior to the day you are scheduled to meet, be sure to call to confirm the time and location.

When meeting with Poles, a very important component of the business relationship is the trust they have in you personally. For that reason, the rapport that you develop at the very beginning of your association will be key to any long-term business relationship.

Poles are very hospitable, and will offer you a beverage when you first arrive at the meeting. This is the time to establish rapport with them before getting down to the business at hand. Allow your Polish contact to bring up the topic of business, rather than rushing into it. Don't be surprised if you leave the meeting wondering if anything was accomplished. Even if your Polish contact never got around to discussing business, the personal relationship that was developed will have laid a good foundation for subsequent meetings.

When delivering a presentation to your Polish contacts, be sure it is clear, concise, and has been translated into Polish on paper. This will allow them to follow along with you as you deliver your presentation, using graphs and charts. It will also allow them to have information to pass on to the final decision-maker, who may not be present.

Prepare for the questions you will be asked during your presentations, and especially the manner in which those questions will be asked. This nationality is used to making inquiries in a very direct way that you might find startling. You should not act upset by their bluntness.

You should also prepare for meetings to run longer than you might expect. For that reason, avoid scheduling more than two meetings a day, and allow at least three hours from the projected end time of the first meeting to the start time of the second one.

Punctuality

You will find a mixed attitude about time in Poland. Many Poles are sticklers about it and place great importance on punctuality, whereas, others are more lax in their attitudes about time.

As an individual from abroad, you should always be punctual for meetings. However, take plenty of reading material, because you may be kept waiting for as long as half an hour.

Seating Etiquette

Polish etiquette dictates that the guest of honor be given the most respected seat at the head of the table.

Tipping Tips

Restaurants typically will include a 10-percent gratuity charge in your bill. If it is not included, then leave a tip of 10 to 15 percent. Be sure to give your server the tip at the same time you pay the bill.

When porters assist you with luggage, give them zl300 to 500. Chambermaids should be given approximately zl500 each day. Taxi drivers should be given an extra 12 to 15 percent of your cab fare.

Toasting Etiquette

Poles take great pride in serving the highest-quality beverages during meals, considering it an important part of extending hospitality. Since vodka was first created in Poland, it is consumed frequently and with gusto. You are also likely to be offered other liquors, such as brandy. However, don't expect to be served wine, because it is not made in Poland and is therefore very costly. You may be served beer. If this is the case, prepare for it to be warm.

Of all these beverages, toasts are typically made with vodka. The host usually proposes a toast to his or her guests, wishing them good health. The most senior guest should then propose a toast in return to the individual(s) hosting the meal.

Toilet Etiquette

Because it is likely that you will have to pay for toilet paper in Poland's public restrooms, prepare yourself by carrying some with you at all times.

If you are at a train station, restaurant, hotel, or museum, the door marked with a triangle is the men's room, while the room marked with a circle is the women's room.

When You Are Invited to a Polish Home

When you are invited to a Polish home, be sure to go with a gift in hand. Flowers, tea, coffee, or a perfumed soap make great gifts.

You will be treated to quite a feast. Be sure to take small portions initially so that you can accept a second helping. Compliments will also be in order for the hostess.

It is most likely that conversation will continue after the meal has finished, so prepare to stay and enjoy yourself for a while.

Women in Business

Women traveling from abroad will quickly see that male Poles make up the majority of the Polish work force. Women have not yet made significant inroads in this country and tend not to be in high-ranking positions.

As a woman from abroad, you will be treated by Polish men with the respect accorded all women. Thus, you can expect to have doors opened for you, compliments paid to you, and restaurant bills paid by the men. Accept these courtesies graciously, maintaining a professional demeanor at all times. By doing so, you will be accepted as a businessperson.

Whatever You Do...

- Don't correspond in English with your Polish counterparts. Instead, your material should be translated into Polish.
- Don't assume that anything you fax to your Pole contact has been received. Just as with any faxed correspondence, always confirm that it has been received.
- Don't take a taxi until you check with the hotel concierge about what you should expect to pay. Then, before entering the cab, agree upon a fare with the driver. By doing so, you will be charged the proper amount and avoid the risk of being overcharged.

- Don't show up for a meeting unless you have confirmed it at least 24 hours in advance.
- Don't arrive in Poland without having made a hotel reservation. As with meetings, be sure your hotel is confirmed before your arrival.
- Don't drink in excess. Although Poles are big drinkers, make sure you control your alcohol consumption, rather than allowing it to control you.
- Don't walk on a lawn in Poland. Believe it or not, you can get a ticket for doing so.

Chapter 18

Portugal

The Republic of Portugal (or Portuguese Republic) is one of the westernmost countries in Europe, lying on the Atlantic Ocean side of the Iberian peninsula. It is bordered by Spain on the east and north. The islands of Madeira and the Azores, which lie in the Atlantic Ocean, are a part of Portugal, and their inhabitants are of Portuguese descent. In addition, the Asian territory of Macao is under Portuguese control.

The Tagus River effectively bisects Portugal, dividing it into the highlands of the north and the lush lowlands of the south. The country's capital, Lisbon, is a harbor situated at the mouth of the Tagus, near where it empties out into the Atlantic. The northern part of the country is home to an abundance of forests that provide resources for a good portion of the Portuguese industry. Natural mineral resources, however, are scarce in this country, and only tungsten is mined and exported in any quantity. One-third of the land, mostly located in the south, is arable and produces a large quantity of cereal crops, such as wheat and corn. However, agriculture is not a major contributor to the Portuguese economy, which is largely industrial in nature. Shipbuilding, fishing, and the manufacture of textiles, clothing, footwear, paper and wood products, and chemicals are among Portugal's biggest industries. With more than 16 million visitors every year, tourism is also a major contributor to the Portuguese economy. The Algarve coast in the south is one of the most popularly visited places in Europe.

Portugal's population of approximately 10.5 million still lives largely in rural areas; only about 30 percent consists of urban dwellers. Originally settled by Celtic tribes, the country was once subject to invasions from the Romans, Visigoths, Moors, and a Germanic tribe known as the Suebi. In time, a monarchy was established, and Portugal had achieved its present boundaries by the late 1200s, under the rule of King Alfonso III. For a time in the early 1600s, Spain took control, but a revolt in 1640 reestablished the monarchy. By the 1800s, political dissension had created internal strife that eventually resulted in the overthrow of the monarchy in 1910. There followed a long dictatorship under the iron hand of Antonio de Oliveira Salazar, who implemented a Marxist-leaning government with harsh colonization policies. In 1974, military leaders staged a coup and from that point on, Portugal worked towards more centrist policies that encouraged and promoted free enterprise. Businesses that were once owned by the state are now largely privately owned. Portugal is a member of the European Union.

Statistics and Information

Air Travel

Portugal's main airport is the Portela International Airport, located only a few miles from Lisbon. It takes less than half an hour to travel from the airport to the center of the city by taxi or hotel shuttle.

Country Code

Portugal's country code is 351.

Lisbon's city code is 1.

Currency

Portugal's currency is known as the *escudo* (abbreviated EsC). One *escudo* is equivalent to 100 *centavos*. Notes come in the following denominations: EsC10,000, 5,000, 1,000, and 500. *Escudos* are also available in coin form of EsC200, 100, 50, 20, 10, and 5. Coins are available in 50 *centavos*.

Banks and electronic currency exchange machines, found in airports and train stations, provide the best rates for exchanging your money.

Dates

As in most European countries, dates are written in the standard European form. The number representing the day is written first, followed by the month, and then the year. For example, June 22, 2010, would be written as 22/6/10.

Ethnic Makeup

The vast majority of the population living in Portugal is of Portuguese descent.

Holidays and National Celebrations

The following is a list of Portugal's religious holidays and national celebrations. Because offices and stores close on these dates, meetings should not be scheduled at these times.

January 1	New Year's Day
Late March/ April	Good Friday, Easter
March 19	St. Joseph's Day
April 25	Liberty Day
May 1	Labor Day
June 3	St. Anthony's Day
June 10	National Day
June 12	Feast of St. Anthony

August 15	Assumption Day
October 5	Proclamation of the Republic
October 12	National Day
November 1	All Saints' Day
December 1	Independence Day
December 6	Constitution Day
December 8	Day of the Immaculate Conception
December 25	Christmas Day

Language

Portuguese is the country's official language. Individuals from abroad may also hear many people speaking French and English.

Religion

Religious freedom is guaranteed in Portugal. The vast majority of the population practices Roman Catholicism.

Time Zone Differences

Portugal is one hour ahead of Greenwich Mean Time and six hours ahead of U.S. Eastern Standard Time.

Weather

Portugal's climate is predicable. Typically, the winters are mild and somewhat humid, with temperatures usually between the mid-30s and the mid-50s Fahrenheit. Summer weather can be fairly dry, with temperatures in the low-70s.

Etiquette

Business Attire

The Portuguese are class acts when it comes to dressing, and will attire themselves as business professionals no matter where they are going. The Portuguese also enjoy wearing designer accessories and will notice what you are wearing. This alone tells you that they are a very fashion-oriented group of people. Thus, when visiting Portugal, make a point of leaving your business-casual wear at home.

For men, proper attire means a business suit with a shirt and tie. Women should wear a suit, elegant dress with heels, or tailored pants suit. Both men and women will also do well to take formal clothes to Portugal for evening events, such as the theatre or a concert.

Business-card Etiquette

Business cards will inevitably be part of all introductions in Portugal, so take plenty with you to Portugal.

Because English is a commonly spoken language in Portugal, you may not need to have your business card translated into Portuguese. It may be a good idea, however to find out if the individuals with whom you will be meeting are fluent in English before deciding what is appropriate.

Business Entertaining/Dining

As in many European countries, the mid-day meal is the one at which business may be discussed. You may enjoy dinners with your Portuguese hosts, but those will be strictly social events that will include spouses. In either case, most entertaining takes place in restaurant settings.

Although meat is enjoyed in Portugal, fish is by far the most commonly consumed main course. This protein is usually accompanied by a starch, such as potatoes or rice. These foods are also enjoyed in the form of stew. Salad may be served on the same dish as part of the main course, rather than being offered separately, and bread is also served during meals.

As in most countries, hands should always be showing and above the table (as well as out of your pockets).

Napkins should remain on the left-hand side of the table when you are not using them, as well as when you have to leave the table for a fleeting moment. (This differs from most other European countries.) When you are finished and/or are ready to leave the table following a meal, the napkin should be placed neatly on the *right* side of the place setting.

You will notice that food is served "family-style" in Portugal—that is, community platters will be offered to you from which you may serve yourself. Keeping that in mind, it is best to remain conservative with the amount of food you take the first time around so that you are able to accept more food the second or third time platters are passed to you.

It goes without question that everyone at the table should be served before anyone begins to eat. It is also appropriate to wait for the person hosting the meal to invite you to begin eating.

The majority of food you will enjoy in Portugal is considered utensil food, rather than "finger food." This includes the fruit and cheese that may be served following the entree.

Conversation

The Portuguese are an outgoing people by nature and enjoy conversing with visitors from abroad. While English will likely be understood by those with whom you interact, acronyms and slang should be avoided as a way of keeping the lines of communication open.

Good topics of conversation would include your trip to Portugal and the parts of the country you have visited, as well as your travels to other countries, and sports. Because families are an important part of Portuguese life, they will also enjoy learning about your family (and telling you about theirs).

You will soon learn that "small talk" topics are much safer bets for conversing than getting into such personal areas as what one does for a living, his or her income, inflation, and so on. You should also be sure to stay away from topics that involve government issues or the political arena.

Gestures and Public Manners

When in Portugal, do as the Portuguese do and play down your hand motions. Your words, rather than your body language, should convey what you mean.

Do not use your index finger to indicate when you want someone to approach you. Rather, put your hand down with your palm facing you and move your fingers back and forth.

On the move: Although most people think nothing of it, it is considered inappropriate in Portugal to eat food or drink beverages while you are walking around. Instead, sit down whenever you want to enjoy a food or drink.

Gift-giving Etiquette

While gifts are not part of the initial relationship-development process, they are generally exchanged following negotiations. You should use your judgment as to when it is appropriate to exchange gifts with your Portuguese business colleagues. If you are presented with a gift, open it immediately, in front of the giver.

Gift-giving is also appropriate if you are in Portugal during holiday festivities.

Some suggestions for appropriate gifts include desk items, crystal, fine chocolates, or anything with your company's logo. Stay away from gifts of wine or liquor.

Greetings and Introductions

The Portuguese are very warm and hospitable individuals, as well as high-contact people. Thus, you can expect them to stand fairly close when greeting you.

When meeting new Portuguese contacts, extend your hand and as you look at the person, offer a "*Bon dia,*" which is the equivalent of "Good Day" or an American "Hello."

Although it is appropriate for women in the United States to stand when meeting a man, they may remain seated in Portugal.

If a rapport has been established after an initial meeting, then subsequent encounters between men may consist of an embrace and pat on the back, rather than a handshake. A second greeting between women may be comprised of a brush of the lips on both cheeks.

Proper forms of address: When meeting a Portuguese individual, make a point of addressing the person using the equivalent title of Mr., Mrs., or Miss, followed by the individual's last name. This is a polite and necessary formality. However, if a person has earned an academic or professional title, use that instead, followed by the person's surname(s). Otherwise, use the following courtesy titles:

- *Senhor:* Mr.
- *Senhora:* Mrs.
- *Menina:* Miss.

If the person has a professional title, such as doctor or professor, you may leave out the surname entirely and address the person as "Mr. Engineer" or "Mrs. Professor."

Hierarchy Is Important

In order to successfully do business with the Portuguese, it is very important to develop strong personal relationships with them. To do this, it is necessary to understand the strict hierarchy followed by Portuguese companies.

If companies are government operated, they follow a hierarchy based on rank and file. However, if a company is privately owned and/or operated by a family, the hierarchy tends to be more personal than systematic. In other words, rather than assigning certain responsibilities based on title, the person who may be asked to handle an assignment is likely to be the one who has a strong personal relationship with the decision-maker(s). For that reason, it is important to get connected with the right people and to develop personal relationships so that a strong professional one will follow.

How Decisions Are Made

Understanding the hierarchy is crucial in Portugal (see "Hierarchy is Important" section), and you may or may not have direct contact with the decision-maker. Because of this, and because all decisions are discussed in private, this process will entail a great deal of time before deals are finalized—which means you must be patient when waiting for a decision from your Portuguese contacts.

Meeting Manners

You may find a double standard in Portugal when it comes to punctuality. Although you may be forced to wait, you will be expected to arrive on time and make no mention of having been kept waiting yourself.

You will be offered a beverage and small talk will be made before the meeting begins. Note that although there will be an agenda, it may not be followed.

Keep in mind that decisions will be made in private, rather than at any time during a meeting. The meeting itself is primarily just for gathering information and as a forum for discussion. Frequently, the managing director may not be present and those participating in the meeting will need to have materials to take back to him or her.

Prepare to be asked many questions at the meeting. Many of them will be of the "What if" variety. You should be prepared to overcome any obstacles posed by such questions.

Punctuality

For prearranged business meetings, you should be sure to arrive on time. However, when you are invited to your Portuguese contact's home, it is appropriate to arrive about 15 minutes after the time specified on the invitation.

If you are kept waiting by your Portuguese contact, avoid acknowledging it, so that you don't embarrass the person.

Seating Etiquette

Seating etiquette in Portugal dictates that the individuals hosting the meal sit at the head of the table. The male guest of honor will be offered the seat to the immediate right of the hostess, while the female guest of honor will sit to the immediate right of the host.

Tipping Tips

In most cases, restaurant bills will have a built-in 15-percent service charge. If a server has gone above and beyond the call of duty, or if you have stayed at the table longer than most patrons, be sure to leave additional change (for example, 150 to 200 *escudos*).

When hotel porters assist you with luggage, tip the person something in the range of 100 *escudos* for the service rendered. Be sure to give chambermaids up to approximately 50 *escudos* per day.

When riding in a taxi, you should base your tip on the distance you have been driven. For instance, when you are driven short distances, add a 10-percent tip to your fare. On the other hand, when you are driven longer distances, be sure to add a 15-percent tip to the final fare.

It is also appropriate to acknowledge theater ushers, washroom attendants, and coatroom clerks by giving a small tip.

Toasting Etiquette

In Portugal, wine is commonly taken with dinner. Beer is also enjoyed and sometimes even substituted for wine when the weather is hot and one's thirst needs quenching.

Portuguese toasting etiquette follows universal toasting rules—that is, guests should lift their goblets only after the host has initiated a toast to the person being honored.

It is acceptable for women to offer toasts.

If your host lifts his or her goblet or glass and says, "*Á sua Saúde*," then you know that the person has proposed a toast to you.

When You Are Invited to a Portuguese Home

When you are invited to someone's home in Portugal, be sure to arrive on time and go with something in hand as a way of extending your thanks for the invitation. Good gifts include fine chocolates or a bouquet of flowers (other than chrysanthemums).

When you arrive, you will most likely be offered a before-dinner beverage. Later, after dinner has ended, do not leave within an hour or so, as is appropriate in some other European countries, but prepare to stay until shortly before the clock strikes 12.

Be sure to express your compliments to the hostess throughout your visit, making special note of the evening's food and hospitality.

Women in Business

Although women are in the work force, especially in cities, women in management are by far the exception rather than the rule. If anywhere, women will be in higher-ranking positions in family-owned businesses.

Although Portuguese men will accept a lunch invitation, if a woman initiates the invitation and plans to pay, she should do so inconspicuously, to keep her Portuguese male guest from attempting to treat her.

When extending a dinner invitation, be sure to include spouses.

Whatever You Do...

- Don't make reference to the Portuguese or other things in Portugal as being Spanish. Although Portugal was ruled by the Spanish at one time, its citizens dislike being thought of as Spanish.
- Don't wait to be seated in most restaurants. It is perfectly acceptable and even necessary for you to seat yourself in almost any restaurant. Only the finest quality restaurants require you to wait to be seated.

- Don't schedule meetings during the middle of July through September. This is the time that many Portuguese will go on holiday.
- Don't expect first-class travel and a stay at the finest hotel to provide the Portuguese with a good impression of you and your company. They are less likely to be impressed with your lodging; you will be better off displaying your knowledge about the service or product you represent.
- Don't dress casually if you are going out after work. The Portuguese believe in dressing up even if they are going for coffee.
- Don't take wine as a gift. Many Portuguese have wine cellars, so there is plenty to be had already, and it is not considered a special gift.
- Don't give chrysanthemums as a gift. These flowers are associated with funerals.

Advice From the Experts

"Take a conservative approach to negotiations. Clearly communicate prices and delivery dates. If faced with an ultimatum, don't be afraid to walk away, rather than accept less than face value. The Portuguese will look upon such a decision with respect."

—Barbara G. Toms, Traffic Manager, Goettsch International, Inc.

Chapter 19

Romania

Romania (which is also spelled Rumania) is a former Communist country located in southeastern Europe. Its southeastern border lies on the Black Sea. It is bordered on the north and northeast by Ukraine and Moldova, on the northwest by Hungary, on the southwest by Serbia, and on the south by Bulgaria. This country's landscape is distinguished by the Carpathian Mountains that run across a large portion of the country (creating a northeastern region called Moldavia), as well as a plateau to the west of the mountains (the region called Transylvania) and low, arable lands in the east and south (Wallachia). The Danube River flows along Romania's southern border. The capital is Bucharest, located in the southern region of Wallachia.

Romania's three distinct regions were at one time separate states that formed part of the Ottoman Empire. Russia took control of a portion of Moldavia, called Bessarabia, in 1812. Following the Crimean War of 1853-1856, Wallachia and Moldavia became independent principalities. They united in 1861 to create the nation of Romania, which was internationally recognized in 1878. Following World War I, during which Romania sided with the Allies, it regained Bessarabia, as well as Bukovina, and was also united with the state of Transylvania to form the country that is Romania today. During World War II, Romania, which had formed an alliance with the Germans, was invaded by troops from the Soviet Union. By 1948, the monarchy that had ruled the country was abolished and a Communist government was set up under the name of the Romanian People's Republic. While closely linked to the Soviet Union, the nation took an independent route under the unpopular leadership of dictator Nicolae Ceausescu, who was ousted in 1989 and ultimately executed. Thereafter, the country was ruled by coalition governments composed of Communists and non-Communists, and free elections have been implemented. It is now a republic led by a prime minister who oversees a bicameral parliament and a cabinet called the Council of Ministers. There is also an elected president, who serves as chief of state.

Since 1990, Romania's economy has gradually changed from a centrally planned one based on agriculture to a more free-market society, putting the emphasis on industrialization and private ownership. Its major exports today include steel, machinery, fuels, and chemicals. Primary crops are corn, sugar beets, potatoes, and cereals such as rye, barley, and wheat. Romania is, in fact, one of the major cereal producers in Europe, in addition to fruits and vegetables. Mineral resources include coal, iron ore, bauxite, lead, and copper, among others, as well as petroleum and natural gas. Romania has undergone tremendous economic and social struggles since the collapse of the Communist regime, and it is one of the poorest countries in Eastern Europe, but it is slowly getting on its feet and gaining a position of respect and importance.

Statistics and Information

Air Travel

Most individuals arriving from outside the country fly directly into the Otapeni Airport, which is about 9 miles north of Bucharest. Buses, shuttles, and taxis are the available means of transportation into the city, costing about $.50, $10, and $30 respectively.

Country Code

Romania's country code is 40.

Bucharest's city code is 1.

Currency

Romania's currency is the *Leu* (abbreviated L; *lei* is the plural form). Notes are available in denominations of L10,000, 5,000, 1,000, and 500. Currency also comes in coin form of L100 and 50.

In order to get the best buys, be sure to make as many purchases as you can using the *lei*.

Be sure to keep the receipts you are given when exchanging currency. The reason is that they will be needed for proof that you did not convert currency on the black market.

Dates

Romanians follow the European standard format when writing dates, with the number referring to the day listed first, followed by the month, and then the year. September 21, 1999, would be written as 21/9/99.

Ethnic Makeup

More than 80 percent of the population in this country has Romanian roots. Almost 10 percent is Hungarian, while less than 2 percent of the population is of German descent.

Holidays

January 1/2	New Year's Celebration
May 1	May Day
August 23/24	National Day Celebrations
December 1	Union Day
December 25/26	Christmas

Language

The country's official language is Romanian. It is a Latin-based language that contains sounds similar to French, Spanish, Italian, and Portuguese. This distinguishes Romanian from other Eastern European languages, which are of Slavic origin. Many of the people in Romania also speak Hungarian and German, and there are pockets of Serbian and Turkish, as well. While French is commonly used in the business arena, you will also will hear German and English.

Religion

Approximately three quarters of the inhabitants of this country belong to the Romanian Orthodox Church. Many people also follow either the Calvinist Protestant religion or the teachings of the Roman Catholic Church. There are also small minorities of Jews, Muslims, and Lutherans.

Time Zone Differences

Romania is:

- Two hours ahead of Greenwich Mean Time.
- Seven hours ahead of U.S. Eastern Standard Time.

Weather

Temperatures will vary in Romania, based on the part of the country you're visiting. The climate also fluctuates throughout the year. Temperatures in Bucharest drop to –25 degrees Celsius in the winter, with much snow and fog. Summers are sunny and rainy with temperatures at 25 degrees Celsius.

Etiquette

Business Attire

Taking care is the rule in Romania. While it is important to always present yourself as polished, you should not overdo it by wearing clothes or accessories that may be equated with wealth. Business attire should be modest and conservative, instead. Men should wear dark suits, white shirts, and plain ties. If the weather is hot, they may remove their jackets on their host's cue. Businesswomen should wear dark suits or classic style dresses with modestly cut skirts, blouses, and heels.

It is acceptable to wear business attire to evening events, rather than tuxedos or evening gowns.

Business-card Etiquette

Be sure to take plenty of business cards with you, because you will be expected to give them to every business contact you meet.

It would be appropriate and appreciated if you arranged to have your business card translated into Romanian on the reverse side. Be sure to have your title printed in larger type than usual so that it stands out on the card. Titles are of great importance to the Romanians.

Business Entertaining/Dining

Entertaining is a very important part of establishing business relationships with Romanians. Believe it or not, dinners can be comprised of as many as seven courses.

If you receive an invitation to dinner, you may be asked to arrive around 7 p.m. or later. Because meals can be prolonged, you should be prepared to stay for several hours.

Although it may seem unusual to some Westerners, your napkin should remain on the table throughout the meal, rather than being placed on your lap after everyone has been seated.

Be sure to accept a little of everything, rather than refusing a particular food. Food is an important part of Romanian hospitality, and you may risk offending your host if you choose not to taste a particular dish.

Salad will not be served as a separate course, but instead will be put directly on your main course plate with your other food.

Many Romanian meals center on meat, so there's a good chance you will be served pork, beef, and chicken. A few favorite Romanian dishes that you may be served include grilled meatballs, *sarmale*, which is cabbage filled with seasoned meat and rice, and *mamaliga*, a dish of ground corn mixed with butter, sour cream, and cheese.

Excellent wines abound in Romania and can be bought at very low prices. Local beer is popular and cheap, but you can expect to pay heavily for an import.

Get ready for toasts to be proposed at nearly every meal. As glasses are raised, you will hear common toasts, such as "Good luck."

Conversation

Romanians welcome visits from Westerners and are most interested in learning about their lives in the United States, so expect this to be a topic of conversation. They will also ask you many questions about both your business and personal life. Their questions are true reflections of their interest in what it's like to be living in the land of opportunity.

Other safe topics include your travels in Romania, other countries you have visited, sports, art, and even the Dracula legend.

Most Romanians make a point of remaining very current about what's going on internationally and will encourage you to share your thoughts on world affairs. While it is considered acceptable to discuss politics about your own country and other nations, stay away from Romanian politics.

Gestures and Public Manners

Romanians are very warm, open, and expressive people. You will see friends of both sexes embracing, exchanging kisses, and talking with great emotion. As a Westerner, you will be given the same sort of treatment, so be prepared to be hugged and kissed, and to have people stand closer than two arms' lengths to you.

Romanians are known for making very direct eye contact. In fact, some individuals from abroad may misinterpret this directness as staring. This is not the case, however, and you should reciprocate by mirroring the person looking at you with smiles and eye contact.

While you will have access to public restrooms in hotels, restaurants, and train stations, you may be surprised to find that you will have to pay for items such as toilet paper and even soap. If you prefer not to pay, go prepared with your own supply of these materials.

Gift-giving Etiquette

Romanians are a very hospitable people, and love to both give and receive presents. Thus, you should be sure to go to Romania with gifts in hand.

It is considered appropriate to give a gift at many different times, including when you first meet your Romanian contact, after you have completed a business deal, when you have been invited to another's home, and even prior to leaving Romania.

Because the salaries Romanians earn are considerably lower than U.S. incomes, be sure to give moderately priced gifts. Suggested presents include a bottle of liquor, items for the office or desk, a paperweight with your company logo, or something from the city you represent.

Greetings and Introductions

Romanians are fond of meeting individuals from abroad, yet may maintain an arms'-length distance when first becoming acquainted. You should shake hands with others both at the initial meeting and upon departure.

Romanian etiquette encourages men to greet a woman by kissing her hand. Women from abroad should accept this gesture graciously. On the other hand, when men from abroad meet a Romanian woman, there is no need to kiss her hand. Instead, hands should be shaken, but only after she has initiated the handshake.

Titles are an important part of a Romanian greeting. For that reason, when meeting a person who is a doctor, engineer, or lawyer, or who holds another academic or professional title, be sure to address the person by his or her title and last name.

Hierarchy Is Important

Recognizing the appropriate hierarchical order is an important part of successfully conducting business in Romania. When possible, become acquainted with the titles of the individuals you will be meeting so that you are able to determine who is responsible for making the final decision.

How Decisions Are Made

As a result of Romania's long history of Communism and continued bureaucratic red tape, you should prepare for a decision-making process that is very slow and deliberate. Usually, an organization's top executive will be the person who will ultimately have the final say on a project.

Meeting Manners

Taking time to establish rapport is an important part of developing a business relationship with Romanian businesspeople. Like people of most other nationalities, Romanians appreciate individuals who are down-to-earth in their approach. Therefore, be sure to add warmth to your presentation, along with making it factual and easy-to-understand. Any form of documentation you can provide will be appreciated, especially if it is translated into Romanian.

Romanians are unlikely to accept the first offer you make to them. Part of the way they conduct business is through the bargaining process. Allow your Romanian contacts to set the tone and mirror their indirect negotiating style, rather than risking being perceived as too direct in your approach.

Punctuality

As in many countries, time is fluid in Romania. For that reason, be sure to take plenty of reading material with you to a meeting, as you can expect to be kept waiting for as long as 60 minutes. However, understand that you will be expected to arrive at the appointed time. In addition, meetings may run much longer than expected. For that reason, avoid scheduling meetings close together.

Seating Etiquette

Contrary to the seating etiquette in many European countries, the most senior guest of honor will be seated across from the host at the other end of the table.

Tipping Tips

Most Romanian restaurants add a gratuity to your bill. If you have received outstanding service, however, servers will appreciate any additional amount that you may choose to leave.

When porters assist you with luggage, it is appropriate to give them 35 to 55 *lei* per bag. Taxi drivers should be tipped 10 percent of your fare.

When You Are Invited to a Romanian Home

While most entertaining is conducted in restaurants, you can be sure that you will be treated like royalty when you are invited to your Romanian contact's home. It is in order to arrive on time, rather than showing up fashionably late. You should dress as you would during the business day, in business professional attire.

Be sure to show your appreciation by going with chocolates, liquor, or a bouquet of flowers in hand. If you bring flowers, make sure they are an odd number, as even numbers are associated with funerals. If there are children in the family you are visiting, bringing a few small gifts for them will be very much appreciated.

The evening itself will center on food. You will most likely be offered second and third helpings, and if you refuse, your Romanian contacts will interpret it as your merely being polite, rather than not caring for more.

When you are satisfied and do not care for more of a particular food, be courteous but insistent in your refusal. You should express how excellent the food is, yet how satisfied you are.

Following dinner, conversation will take place while you enjoy coffee and dessert.

Women in Business

It is refreshing to know that chivalry is alive and well on the Romanian front. For that reason, women traveling from abroad will be treated with the utmost respect.

Although few Romanian women hold high positions of authority in the business arena, women from abroad will be taken seriously by dressing and acting conservatively and putting their best professional selves forward.

Whatever You Do...

- Don't flaunt what Romanians may perceive as wealth. The people of this country are among the poorest in Eastern Europe.
- Don't order food in a restaurant without first asking to see the cost of each item. This will prevent your paying more for the meal than you should.
- Don't get into a taxi without first agreeing on the fare.
- Don't misplace the receipts you are given when you exchange currency. You will need these receipts as proof that you did not exchange money on the black market.
- Don't expect to seal a business deal during your first trip to Romania. Instead, be prepared for your Romanian contacts to take even longer than the Germans in reaching a decision about how they would like to proceed.

Chapter 20

Russia

Russia—once known as the Russian Empire, the Russian Federation, and the Russian Soviet Federated Socialist Republic—is the largest country in the world. Located in eastern Europe and northern Asia, its territory at one time (c. 1914) comprised almost one-sixth of the earth's land area. This territory included large portions of Europe then under its control, as well as massive amounts of Asia. Russia also formed the greatest part of the Union of Soviet Socialist Republics in the days prior to the downfall of Communism in that nation. Like other countries of the Soviet Union, it is now a separate, independent, self-governing nation, working to instill democratic principles and a free-market economy.

Russia today borders the following countries: Finland, Estonia, Latvia, Lithuania, Belarus, and Ukraine on the west, and Georgia, Azerbaijan, Kazakhstan, Mongolia, China, and North Korea on the south. It also touches the Baltic and Black Seas on the west, the Pacific Ocean on the east, and the Arctic Ocean on the north. The capital is Moscow. The country's economy has always been dependent on industrial development, although the natural resources of the land have also provided a great source of income. Russia is rich in a vast number of mineral resources, and also relies on fishing as one of its biggest industries. Agriculture does not contribute greatly to the GNP, because only about a sixth of the total land area is arable. Meanwhile, since the Soviet Union was abolished, businesses that were run by the government have found their way back into private hands and such industries as the production and export of chemicals are on the rise.

Russia's history extends back for centuries. It was conquered by Mongols in the mid-1200s, after which it slowly began a rise to primacy in Asia and eastern Europe. By 1533, Ivan IV the Terrible had begun his reign as Russia's first tsar, and by 1613, Michael Romanov had begun a tsarist dynasty that would last until the Russian Revolution of 1917. Although the country was to benefit under the leadership of tsars, such as Peter I the Great, and empresses, such as Catherine II the Great, both of whom expanded Russian territory and power during their reigns, the Russian people chafed increasingly under a royalist regime. Devastated by its participation in World War I, the country went into revolt soon thereafter. The Romanovs were overthrown and a democratic government was established, but this, too, was soon supplanted by the Bolshevik uprising of 1918. The Union of Soviet Socialist Republics thereupon came into effect, a Communist government that gained in strength over the years. Vladimir Lenin and Josef Stalin became infamous for their iron-fisted control and suppression of the Russian people. By the time Nikita Krushchev came to power in the 1950s, the U.S.S.R. had become a dominant power that had entered into a Cold War with the world's other dominant power, the United States. However, with the failure of socialist policies and the reformist government of Mikhail Gorbachev in the 1980s, Communist policies experienced a downfall that would ultimately lead to a complete overhaul of the government, free elections, and the dissolution of the Soviet Union. Russia is now a republic with an elected president (currently Boris Yeltsin) and a legislature in the form of the Congress of People's Deputies. The current population numbers close to 150 million people.

In addition to its political prominence in global affairs, Russia has made numerous contributions to the arts, and has given the world some of its greatest writers, dancers, and musicians, including Peter Ilich Tchaikovsky, Nikolai Rimsky-Korsakov, Rudolph Nuryev, Mikhail

Barishnikov, Leo Tolstoy, Fyodor Dostoyevsky, and Anton Chekhov, among countless others.

Etiquette

Air Travel

Most people traveling to Russia fly into either Moscow's Sheremetyevo Airport or St. Petersburg's Pulkovo Airport. Taxis for the journey into either city are costly. An alternative is to travel from the airport to Moscow or St. Petersburg using the excellent metro bus system, which costs only the equivalent of a few dollars.

Country Code

Russia's country code is 7.

City codes include:

- 095 for Moscow.
- 812 for St. Petersburg.

Currency

Russia's currency is the *ruble* (Rub). One *ruble* is equal to 100 *kopecks*. Bills come in denominations of Rub100,000, 50,000, 10,000, 5,000, 1,000, 500, 200, and 100. Coins come in units of 50, 20, 15, 10, 5, 3, 2, and 1 *kopecks*, as well as 1 *ruble*.

You will find the best exchange rate at the state-run bureaus, where exchange booths are located.

Dates

As in other countries of Europe, Russians write the date by listing the day of the month first, followed by the month, and then the year. June 30, 1999, would therefore be written as 30/6/99.

Ethnic Makeup

The majority of Russia's population is comprised of Russians. However, there are more than 60 other nationalities represented, including a small percentage of Tatars and Ukrainians.

Holidays and National Celebrations

As in other European countries, holidays and national celebrations are an integral part of the culture. For that reason, meetings should not be scheduled on these dates.

January 1	New Year's Day
January 7	Orthodox Christmas
March 8	International Women's Day
May 9	Victory Day
June 12	Russian Independence Day
October 7	Constitution Day

Language

Russian is the language of Russia. It is a Slavic language and its alphabet is called the Cyrillic alphabet. Many people also speak English. Numerous different dialects and languages can be found in different regions of the country.

Religion

After almost a century of Russian leaders declaring the country to be atheist, religion is becoming more popular and visible. Most Russians follow the Russian Orthodox Church. Islam has the second largest following, with Catholicism and various Protestant religions also practiced.

Time Zone Differences

Russia is:

- Three hours ahead of Greenwich Mean Time.
- Eight hours ahead of U.S. Eastern Standard Time.

Weather

Because of its vast size, Russia's climate can vary from region to region. However, it is generally similar to the weather in the U.S. Midwest. Winters are known to be dreary and cold, with snow and ice, and temperatures that often fall below freezing. Summers are warm, with frequent rain showers. Temperatures at this time of year average in the mid-70s Fahrenheit. The autumn and spring seasons are usually mild. Meanwhile, regions in the far north can experience long, harsh winters that make those areas almost uninhabitable.

Etiquette

Business Attire

People dress in a variety of ways in Russia. Older generations are still very conservative in their attire, while younger people have adopted a more Western-style of dressing. However, a lack of resources and large demand for clothing make it challenging for many Russians to have a lot of clothes. In fact, it is more the norm than the exception for individuals to wear the same outfit several times during the course of the same week. With this in mind, be sure to dress conservatively. By doing so, you will blend in and will also not cause the envy of any of your Russian contacts. You will also allow your contacts to focus on the business at hand, rather than on what you have and what they don't have.

For business, men should wear dark-colored suits and white shirts with conservative ties. Women should wear tailored suits, also in dark colors, with skirts of modest length.

Business-card Etiquette

Be sure to take an ample supply of business cards with you. Although many of the individuals with whom you will be meeting have a command of the English language, it still is a good idea to have the back side of your card translated into Russian.

Note that some people you give your cards to may not be able to reciprocate because they do not have business cards of their own. To help them get over any feelings of discomfort about this, simply jot down information about them in your planner.

Business Entertaining/Dining

When you are invited out by a Russian, get ready to be treated like royalty. Most entertaining situations will be in restaurants. It is rare that spouses will be part of this type of gathering. Because your Russian contacts will have made a rather hefty investment to entertain you, be sure not to waste any food.

Food is served "family-style" in Russia, with community platters set on the table and each person serving himself or herself after the host initiates the invitation to do so.

Note that Russians use the continental-style of holding utensils, with the fork held in the left hand, tines down, and the knife in the right hand at all times. You will also note that Russian desserts are enjoyed with a spoon, rather than with a fork.

Russian cuisine is very good and will contain several starches. You may be treated to caviar, followed by meat and vegetables and accompanied by potatoes and bread.

Conversation

You can expect your Russian contacts to have a lot of questions for you about what it's like living on the Western front. While questions may appear personal by Western standards, they will appreciate some answers from you, even if you reply in a general way.

You will find Russians to be enthusiastic about discussing politics and the trials and tribulations of living in Russia. When you are involved in this type of conversation, the best way to participate is by being a good listener, rather than by expressing your views and risking possible offense.

Safe topics of conversation include books, art, films, and current events.

Don't be surprised if a compliment you've expressed is downplayed. Like most people, Russians enjoy hearing flattering words. However, it is thought to be more appropriate to accept compliments by downplaying them.

Gestures and Public Manners

Rules that govern personal space and autonomy are quite different in Russia from what they are in the United States. For instance, Russians are high-contact people when interacting with their friends and acquaintances. While shaking hands is common, so are embraces, pats on the back, and kisses on the cheeks and lips.

A Russian's comfort level as it relates to distance is to stand no more than one arms' length from the person he or she is talking to. Russians are used to being in very close contact with each other, as is the case on public transportation, for instance. Even if you feel as though your space is being invaded, accept it when a Russian stands closer to you than your comfort level allows. If you try to back away, you could risk offending the person.

Besides being high-contact people, Russians are very open about their personal lives and will expect you to reciprocate.

Don't think a Russian is being rude if he or she appears to be glaring at you. Staring is a very common Russian form of nonverbal communication.

When Russians are pleased with a performance, they may clap and shout "Bravo." If they are displeased with anything, they will express it by whistling.

When you are in a theater environment and need to pass someone in your row, Russian etiquette dictates that you do so facing the person, rather than having your back towards the individual.

When sitting, be sure to keep the soles of your shoes facing the ground.

Two gestures that are considered extremely rude in Russia are the "okay" sign and the "V" for victory. You should therefore avoid making these gestures.

If you are on the hunt for a public restroom, be sure to have plenty of tissues with you. Once you do find a toilet, you may be surprised to find that it consists of a mere hole in the ground. You will find more modernized facilities in restaurants and hotels.

Gift-giving Etiquette

Russians greatly enjoy both giving and receiving. For that reason, be sure to go to Russia with several gifts in hand. Practical items will be most appreciated. Recommended gifts include liquor, fine chocolates, flowers, perfume or cologne, desk items, and clothing.

Russian protocol does not require gifts to be wrapped, so be sure to present yours "as is" in a box or bag. In addition, you will note that the person receiving your gift will wait until after you have left to open it. Be sure to follow suit, and wait until you are in private to open any gifts you receive.

Greetings and Introductions

Be sure to shake hands when meeting and greeting Russians. Once rapport has been established, expect to be greeted during subsequent get-togethers with an embrace and a kiss.

To avoid being perceived as too aggressive, men from abroad should allow Russian women to initiate any handshakes.

Proper forms of address: Part of a Russian greeting includes addressing the person by his or her full name. This is comprised of three parts, as per the following examples:

- Mikhail Ivanovich Glinka (man).
- Mikaila Ivanovna Glinka (woman).

The person's first name is called the given name—for instance, *Mikhail* for a man and *Mikaila* for a woman. This is followed by the first name of the person's father and the appropriate ending according to sex. For example, if the father's name is Ivan, then this person's middle name would be *Ivanovich* for a man (meaning "son of Ivan") and *Ivanovna* for a woman (meaning "daughter of Ivan"). Finally, the last name is spoken.

After the initial greeting, the appropriate way to address a Russian is by the person's first and second names, leaving off the last name.

Hierarchy Is Important

Business life in Russia is formal and hierarchies play an important role in internal relations and decision-making. For that reason, it is important to remember that the person at the highest level within the organization is the most powerful.

How Decisions Are Made

Be prepared—it will take a long time for decisions to be made in this country. One reason is that your Russian contacts will want to get the total picture. Another is that the head person will be the sole decision-maker and will need time to assess the situation. Stalling on decisions may also be part of the Russian negotiating strategy.

Once a contract is signed, don't be surprised if terms in the contract are not met. It is quite common for Russians to attempt to modify contract specifications after the fact.

Meeting Manners

Although there have been a lot of positive changes within Russia during the last several years, there is still a great need for improvement. Thus, it is important to always bear in mind that it will take time to develop a business relationship with a Russian company.

A crucial part of building and strengthening a Russian business relationship is by becoming acquainted with your contact on a one-to-one basis. Let the person see and know the "personal you" as a way of developing a healthy foundation for the business relationship itself. By letting your Russian acquaintance see you as a down-to-earth and sincere person who does what you say you're going to do, you will be on your way to earning his or her trust. Once again, try to avoid flaunting opulence in your clothes, jewelry, and accessories (including your pen).

Be sure to arrange for a translator to be part of any meeting you plan.

A typical Russian meeting consists of small talk before getting down to business. Once you begin, prepare for the meeting to be interrupted by phone calls and/or visitors. Also, don't be surprised if your Russian contacts smoke during the meeting.

Your presentation should be detail-oriented, as well as clear, concise, and easy to understand. Be sure your material includes background information about your organization, in addition to what your company has to offer your Russian contacts that other similar companies may not be able to offer.

Be sure your presentation material is translated into Russian, so that those attending can follow along with your presentation, in addition to having material to review following the meeting.

During the initial meeting, your Russian contacts may appear to be taking a low-key approach. In fact, this is their time for absorbing the information you are providing. During subsequent meetings, you are likely to see them verbalizing their thoughts in a very emotional way. Being direct is very much a part of the Russian manner. However, rather than mirroring this emotional approach yourself, you should stay calm.

Although time is fluid with Russians, when they have arranged a business meeting, they try to arrive close to the appointed time. You should always make a point of arriving on time yourself. Also, take reading material with you so that if you are kept waiting, you will be able to use your time wisely.

Seating Etiquette

Russian seating etiquette dictates that the center seats be reserved for the most senior officials. You should sit on the opposite side of the table from your Russian contacts and be seated across from your peer according to rank.

Tipping Tips

Tipping those in what Westerners call the "service industry" is not commonplace in Russia. You should feel free to tip according to what you feel is appropriate. However, recognize that it is acceptable to leave a lesser rather than greater amount in your gratuity. For example, no more than a little change is considered an acceptable tip for servers. The same applies to washroom attendants and coatroom clerks.

Toasting Etiquette

Russians definitely enjoy their alcohol. In fact, vodka is one of the most commonly consumed hard liquors in this country. With drinks in hand, toasts will inevitably follow. Not only are they initiated by the host at the beginning of a meal, they continue throughout the evening.

Common Russian toasts include "To you," "To us," and "To your health."

Guests should prepare to offer toasts in return for having one or more toasts proposed to them.

When You Are Invited to a Russian Home

Even though many Russians live in apartments with limited space, they enjoy entertaining and also have a knack for it. Thus, if you are invited to a Russian home, you will be treated with the greatest of hospitality.

Hospitality dictates that you go with a gift in hand for the hostess (for example, flowers or chocolates) and any children who may be part of the family (toys or games).

If it appears that your Russian hosts are wearing slippers, emulate them by removing your shoes and putting on the footwear you are offered.

You should arrive on time. Do not expect to have pre-dinner drinks and appetizers, as the meal is typically served within minutes after you arrive.

Women in Business

Russian women do not occupy many ranking positions in the Russian work force. Russian men still have a gallant, chivalrous attitude toward women. Women traveling to Russia from abroad will be respected and taken as seriously as they look and act.

Whatever You Do...

- Don't expect to be seated in a restaurant without reservations.
- Don't schedule your trip to Russia near the end of July or during the month of August, because this is the time of year many people go on holiday.
- Don't send correspondence addressed in English. Instead, be sure it is keyed in Russian, as this will expedite your letters being received and read.
- Don't request ice cubes in your beverages, because they may have been made from water that has not been purified.
- Don't speak in a loud voice in public.
- Don't hesitate to introduce yourself to another person if your Russian contact does not introduce you.

Advice From the Experts

"Good manners in Russia means allowing your dinner partner to refill your glass. In turn, it means observing your table partners' glasses and replenishing them accordingly. Typically, there are four bottles placed at every seat—vodka, champagne, brandy, and a nonalcoholic beverage."

—Anne Wood Schlesinger, Ph.D., President of Execuspeak, Author of Put Your Mouth Where Your Money Is

"Be very punctual. Be ready for long negotiations. Never compare Russia to other developing countries."

—Enzo Ferraris, Manager, International Trade Relations, The Procter & Gamble Company

Chapter 21

Scotland

A member of the United Kingdom, Scotland is located on the northernmost part of the island of Great Britain, which includes England and Wales to its south. The Atlantic Ocean lies on its west and north coasts, with the North Sea on the east. Scotland also includes more than 780 islands, most of them less than three square miles in area. The best known of these are the groups known as the Hebrides, Orkney, and Shetland islands. Scotland's major cities are Glasgow, Edinburgh, and Dundee. The current population numbers approximately 5.1 million.

Originally called Caledonia, Scotland's current name was derived from a Celtic tribe called Scots who migrated from Ireland and settled on a tract of land in the western part of the island, which they named Scotia. A Celtic monarchy eventually evolved from a conglomeration of tribes, and Scotland existed largely as an independent nation until well into the 13th century, when King Edward I of England attempted to force English rule on the country. A series of revolts finally led to the official recognition of the Scottish kingdom under Robert the Bruce and the establishment of the Stuart monarchy. In 1603, upon the death of Queen Elizabeth I, King James VI of Scotland succeeded her, thus uniting the two kingdoms into a peaceful alliance that has been shaken by rebellion on a few occasions (including the Jacobite revolts of 1715 and 1745), but has remained stable since the mid-1700s. In 1707, the Act of Union was passed, uniting England, Scotland, and Wales into the Kingdom of Great Britain, at which, Scotland dissolved its parliament (and received guarantees that its laws and courts and the Presbyterian Established Church—now the Church of Scotland—be allowed to remain autonomous). Scotland holds 72 seats in the U.K.'s House of Commons and maintains separate administrative, legal, banking, and educational systems.

Scotland is geographically divided into three regions: the Highlands, which are marked by mountains and numerous lakes called lochs (for which the country is famous); the Lowlands (also known as the Midland Valley), an area of hills, moors, and farmland; and the Southern Uplands, with flat valleys, table mountains, and very rich, arable land. The Scottish countryside is known for its abundance of peat, heather, and bracken. The country has numerous natural resources that provide important contributions to the economy, including coal, forests, and an abundance of petroleum offshore in the North Sea. At one time, shipbuilding and the production of steel were two of Scotland's major industries, but these businesses are now in a decline. Agriculture, forestry, and textile manufacturing remain strong, however, and the manufacture of automobiles and other machinery has flourished in recent years. Scotland is also home to one of Europe's largest marine fishing industries.

Statistics and Information

Air Travel

Scotland's major international airport is the Glasgow Airport, located 9 miles outside the city. Taxis and shuttles are available and can get you to the city in about 20 minutes.

Country Code

Scotland's country code is 44.

City codes include:

- 131 for Edinburgh.
- 141 for Glasglow.

Currency

Although it maintains its own banking system and manufactures its own banknotes, Scotland's currency is the English *pound* (£). One *pound* is equal to 100 *pence* (p). Notes are available in denominations of £50, 20, 10, and 5. Coins come in p50, 20, 10, 5, 2, and 1, and £1.

Banks provide the best currency exchange rates.

Dates

Dates are written following the European standard format, with the number representing the day preceding the number representing the month, followed by the year. For example, December 29, 2015, would be written as 29/12/15.

Ethnic Makeup

The vast majority of the country's population is of native Scottish descent.

Holidays And National Celebrations

As in most countries, many holidays and national celebrations are observed in Scotland. For that reason, be sure to avoid requesting meetings around these days.

January 1	New Year's Day
Late March/ Early April	Easter Monday
First Monday in May	May Bank Holiday

Last Monday in May	Spring Bank Holiday
Last Monday in August	Summer Bank Holiday
November 30	St. Andrew's Day
December 25	Christmas Day
December 26	St. Stephen's Day

Language

The country's official language is English. However, accents and the use of different terms for the same thing may cause communication problems. Be sure to listen carefully to avoid misinterpretation.

You will also find Gaelic spoken in the north and west regions of the country, and Scots spoken in the Lowlands.

Religion

A large number of the population belongs to the Church of Scotland, which is Presbyterian. The remainder of the population practices other Protestant faiths.

Time Zone Differences

Scotland is:

- On Greenwich Mean Time.
- Five hours ahead of U.S. Eastern Standard Time.

Weather

Scotland's climate is rather mild and changes little throughout the year. Winters can be chilly, yet it rarely gets colder than the low-40s Fahrenheit. Summers are pleasant, with temperatures reaching into the high 60s. Rainfall is common year-round.

Etiquette

Business Attire

Business dress follows American tradition, but colors are dark and fabrics are heavier. Men should wear suits with starched shirts and ties. Avoid wearing striped ties, because these are associated with military regiments. Women should wear classic-styled suits with heels. Slack suits are not as common in Scotland as they are in the United States.

Scotsmen may also be seen wearing their traditional kilts, which are a very important part of this country's tradition.

Business-card Etiquette

English is the national language, so business cards need not be translated into another language on the reverse side. However, be sure to take plenty of cards with you, as you are likely to be presenting them to a great many people.

Business Entertaining/Dining

Scots entertain business associates at lunch and dinner. Dinner parties are often held in private homes, rather than in restaurants. Spouses are generally included when a function is to be held in a home.

Scottish food can be rather plain, yet excellent. A well-known dish is lamb stew. You will be served a variety of meats, fish, and vegetables. *Haggis* is another well-known Scottish dish. This is a sheep's stomach containing other parts of the animal's internal organs and prepared with spices, oatmeal, and suet. This may not seem appealing to Americans, but it is quite a delicacy in Scotland.

The Scots eat using the continental-style of dining, with the fork kept in the left hand, tines down, and the knife in the right hand at all times. Like other Europeans, the Scots see this as a very efficient way of eating.

Be sure to keep your hands above board at all times. As in other European countries, it is a *faux pas* for hands not to be showing.

Food is typically served "family-style" in Scotland. When this is the case, platters are passed around, allowing you to help yourself to a portion of the food.

One way to demonstrate that you are satisfied is to leave a small amount on your plate, thus demonstrating that you have had more than enough to eat.

Conversation

It may take a while to establish rapport with the Scots, because they are soft-spoken and private by nature and tend not to be open with people they have just met. However, you will also find them to be very interested in meeting you, and once they've become acquainted with you, their tone will change and you are sure to see the friendlier side of them.

Small topics provide a good way to warm up a conversation. Appropriate subjects include your travels in Scotland and throughout Europe, outdoor activities, and the weather conditions.

Avoid any conversation that involves politics, religion, and Northern Ireland. You should also not ask about a Scot's family, nor what the person does for a living. In Scotland, an individual's personal life is considered private.

Gestures and Public Manners

When in Scotland, be sure to speak in a low voice. Talking too loudly in public is considered offensive and will cause both you and those around you a lot of embarrassment.

Scots are also low-keyed when it comes to using nonverbal forms of communication. They rely on their words, rather than using their hands to express themselves.

Keep your hands out of your pockets. Just as hands should be showing when you are eating, the same rule applies to standing and walking.

Scots are low-contact people. Rather than touching or getting too close, it is more appropriate to remain at least one arms'-length distance from your Scottish contact.

Queuing: Contrary to some countries where pushing and shoving is the norm, Scots are very respectful about standing in line. It can also be a social occasion; some persons around you may even ask you questions. Be sure to limit your conversational small talk to your immediate environment. You may also want the person who initiated the conversation to set the tone of the topic as the line moves forward.

Gift-giving Etiquette

While you may want to go to Scotland with gifts in hand, you do not need to present anything until after a business deal has been solidified. When the time is right, you may give items such as desk accessories, a coffee table book about your homeland, a paperweight with your company logo, or even a bottle of good whisky.

Greetings and Introductions

The most appropriate form of greeting in Scotland is to exchange handshakes with the person you are meeting and say, "How do you do?" Rather than "pumping" the other person's hand, make sure you retain a light grip. A handshake should also be offered when leaving. A man should wait for a Scottish woman to initiate any handshakes.

While eye contact is an important indication of listening in some cultures, in Scotland it should be broken off after a few seconds as a sign of politeness.

When you are speaking about the citizens of Scotland, the proper terms to use are Scotsmen or Scots.

Proper forms of address: As in other countries, you should not use a Scot's first name unless you are invited to do otherwise. Use the last name with the appropriate title, such as Mr., Mrs., or Miss, or the person's academic/professional title. Note that while the term "doctor" is used in many countries to describe a person who has earned a doctorate in graduate school, in Scotland this term is used only for people who have earned a medical degree.

The title Sir should be used when addressing someone who has been knighted by the Queen, followed by the person's first name. For instance, Sir Andrew Carnegie would be addressed as "Sir Andrew."

Hierarchy Is Important

The best way to determine who's in charge is to watch the corporate deference that is given to others during a meeting. Although it will be apparent that the managing director will have the final word, by observing how people treat each other, you will be able to understand the pecking order in an organization.

How Decisions Are Made

The most senior executives in the majority of Scottish companies are called "managing directors." These are the individuals who are ultimately responsible for making final decisions.

Meeting Manners

As in any other meetings, you should be well-prepared by having presentation materials with you, along with charts and graphs. Also allow time for the individuals in attendance to ask questions. The meeting may get informal at times, but avoid letting down your guard.

Soon after a meeting has ended, be sure to summarize the results and send your summary to your Scottish contacts. This will be one way to demonstrate your follow-through.

Punctuality

Unlike their English neighbors, Scots value punctuality. Be on time for both business and social functions. If you have extenuating circumstances and will be arriving late, be sure to call ahead and explain your situation.

Seating Etiquette

The host and hostess will be seated at opposite ends of the table, facing one another. The male guest of honor will be seated to the right of the hostess and the female guest of honor will be placed to the right of the host.

Tipping Tips

Restaurant bills usually include gratuities of 10 to 15 percent. Leave some change if the tip is included. If you find the gratuity is not part of the bill, then leave a tip of 10 to 15 percent.

Tip hotel porters approximately 25p for each bag handled. Chambermaids should be given £1 for each day of your stay. Taxi drivers should be tipped 10 to 15 percent of the fare.

Toasting Etiquette

Scotland's national drink is whisky (spelled without an "e"). Scots tend to enjoy it straight or with a mix of water. As in many European countries, ice is not a regular part of drinks.

The traditional Scottish toast—and the most common one you will hear in Scotland—is "*Shlante,*" which means "To your health." As in other countries, it is appropriate for the host to propose a toast at the beginning of the meal.

When You Are Invited to a Scottish Home

Scots are a very hospitable people, and you may expect to be entertained in a Scot's home, as well as in a restaurant. You should arrive on time, and also go with flowers in hand for the hostess. Fine chocolates and wine also make good gifts.

Women in Business

Although Scottish women do work outside the home, few have made it up that slippery ladder of managerial success. For that reason, women from abroad doing business in Scotland should put their most professional selves forward. That includes both attire and demeanor. By maintaining a high degree of professionalism and displaying a strong knowledge of the business, women will clearly demonstrate their competence to Scotsmen.

Whatever You Do...

- Don't make comments that group the Scots with the English. Scots are very proud of their country's history and tradition.
- Don't wave your hand in the air when you would like to request the bill from the server. The proper way is to lift your hand and pretend you are writing on it.
- Don't refer to slacks or trousers as "pants." To a Scot, this word means "underwear."
- Don't be offended if you are a woman and are referred to as "deary" or "love." While it may not be the case in the United States, in Scotland these terms are commonly used and are considered acceptable.
- Don't attempt to schedule business meetings during the summer months. This is when, like most Europeans, Scots go on holiday.
- Don't invite a businessman to dinner if you are a woman; extend a lunch invitation instead.
- Don't refer to objects or other things in Scotland as being "Scotch." The correct term to use is "Scottish."

Chapter 22

Spain

One of the largest countries in Europe, the Kingdom of Spain occupies approximately 85 percent of the Iberian peninsula, in the southwest corner of the continent. It shares borders with France and Andorra on the north and with Portugal on the west. The northwest and southwest borders of the country lie on the Atlantic Ocean, while the eastern and southern coasts touch the Mediterranean Sea. The island of Gibraltar, which belongs to England, lies off Spain's southernmost coast. There are several islands that belong to Spain, including the Balearic Islands, which lie off the eastern coast, and the Canary Islands, found off the coast of North Africa. In addition, Spain owns two cities in northern Morocco, Ceuta, and Melilla. The combined population of Spain and its territories is well over 40 million people. The capital is Madrid, located in the center of the country. Other major cities include Barcelona and Seville. Total population of Spain is more than 38.8 million people, 78 percent of whom live in urban areas. Nearly 3 million people live in Madrid alone.

A country of mountains and valleys and beautiful countryside, Spain has long held a position of historical, political, and cultural importance in Europe. Invaded by the Celts, Romans, and Germanic tribes in early centuries, it was eventually the Visigoths who attained control of the peninsula and established a kingdom there. Muslim tribes conquered large areas during the early part of the 8th century, but by the 13th century, the Christian kingdoms of Aragon and Castile had driven out the Muslims and reacquired most of the land. After Ferdinand II of Aragon married Isabella I of Castile in 1469, their kingdoms were united and Spain as a country came into being. They were later succeeded by the Habsburgs, then the Bourbons. Spain colonized many parts of the world, but lost most of its overseas possessions after the Spanish American War of 1898. The monarchy was finally abolished in 1931, when Alfonso XIII abdicated and a republic was formed. There followed a period of civil unrest led by General Francisco Franco, who took control of the country in 1939 and remained in power until his death in 1975. His designated heir, Juan Carlos de Borbón y Borbón, was thereupon crowned King of Spain, thus restoring the monarchy and reestablishing a true democracy in the country. Led by a prime minister, the government now consists of a bicameral parliament, with a system of autonomous regional communities. There are 50 provinces altogether in 17 regions.

Spain's economy depends largely on the service industry. Agriculture, livestock, forestry, fishing, and manufacturing are also contributors to the GNP. Spain's major exports include wine, wheat, grapes, sugar beets, barley, potatoes, fish, and heavy and light machinery. Spain is also a leading manufacturer of automobiles. Its mineral resources include coal, copper, iron ore, mercury, potash, salt, tin, and zinc.

Spain is well-known for its beautiful architecture. Many of its natives have achieved renown for their contributions to the arts and humanities. These include painters such as El Greco, Velázquez, and Picasso, as well as musicians such as Pablo Casals and Andrés Segovia and writers such as Miguel de Cervantes and Frederico Garcia Lorca.

Statistics and Information

Air Travel

The primary international airport is Barajas Airport, located approximately 25 minutes from downtown Madrid. Both taxis and buses are readily available forms of transportation.

Country Code

Spain's country code is 34.

City codes include:

- 3 for Barcelona.
- 1 for Madrid.
- 54 for Seville.

Currency

The *peseta* (Pta) is the Spanish currency. Notes are available in Pta10,000, 5,000, and 1,000. Coins are also available in denominations of 500, 200, 100, 50, 25, 10, 5, and 1 *pesetas*.

You will find money exchange offices and automated machines in airport terminals and baggage claim areas.

Dates

Dates are written in the standard European format, with the number representing the day of the month written first, followed by the month, and then the year. For example, November 13, 2005, should be written as 13/11/05.

Ethnic Makeup

Nearly three-quarters of the individuals living in Spain are native Spanish. Individuals from northeast Spain or Catalonia make up just under 20 percent of the population, while people from northwest Spain (more specifically, Galicia) comprise a tenth of Spain's population. Basques living in the northern most part of the country make up approximately 2 percent of the population. There is also a small minority of Gypsies.

Holidays and Religious Celebrations

The following is a list of Spain's national holidays. Because Spaniards are likely to be off work on these days, avoid scheduling meetings around these times.

January 1	New Year's Day
January 6	Epiphany
March 19	St. Joseph's Day
Late March/ Early April	Maundy Thursday
Late March/ Early April	Good Friday, Easter
May 1	Labor Day
Two months after Easter	Corpus Christi
July 25	St. James Day
August 15	The Assumption
October 12	Virgin of Pilar Day
November 1	All Saints' Day
December 8	Immaculate Conception
December 25	Christmas Day

Language

Castellano or Castilian (also known as modern standard Spanish) is Spain's most common language, while gallego or Galicia is spoken by less than 10 percent of the population. There are several regional dialects, including those spoken in Catalan and in Basque country.

Religion

The vast majority of Spain's population practices Roman Catholicism. There are also small pockets of Protestants, Jews, and Muslims.

Time Zone Differences

Spain is:

- One hour ahead of Greenwich Mean Time.
- Six hours ahead of U.S. Eastern Standard Time.

Weather

The climate in Spain will depend on where you are visiting. The northern and eastern coasts enjoy a mild climate, with temperatures going only as low as 48°F in the winter and as high as 64°F in the summer. The central plateau, where Madrid is located, experiences more continental conditions, with temperatures ranging from 75°F in the summer to 40°F in the winter. Along the Atlantic and Biscayan coasts, the climate tends to be damp and cool, while mountainous areas will see colder temperatures year-round. Annual precipitation can range anywhere from 15 to 45 inches, depending on the region.

Etiquette

Business Attire

Clothes are a tell-tale sign of importance and respect in Spain. The quality and style of clothes you wear will also signify the position you hold within your company. For that reason, what you wear should be both professional and stylish in appearance.

Keep in mind that Spaniards dress more conservatively than individuals from the United States. They invest in designer clothes as a way of putting their best professional and personal selves forward.

Dressing *con elegancia* means that men should wear dark suits with starched white shirts and ties. Suit jackets should be kept on at all times, unless a Spanish contact invites you to do otherwise and also removes his jacket.

Women will do well by also wearing designer suits or business dresses made of high-quality fabrics. While tailored slack suits may not be the typical order of the day, dressy pants are acceptable for evening engagements.

Business Entertaining/Dining

It won't take long to see that Spaniards enjoy entertaining and also see it as an integral part of conducting business. Lunch is the main meal of the day for most people, and is more casual in nature than dinner. Business lunches are commonly enjoyed around 2 p.m., during which time business may be discussed.

In contrast to lunches, dinner engagements tend to be more formal and entail more of a social nature. While this meal is typically the lighter of the two, it may include three or more courses during business engagements. Because dinner is usually taken around 9 p.m. or later, lighter fare may be served. Business topics should only be brought up if your Spanish host initiates it.

When you are hosting a meal and would like to include your spouse, first extend an invitation to your Spanish contact's spouse. If she or he is able to join you, then you can feel free include your spouse.

When your Spanish contact is hosting a meal and suggests that you stop at a *tapas* bar prior to dinner, this is the signal that you will be beginning the evening with a before-dinner drink. Following the *tapas* bar experience, you will move onto the restaurant for dinner.

Unusual foods: If you like garlic and olive oil, you will love Spanish cuisine. A very common and favorite Spanish dish is *paella* (a word that originated from the phrase *para ella*). This popular meal consists of rice with saffron, a variety of seafood, sausage, and vegetables.

The Spanish follow the continental-style of dining—the fork in the left hand and the knife in the right at all times. Both utensils may rest on your plate in an "X" position when you are resting or drinking a beverage. When you have finished eating, place your knife and fork next to each other on your plate.

Note that bread plates are not common protocol in Spanish restaurants. Therefore, don't be surprised if one is not available. In addition, butter is not commonly served with bread at lunch and dinner.

Business-card Etiquette

While the business card exchange is not quite as ceremonious an event as you will find in many Asian countries, it is very much an important part of the Spanish meeting. You should go that extra mile by having your business card translated into Spanish on the reverse side.

When you arrive at an appointment, the most appropriate way to announce yourself is to present your card to the receptionist, who in turn will let your Spanish contact know that you are there.

Conversation

The Spanish are very animated individuals. Unlike what you may find in many other cultures, you should expect to be interrupted while you are talking. Don't take this as a personal affront, but recognize it as part of the conversational process in Spain.

Appropriate topics of conversation include politics, soccer, your home country, and current world events.

Although Spaniards are very hospitable, there are certain times when you will do better in keeping your distance, and that is especially true with certain topics of conversation. For instance, avoid asking a Spaniard what he or she does for a living. You should also never ask another person about his or her family life, unless that individual initiates the conversation first. Allow your Spanish friends to disclose this information when they feel comfortable.

Other topics of conversation to avoid include religion and war.

Gestures and Public Manners

Although the "okay" sign means that all is well when communicating with some cultures, in Spain, it is considered to be an obscene gesture, so it should be avoided.

To indicate that you would like someone to come near you, extend your hand with your palm down and open and close your hand.

Spain is composed of many autonomous regions, and the people in those regions take great pride in their origins. Thus, when talking with Spaniards, it is important to place emphasis on them as individuals and the region they represent, rather than categorizing them as Spaniards in a general way. For instance, a Catalonian would not want to be misrepresented as a Sevillano, any more than a Sevillano would want to be labeled as an Andalucian.

Spanish men are quite the charmers in the eyes of some, but may be considered rather forward by others. When they see a lovely woman walking down the street, they will more often than not whistle at her as a form of "applause."

Queuing: Conformity is not the norm for Spaniards, and individualism is a much-valued trait. Because of this, you can expect Spaniards to attempt to cut in front of you when you are standing in line.

Before getting into a taxi, be sure to negotiate the fare. This will ensure that you are being treated equitably.

Gift-giving Etiquette

While gifts are typically not exchanged during initial meetings, you should be prepared to give one at the conclusion of a series of meetings that have yielded a successful partnership. When you receive a gift, the proper protocol is to open it in front of the gift-giver.

Gifts engraved or printed with your organization's logo, such as desk items or pens, are appreciated. The Spanish also enjoy audiotapes, CDs, and pictorial books about the city you represent.

Greetings and Introductions

First-time introductions with Spaniards should be made in a formal manner. Extend a brief but confident handshake, while maintaining eye contact during the greeting. A "*Buenos dias,*" "*Buenas tardes,*" or "*Buenas noches*" should accompany your greeting. In addition to being polite, it is a great way to establish rapport.

The Spanish are high-contact people. Once rapport has been established, prepare for an *abrazo* (embrace) and be sure to give one in return. Air kisses are also a common form of greeting with individuals whom you have met and with whom you have developed a relationship. Even if you are a low-contact person, you should mirror your Spanish contact's greeting so that the other person does not take offense.

Proper forms of address: Most Spaniards have two last names, which may be hyphenated. The first of these is the individual's father's name, while the second is his or her mother's maiden name. When speaking to a Spanish man, it will only be necessary to address him by Mr. and his father's last name. However, when corresponding with someone in writing, the person's full name should be used, including the first name and both last names. Whatever you do, avoid addressing the person by his or her first name alone without first being invited to do so.

The titles of *Señor, Señora,* and *Señorita* should be used during the period of time when you are developing a relationship. Once a comfort level has been established and you have been asked to address someone by their first name, then place *Don* (for a man) or *Doña* (for a woman) before the name as a sign of respect (for example, "Don Carlos" or "Doña Elena").

Hierarchy Is Important

You should be aware of the importance that hierarchy and position play in Spanish business. It would be frowned upon for you to invest a great deal of time and attention on someone who is of lesser rank than you. Focus on those with equal rank in the company.

How Decisions Are Made

Spaniards make decisions more on intuition than they do on facts and figures. For that reason alone, many business relationships are built on trust and the rapport that is established on a personal basis. If Spaniards feel as though they can count on you, and they see that you are a person of your word, your chances for building a business relationship with them will be much higher.

In general, final decisions are made by the most senior-level person making the final decision. Although this individual may not take part in your meetings, the middle managers in attendance will most certainly be acting as liaisons for the person making the final decision. For that reason, understand that the rapport you establish with these individuals will be contingent upon the company that is chosen in the final process.

Meeting Manners

When scheduling meetings, do so during the mid-morning hours or after 3 p.m. Most businesses are closed between noon and 3 p.m. for the lunch hour, followed by an afternoon break.

Once a meeting does begin, prepare for many people to be talking at once and overlapping each other in conversation. Be patient with this and understand that it is very much part of the culture.

Rather than expecting Spaniards to tune into your way of doing things, you should be the one to mirror their behavior. This demonstrates your respect for their culture, and also tells others that you are adaptable. In addition, be sure to answer any questions you are asked about your background and family life during a first meeting. Questions like these are asked because Spaniards want to first become acquainted with you before getting down to business.

Be sure to take plenty of literature about your company with you. Spaniards are tactile people and will also appreciate receiving samples of your products and/or demonstrations of your service.

Keep in mind that this culture is a very proud group. Therefore, be sure to make your presentation comprehensible, so that your Spanish contacts will not be made to feel incompetent by telling you that they do not understand.

Punctuality

The Spanish are much more relaxed about time than others in Western Europe. Starting times for appointments and social engagements alike will be considered flexible. However, it would be wise for you to arrive on time for business engagements and only moderately late for social affairs. Do not mention your associates' tardiness when they do finally arrive.

Although you should be punctual yourself, keep in mind that "*el tiempo is como el espacio*" in Spain—or, "time is space." Thus, don't be alarmed if you are kept waiting for anywhere from 15 to 30 minutes prior to others arriving and a meeting actually getting off the ground.

Seating Etiquette

Spain follows the traditional Western seating arrangement for social events. The host and hostess will sit at opposite ends of the table. The male guest of honor will be seated to the right of the hostess and the female guest of honor will be placed to the right of the host.

Tipping Tips

In Spanish restaurants, a gratuity is usually added to the bill. If it is not included, then be sure to leave a minimum tip of 15 percent. If servers go above and beyond the call of duty, acknowledge it by leaving an additional 5 percent.

Hotel porters should be tipped about 50 *pesetas* per bag, while chambermaids should be given a tip of between 15 to 20 *pesetas* per day. When traveling by taxi, give a 10-percent tip to drivers with meters.

Toasting Etiquette

Toasting etiquette consists of a host raising his or her goblet and saying "*Salud.*"

Toilet Etiquette

When a public restroom is needed, men should look for a door marked "*Caballeros,*" while women should look for a door marked "*Señoras.*" In smaller towns, rooms marked "W.C." (for "water closet") are bathrooms used by both men and women.

When You Are Invited to a Spanish Home

Although Spaniards take great pride in their homes, it is much more common to be entertained in restaurants, rather than in a personal setting. If you are asked to visit your Spanish contact's home, it may be simply to stop in for a beverage prior to going to dinner.

As in other Spanish settings, "time is fluid" in a social setting. For that reason, it is considered more appropriate to arrive 30 minutes after the hour you were asked to be there, rather than early or on time.

Be sure to bring a small gift, such as chocolate, wine, or flowers for the hostess. Because children are usually part of evening or weekend gatherings, they should also be remembered with gifts.

Women in Business

Although only a handful of Spanish women hold management positions, businesswomen traveling to Spain will have few if any problems being taken seriously. The most important advice for women is to both look and act the professional part. By doing so, they will be perceived as "I mean business" individuals.

It is important for women from abroad to recognize that Spanish men are inherently machismo and like to be in control of situations. By knowing this up front, it will be easier to understand the Spanish mind-set and to allow men to feel as though they are in control.

Men will be comfortable accepting a lunch or dinner invitation from a businesswoman. As in most countries, whoever extends the invitation picks up the check.

Whatever You Do...

- Don't criticize or embarrass a Spaniard, especially a male. Honor is a top value and of great concern to the Spanish.
- Don't be shocked if you are greeted by kisses on the cheek. This will most likely happen with men or women whom you have previously met.
- Don't forget that many businesses are closed from 1 to 4 p.m. daily. This is the time designated in Spain for individuals to return home to enjoy their main meal with their families and also for an afternoon *siesta*.

- Don't leave food on your plate, because it is considered unacceptable to waste food. Make a point of eating everything on your plate and avoid accepting a second helping unless you know you can finish it.
- Don't use foul language. Spain is a highly religious country and your Spanish contact will be offended to hear remarks that take the Lord's name in vain.
- Don't expect to have Spaniards maintain any distance from you when they are talking. Spaniards are high-contact people and may not only stand closer to you than what you are comfortable with, they may also pat your arm or shoulder when conversing with you.
- Don't make offensive comments about bullfighting. The Spanish people enjoy this sport and place much value on it.

Advice From the Experts

"Be very formal. Be ready to go to dinner at 9 p.m. at the earliest. Peak hour for dinner time in Madrid is 11 p.m."

—Enzo Ferraris, Manager, International Trade Relations, The Procter & Gamble Company

Chapter 23

Sweden

The Kingdom of Sweden is a northern European nation located on the Scandinavian Peninsula. It is bordered by Norway on the west and northwest and by Finland on the northeast. Its coastline meets a number of seas, including the North Sea on the southwest, the Baltic Sea on the southeast, and the Gulf of Bothnia on the east. With an extensive land mass and well over 10,000 islands, Sweden is the third-largest country in Europe. More than half the land is covered with forest, and the countryside is also marked by mountains, plains, lakes, and rivers. Less than 10 percent of the land is arable for farming. At one time an agrarian society, Sweden has evolved in recent years to become one of the most technologically advanced countries in the world. Despite its size, Sweden is also one of the world's most sparsely populated nations. The majority of its population of 8.8 million lives in urban areas in the southern half of the country. The capital, Stockholm, is home to 1.6 million people.

Sweden is one of the oldest continuously existing nations in the world, with a history that dates back more than a thousand years. At one time a stronghold of the Vikings, the country became a major European power during the 17th century, when it had control over Finland, Estonia, Latvia, and part of northern Germany, as well as colonies elsewhere in the world. With its proximity to Russia, it has held a position of strategic importance, as well, both economically and politically. In 1815, Sweden was united with Norway, a union that lasted until its dissolution in 1905. Thereafter, the Swedish nation tried to maintain a neutral status in world affairs, which was not always easy. Following World War II, Sweden joined the United Nations, but not NATO, in its quest to maintain its neutrality. With the collapse of the Cold War, neutrality was no longer an issue, and Sweden has joined the European Community in a spirit of cooperation.

Sweden's governing structure was at one time an absolute monarchy, with a series of kings ruling the country over the centuries. Since the early 1800s, however, a constitution has been in effect, and legislative power resides in the Riksdag, a unicameral parliament. The prime minister is the majority party leader. The leading political party in Sweden is the Social Democratic Labour Party, which has rarely been out of power in this century. Sweden is known for its many programs devoted to social reform and welfare.

Economically, the country depends greatly on forestry and the production of wood products, as well as on mining. Its greatest natural resources include iron ore and copper, and it is a major producer of iron and steel, as well as aircraft, heavy machinery, and electronics and communications equipment. Other industries include chemicals, pharmaceuticals, medical equipment, and processed foods. Sweden is a very prosperous nation, and its people enjoy a comfortable standard of living. This country has given the world much in the way of scientific and technological advancement, producing inventors, engineers, and scientists who have made invaluable contributions to the world's technology and design.

Statistics and Information

Air Travel

Sweden's major airport is Arlanda International Airport, which is located about 25 miles north of Stockholm. Shuttles and taxis are available to transport you to your hotel.

Country Code

Sweden's country code is 46.

Stockholm's city code is 8.

Currency

Sweden's currency is called the *krona* (SEK). One *krona* is equal to 100 *øre*. Notes come in denominations of SEK1,000, 500, 100, 50, and 20. Coins come in denominations of 50, 10, 5, and 1 *øre*.

Banks, post offices, and ATM machines provide the best rates for exchanging your money.

Dates

Dates are written in the standard European style, with the day preceding the month, followed by the year. For example, January 30, 1999, would be written as 30/1/99.

Ethnic Makeup

More than 90 percent of the population is of Swedish descent. Finns and Lapps (also called Sami) make up a small percentage of the Swedish population, along with other European ethnic groups.

Holidays and National Celebrations

The following is a list of Sweden's national holidays. As in most countries, it is wise to avoid these dates when scheduling business meetings.

January 1	New Year's Day
January 6	Epiphany
Late March/ April	Good Friday, Holy Saturday, and Easter
Five weeks after Easter	Ascension Thursday
May 1	Labor Day

Eight weeks after Easter	Whitmonday
June 6	Swedish Flag Day
November 1	All Saints' Day
December 25	Christmas Day

Language

The country's official language is Swedish, which is Teutonic in origin and closely related to Norwegian and Danish. English is mandatory in Swedish schools, creating a population that is also fluent in English.

Religion

Evangelical Lutheranism is the country's dominant religion and is recognized by the government as the official church. While the majority of the population practices this religion, a small percentage is of the Jewish faith and other Christian religions. Religious freedom is the norm in Sweden.

Time Zone Differences

Sweden is:

- One hour ahead of Greenwich Mean Time.
- Six hours ahead of U.S. Eastern Standard Time.

Weather

Like the other Scandinavian countries, Sweden has cold temperatures most of the year, although given its latitude, the climate is fairly mild, especially in the southern and central regions. In the northern part of the country, temperatures range from frigid in the winter to the mid-50s Fahrenheit in the summer. In the southern part of the country, temperatures can range from the high 20s to the low 60s.

Etiquette

Business Attire

When packing for Sweden, be sure to include clothes that are up to date. You will see that Swedes take much pride in their appearance and stay up with the latest fashion trends.

For business purposes, men should wear suits of high quality fabrics with silk ties and dress shirts. Women will do well in designer suits or business dresses that command presence. Slack suits are also acceptable for women in Sweden.

Leave your casual attire at home and pack fashionable but sensible clothes that can be accessorized in such a way that what you wear during the day can take you into the evening. Because it is cold in Sweden, also prepare to dress in layers.

Business-card Etiquette

Most Swedes speak and understand English, so there is no need to have your business cards translated into Swedish. However, be sure to take plenty of cards with you, because you will be presenting them to your Swedish business contacts.

Business Entertaining/Dining

Meals are frequently enjoyed as you are trying to work out business deals. In most cases, the get-together will take place over dinner. If you are hosting a meal, be sure to include spouses in the evening function.

Swedes enjoy a wide array of foods. In fact, a *smörgasbord*—a form of buffet—is most commonly associated with Sweden. Rather than placing a lot of food on your plate at once, it is appropriate to take small amounts so that you can return to the table to enjoy other courses.

Like other Europeans, Swedes use the continental-style of dining, keeping the fork in the left hand and the knife in the right without switching hands while cutting and eating. In addition, hands should always be kept above the table and showing during meals.

Do not cut your entire piece of meat at one time. Rather, you should cut and eat one piece at a time.

As with any buffet, when you are participating in a *smörgasbord*, be sure to use a clean plate each time you return for another course.

It is good manners to try a small portion of everything served. If you must leave some food on your plate, your host would not be offended.

When you have finished eating, place your utensils on your plate in a 10 o'clock-4 o'clock position, with your fork tines up.

Beverage etiquette: While beer is enjoyed at some meals, wine will be offered during more formal events. It is appropriate to take the first sip after your host has said a few words and toasted everyone at the table.

Conversation

Appropriate topics for conversation with a Swede include travel, Swedish culture, hockey, or the fine arts. Any knowledge you have of Swedish history should be shared, as your hosts will find this impressive.

Never criticize the Swedish government, economy, or culture. Your Swedish friends may be very vocal in their negative remarks, but you should refrain from agreeing.

Swedes are not comfortable discussing personal matters, such as family or income. It is also not advisable to pay compliments to people you have only recently met, because the Swedish will view such remarks as insincere.

Gestures and Public Manners

Swedes keep their body language and hand gestures minimal, rather than relying on nonverbal forms of communication. You will also find that they prefer to maintain some space in their interactions. Therefore, you should be sure to maintain a distance of two arms' lengths between you and the person with whom you are conversing.

In conversation, you should maintain eye contact as much as possible and keep the tone of your voice down. Swedes tend to use "indoor" voices even when they are outdoors and you will be expected to do the same.

Queuing: Although the Swedish are not outwardly aggressive, they appreciate being taken care of promptly. For that reason, it is very common for many stores to maintain a semblance of order by utilizing a number system so that people can be helped on a first come-first served basis.

Gift-giving Etiquette

Although exchanging gifts is not common at the beginning of a business relationship, it is appropriate as you are finalizing the details for working together. Choose a practical gift, rather than one that may be perceived as lavish.

A bottle of good liquor is frequently appreciated. In addition, books about your country, as well as desk accessories, all make practical gifts and can also be keepsakes.

Greetings and Introductions

When you are with a group of Swedes, you will typically be introduced to others by a third party. If a third party is not present, it is okay to take the initiative and introduce yourself.

The proper Swedish greeting is to offer your hand as you make eye contact with the person and say, "*God dag*," which literally means "Good day." When a man meets a women, it is appropriate for either one to initiate the handshake. Handshakes are also part of a Swedish farewell.

Once business or social rapport has been established, you may find that the handshake you once received from your Swedish contact will be replaced with an "air kiss" on both cheeks. However, you should allow your Swedish contact to set the tone.

Proper forms of address: Swedes like to begin relationships on a formal level. Once a relationship has been achieved, they move to a more familiar level. Always address your Swedish contacts by their last names and the correct titles, until you have been invited to address them otherwise.

Titles are important to the Swedish. If someone has an academic or professional title, you should address the person by that title. The following courtesy titles should be used for those without professional titles:

- *Herr:* Mr.
- *Fru:* Mrs.
- *Fröken:* Miss.

Hierarchy Is Important

There is a definite hierarchy in Swedish organizations. However, in many cases, the more senior managers will delegate to the mid-level management team. It will be helpful for you to become acquainted with the "pecking order" and understand that even if you are meeting with individuals who are in the bottom line of management, they may be instrumental in communicating your message to mid- and senior-level management.

How Decisions Are Made

You may be surprised to learn that decision-making falls to the lower rungs of the ladder in Sweden, where there is an emphasis on teamwork and compromise. Do not put all your efforts into wining, dining, wheeling, and dealing with top-level executives. Chances are, they will turn over the power to make a decision to their middle managers, who may even pass the buck to lower levels.

Once a deal has been made and signed, you can rest assured that the Swedes will uphold their end of the bargain.

Meeting Manners

Swedes believe in being prompt, so it is important for you to arrive on time for meetings. This nationality also believes in adhering to the scheduled beginning and end times of a meeting. For that reason, it will be appreciated if you respect the agenda at hand, get down to business right away, and avoid small talk.

As you prepare for your meeting, bear in mind that Swedes are very detail-oriented and will place high value on a well-prepared presentation.

Punctuality

Swedes are sticklers for punctuality. They will respect your time and will expect you to do the same and be punctual for scheduled meetings and appointments.

Seating Etiquette

Swedish seating etiquette dictates that the host and hostess sit at opposite ends of the table. The most senior female guest is offered the seat to the left of the host, while the most senior male guest will be placed to the immediate left of the hostess.

As in most countries, couples are seated separately during meals.

Tipping Tips

Restaurant bills will include a 12- to 15-percent gratuity. Many people choose to round the bill up to the nearest *krona* to leave a small additional tip. In the finest restaurants, leave an additional 5 to 10 percent.

Hotel porters should be tipped about 3 to 5 *kronas*. Taxis also include the tip in the fare. If you like, you may give more by rounding out the total amount.

Toasting Etiquette

Toasts are quite an event in Sweden. The traditional toast that you will hear is "*Skål.*" After the host has proposed the toast, each person at the table may take the first sip of his or her drink.

A uniquely Swedish toasting tip is for men to wait until women have set down their glasses before doing so themselves.

Proper etiquette requires that the male guest of honor speak on behalf of everyone present to express his gratitude to the host and hostess. This should be done prior to the end of the meal.

When You Are Invited to a Swedish Home

Swedes are very hospitable and will invite you to their homes both during the week and on weekends. Be sure to arrive promptly and to go with something in hand. Fine chocolates, a bottle of wine, or flowers for the hostess all make good gifts.

Women in Business

Sweden is an advanced country, in that a high percentage of its women are gainfully employed. However, despite a commanding presence in the work force, they are still climbing the managerial ladder, and very few Swedish women have achieved positions of real power.

Women from abroad who are conducting business in Sweden should be professional in both their attire and their demeanor at all times.

Whatever You Do...

- Don't schedule meetings with Swedish businesspeople for the months of June, July, or August, as well as late February through early March. These are very popular times when Swedes go on holiday.
- Don't be shocked if you are at a beach and see people sunbathing in the buff. This act is very common in Sweden.
- Don't use a lot of superlatives when speaking. The Swedes are opposed to stretching the truth.
- Don't use profanity at any time. If you do, you will offend the Swedes.
- Don't accept or help yourself to the last serving on a platter. This is perceived as a rude in Sweden.

Chapter 24

Switzerland

The Federal Republic of Switzerland has occupied a position of historical and political importance in central Europe for centuries. It is bordered on the north by France and Germany, on the east by Austria and Liechtenstein, on the south by Italy, and on the west by France. This beautiful land is renowned for its abundance of mountains, consisting of the Alps in the central and southern regions of the country and the Jura in the northwest. In between lies the Swiss plateau, along with several valleys, rivers, lakes, and waterfalls. Switzerland's capital is Bern. Other major cities include Geneva, Zürich, Lucerne, Lausanne, and Basel, all of which hold positions of political, economic, or cultural importance. The population totals more than 6.9 people, mostly of German, French, and Italian origins—an ethnic combination that has created a culturally diverse and fascinating society.

At one time, Switzerland was a region under Roman rule, called Helvetia, which was, in time, conquered by the Franks. With the dissolution of the Frankish Carolingian Empire in the 9th century, the region was divided into a number of city-states and, later, regions called cantons that related strongly to the ethnic origins of their people. In 1291, these states formed an alliance for purposes of defense that later developed into what became known as the Swiss Confederation. After the Holy Roman Empire failed to force this confederation into submission in 1499, the Treaty of Basel was drawn up, effectively recognizing Swiss independence. During the Thirty Years' War, the confederation adopted a position of neutrality that it continued to maintain in years to come, sometimes with great difficulty. Wars, threats of invasion from neighboring countries, and industrial development all threatened the peace and stability of the confederation. For a brief period, the country was occupied by France and renamed the Helvetic Republic, but the Congress of Vienna in 1815 restored the Swiss cantons and formally recognized Switzerland's neutral status. In the years that followed, cantons and political coalitions clashed with another, until a new constitution in 1848 effectively provided for a national unification of ethnically oriented cantons. Since then, Switzerland's neutrality has protected it from war and made it a leader in the promotion of peace and cooperation, although it is not a member of the United Nations or the European Union, for fear that membership would compromise its neutral status. It is, however, a member of the Organization for European Economic Cooperation and the Council of Europe.

Although three-quarters of Switzerland's population is German, all ethnic groups share equal power in the Swiss government. Surprisingly, despite a society that has been democratically advanced in many ways, women were not granted the right to vote until 1971. The Swiss constitution was revised in 1973 and 1978. The political system allows for a national executive authority, with an elected bicameral parliament called the National Assembly, which in turn, elects the 7 members of the Bundesrat, a federal council from which a president is elected for a one-year term. Switzerland's 23 cantons (three of which are subdivided into half cantons) are self-administrative, in line with Swiss principles of sovereignty.

Statistics and Information

Air Travel

Switzerland has two major international airports, located in Zurich and Geneva. Taxis are available from either of these airports into the cities. Both airports also have train stations that provide easy access into the heart of the cities.

Country Code

Switzerland's country code is 41.

City codes include:

- 31 for Bern.
- 22 for Geneva.
- 1 for Zurich.

Currency

Switzerland's currency is called the *Swiss franc* (abbreviated SFr). One SFr is equal to 100 *centimes*. Notes come in denominations of SFr1,000, 500, 100, 50, 20, and 10. Coins come in SFr5, 2, and 1, as well as in 50, 20, 10, 5, 2, and 1 *centimes*.

Banks and ATM machines provide the best rates for exchanging your money.

Dates

The format for writing dates in Switzerland follows the same standard practiced in other European countries, with the day written before the month, followed by the year. November 13, 2020, would be written as 13/11/20.

Ethnic Makeup

Switzerland is comprised of individuals of diverse backgrounds, representative of the surrounding countries, who settled into the cantons that make up the nation. More than half of the Swiss population is of German descent, while less than a fifth is of French heritage and about a tenth has roots in Italy. With such a background, the country is understandably a model of ethnic acceptance and toleration.

Holidays and National Celebrations

The following is a list of Switzerland's celebrated holidays. Because many of these are national holidays, it is wise not to schedule meetings for these days.

January 1	New Year's Day
Late March/April	Good Friday, Easter
Five weeks after Easter	Ascension Day
Eight weeks after Easter	Whitmonday
August 1	Independence Day
December 25	Christmas Day

Language

Switzerland has four official languages. German is the dominant one and is spoken by more than three-quarters of the Swiss. French and Italian are also commonly heard. Finally, a dialect called *Romansch* (sometimes called *Ladin*) is also spoken in southern Switzerland.

English is frequently heard in southern and western regions, and is most commonly spoken by individuals conducting international business.

Religion

The majority of the country's population is almost evenly divided between practitioners of the Roman Catholic and Protestant faiths. Muslims and Jews also make up a small percentage of the population. Freedom of religion is guaranteed by the Swiss constitution.

Time Zone Differences

Switzerland is:

- One hour ahead of Greenwich Mean Time.
- Six hours ahead of U.S. Eastern Standard Time.

Weather

The temperatures and precipitation you experience in Switzerland will depend on the part of the country you're visiting. For instance, in higher elevations you will naturally experience colder weather and more snow. In the central plateau and lower elevations, the climate tends to be temperate with less precipitation. Generally, winters are very cold and see much snowfall, while summers are humid, with temperatures ranging from cool to warm.

Business Etiquette

Business Attire

Business attire should be formal and conservative. Men should wear finely tailored suits, starched shirts, and ties. Women should wear suits with skirts of a conservative length. Classic pants suits are also acceptable.

Any jewelry that is worn should be simple yet elegant. The rule that should be followed, especially for women, is "less is more."

Business-card Etiquette

Because many Swiss speak English, business cards need not be translated into French, German, or Italian. In addition to the usual data, the Swiss will appreciate it if your card mentions the length of time your company has been in existence. You should be sure that your title is printed in a larger font than normal and that any academic titles you have earned are listed near your name.

Take plenty of cards with you, because there will be numerous occasions when you will be required to present it.

Business Entertaining/Dining

In some Swiss companies, you may be invited to have lunch in their in-house cafeterias. This is an efficient way to use time, both for you and for your Swiss contact.

Dinner engagements will take place in fine restaurants. In many cases, spouses are part of the evening. Allow your Swiss host to be the first to bring up the topic of business.

Swiss cuisine is a reflection of its variety of ethnic backgrounds. Depending on the region of Switzerland you are visiting, you will enjoy excellent German, Italian, or French foods, often prepared with a Swiss twist. Switzerland is also known for its fine chocolates and cheeses.

During the meal, you will be offered red or white wine, as well as beer. Coffee and after-dinner drinks will follow the meal.

As in most European countries, hands should remain above board and in view. Elbows, however, should not be placed on the table.

In many situations, food will be served "family-style," on platters from which you can serve yourself. When this is the case, be sure to take a small amount of each food you are offered, to avoid insulting both your host and the person who has prepared the meal, and to be able to accept seconds, if necessary. Be careful about how much you take, however. While it is acceptable to leave food on your plate in some countries, this is not the case in Switzerland. If you do, you may risk offending your host.

"Finger foods" or utensil foods? In most cases, you should use utensils, even if you are accustomed to enjoying eating the offered food with your hands in your home country (for example, cheese, fruit, or sandwiches). When in doubt, take the cue from your host.

Conversation

Although you may interpret the Swiss as being rather reserved when you first meet them, once you establish rapport with your contacts, you will find them to be very loyal to your cause. The Swiss are honest and dependable people, and you will find it a pleasure to work with individuals of this nationality.

Conversationally and otherwise, the Swiss are a well-rounded people. Good topics of conversation include world affairs, your travels in Switzerland, and sports.

Because the Swiss are reserved by nature, try to avoid asking them questions about their personal lives. For instance, do not ask what they do for a living, what their marital status is, their age, and so on.

Gestures and Public Manners

The way you sit, stand, and project yourself are of utmost importance. You can expect the Swiss to pay close attention to your posture.

Be sure to point with your full hand, rather than only your index finger. Otherwise, you will be displaying an obscene gesture.

Queuing: You will find that the Swiss do not believe in standing in line patiently, so when you are in a queue, get ready for some pushing and shoving.

Toilet etiquette: While it will be fairly easy to find public restrooms, be sure to carry some change with you, because you will be required to pay to get into a stall.

Taxi etiquette: Swiss taxis may be a real treat for you. More often than not, you will find yourself inside the equivalent of what Americans consider to be luxury cars.

Gift-giving Etiquette

Although it will be important to go to Switzerland with gifts in hand, wait until contracts have been signed before you present them to your Swiss contacts. You should allow your contact to initiate the gift-giving procedure so that you can reciprocate.

Be sure your gifts are reasonably priced, rather than expensive gifts that may be perceived as excessive or even as a form of bribery. Appropriate presents would include paperweights, books about your homeland, or a good bottle of whiskey or cognac.

When giving flowers, keep in mind that chrysanthemums are reserved for funerals. You should not give scissors, cutlery, or anything else with sharp points, as such gifts may be interpreted as severing ties.

Greetings and Introductions

The handshake remains the most popular way to meet and greet business contacts in Switzerland. Once you have established rapport with your Swiss contacts, those who are of German descent may continue to shake hands upon both meeting and departing. However, your French Swiss or Italian Swiss contacts may give you an "air kiss" and/or an embrace, based on their comfort level with you.

When you are meeting a group of people, wait for someone else to initiate the introductions.

Proper forms of address: Always address your Swiss contact by his or her last name, preceded by the equivalent of Mr., Mrs., or Miss. Do not use anyone's first name until you are invited to do so.

How Decisions Are Made

The Swiss will take their time making a business decision, so you must let them do so on their own terms and not appear too pushy. The managing director of a company tends to be the person who makes the final decisions. However, keep in mind that the top person will also seek counsel from those under him or her. Therefore, it would be helpful to learn the pecking order and culture of the company with which you are working.

Meeting Manners

Punctuality is key, so be sure to arrive on time for the scheduled meeting.

Cultural differences affect many aspects of life in Switzerland, and that is especially true of the way meetings are handled. For instance, because Germans tend to be "no-nonsense" people, they will cut to the chase and begin discussing business soon after the start of the meeting. On the other hand, those of French and Italian extraction will the take time to establish rapport by offering you something to drink and making small talk.

No matter what the background of your Swiss contacts may be, you should be certain that your presentation is clear and concise.

Punctuality

The Swiss are very respectful of time, and you should be, too. In fact, you will really impress your Swiss contacts if you arrive 15 to 20 minutes ahead of time as a way of displaying the importance you put on meeting with them.

Seating Etiquette

Allow your host or hostess to indicate where you should sit. Often the guest of honor is seated in the middle of the table, on the side that faces the door.

Tipping Tips

When receiving a restaurant bill, you will see that a service charge has been added. If you were extremely pleased with the service, you may round the bill to the nearest *franc* as a way of leaving slightly more for the server.

Hotel porters should receive a *franc* for each bag they carry. Although tips are not required for chambermaids, if you choose to leave a *franc*, it will be highly appreciated.

Toasting Etiquette

Cocktails are not commonplace in Switzerland. However, toasts are very much part of Swiss meals. Frequently, wine and champagne will be offered when a toast is going to be proposed.

Wait until your host has proposed a toast before sipping your drink. An appropriate response to a toast is to raise your glass to the host and say, "To your health."

When You Are Invited to a Swiss Home

If you receive an invitation to your Swiss contact's home, you should feel quite honored. These invitations are few and far between.

Be sure to arrive on time with fine chocolates, liquor, and/or flowers in hand.

Women in Business

A Swiss woman's role in society is viewed as traditional and conservative by both men and women. Few women hold high-level positions and must work much harder than men to achieve success.

Businesswomen from abroad should maintain a high degree of professionalism, both in their actions and dress. An invitation to lunch will be graciously accepted by your Swiss contact. If a dinner invitation is in order, be sure to also extend it to the person's spouse.

Whatever You Do...

- Don't make business appointments between the hours of noon and 2 p.m. All Swiss offices close for lunch and a relaxation period at this time.
- Don't forget to inquire about the English-language proficiency of the Swiss businesspeople you are to meet. Although English is a common business language, French, German, and Italian may be what your Swiss contacts speak and understand the best, and you may need to prepare for this possibility.
- Don't drink water from the tap. Bottled water is both better and preferred.
- Don't wait to be seated in most restaurants. It will be expected for you to seat yourself.

Chapter 25

Turkey

The Republic of Turkey is a Middle Eastern country of which 5 percent extends into southeastern Europe. It is bordered on the east by Georgia, Armenia, Azerbaijan, and Iran, on the south by Iraq, Syria, and the Mediterranean Sea, on the west by the Aegean Sea and Greece, on the northwest by Bulgaria, and on the north by the Black Sea. Two important straits, the Bosphorus and the Dardanelles, are located within Turkey's borders. It can truly be said that East meets West in Turkey, for this country's location provides an important link between Europe and Asia. Its major cities include its capital, Ankara, and Istanbul. Turkey's population totals more than 58.5 million people.

Turkey is a variable land of mountains and valleys, plateaus and steppes, lakes and rivers, forests and pastures. Nearly two-fifths of the land is arable, and agriculture forms an important part of the Turkish economy. Turkey's major exports include textiles, agricultural products, and petrochemicals. Principal crops include fruit, vegetables, cereals, legumes, cotton, tobacco, tea, and poppies. While it does not have too many natural resources, Turkey is a leading exporter of chromite, and also mines iron ore, coal, bauxite, and copper. It is also the leading producer of steel in the Middle East. Although major portions of the country are heavily forested, this is not exploited. In recent years, manufacturing operations have been on the rise, helping to improve the condition of Turkey's economy. Tourism is also a major contributor to the GNP.

The country known as Turkey today had its origins in a region called Anatolia. The area was occupied by several civilizations for centuries, until the Ottomans rose to power and created a dynastic hold that extended through much of the Middle East and Europe, particularly the Balkan territories. The Ottoman Empire went into a decline in the 1500s and 1600s, and by the late 19th century had lost most of its holdings. Efforts to revive the Empire in the early part of the 20th century failed, and Turkey lost still more territory after it sided with Germany in World War I. The Conference of Lausanne in 1923 delineated Turkey's current borders and established a republic, with Mustafa Kemal Atatürk installed as the country's first president. Atatürk implemented a series of political and cultural reforms that shaped the country's future. In particular, he worked to reduce Islamic influence upon the country, including changing the national language from Arabic to Turkish and instituting equal rights for men and women. After his death in 1938, a democratic government was created, complete with a parliament and multiparty system. The parliament is called the Turkish Grand National Assembly, and it elects a president for a nonrenewable seven-year term. While there have been numerous revolts, moments of civil unrest, and challenges to authority over the years (a new constitution was drawn up as recently as 1982), as well as major disputes with Greece over the ownership of Cyprus, the government is essentially stable and the economy is thriving. Turkey is a member of NATO, the OEEC, and the Council of Europe.

Statistics and Information

Air Travel

When flying to Istanbul, you will arrive at the Atatürk Airport. From there, you can take the bus to Aksaray and then the tramway into the city. Taxis are also readily available.

Country Code

Turkey's country code is 90.

City codes include:

- 312 for Ankara.
- 212 for the European side of Istanbul, or 216 for the Asian side.

Currency

Turkey's currency is the *Turkish lira* (abbreviated TL). Notes are available in denominations of TL20,000, 10,000, 5,000, and 1,000. The *lira* is also available in coin form in denominations of 5,000, 2,500, 1,000, and 500.

Although 100 *kurus* is equivalent to one *lira*, it is not currently in circulation because of inflation.

Banks and post offices will provide the best exchange rate.

Dates

Dates are written following the European standard format, with the number representing the day listed first, followed by the month, and then the year. For instance, November 30, 2010, would be written as 30/11/10.

Ethnic Makeup

While the majority of the population living in Turkey is native Turk, approximately 20 percent is of Kurdish descent. Individuals of Armenian, Greek, and Spanish background also make up a portion of the Turkish population.

Holidays

January 1	New Year's Day
Feb./March	The Ramazan
Feb./March	Seker Bayrami

April 23	National Sovereignty/Children's Day
May 1	Spring Festival
May 19	Atatürk Commemoration and Youth Sports Day
August 30	Victory Day
October 29	Republic Day
November 10	Atatürk's Death

Language

The country's official language is Turkish, spoken by more than 86 percent of the population. Although English and German are also commonly heard languages in Turkey, a mastery of a few Turkish phrases will be key to establishing rapport with your Turkish contacts.

Kurdish and Arabic are also languages spoken in this republic.

Religion

Most Turks practice the Sunni Muslim religion. There are also small minorities of Jews and Christians who live primarily in Istanbul, Ankara, and Izmir.

Time Zone Differences

Turkey follows the Eastern European Time (EET). It is:

- Two hours ahead of Greenwich Mean Time.
- Seven hours ahead of U.S. Eastern Standard Time.

Weather

Turkey's weather varies as much as the terrain in this large country. The majority of Turkey experiences a continental climate, with winters being cold and snowy and summers hot and dry with average temperatures in the 70s. Rain is common throughout the year.

Etiquette

Business Attire

Turks take great pride in their appearance and enjoy looking their best. Although some Turks still wear traditional dress, Western-style dressing is common throughout the country.

Men will do well wearing conservatively tailored suits with shirts and ties. Women must be careful about what they wear. This should include skirts that cover most of their legs or tailored slacks, as well as blouses that cover their shoulders and arms at least down to the elbows. Sleeveless tops should not be worn. When visiting a mosque, women should make a point of covering their heads, because this is the custom.

Business-card Etiquette

When meeting and greeting Turkish individuals for the first time, business cards should always be exchanged. For that reason, take plenty with you and offer one of them to everyone you meet.

Although it is not necessary, if you print a translation on the reverse side of your business cards, you will greatly impress the individuals with whom you will be meeting.

Business Entertaining/Dining

An important part of entertaining in Turkey centers on food. Turks enjoy lengthy and lavish meals. Most of this entertaining takes place in restaurants. If you are the one hosting the meal, be sure to ask your Turkish contacts to recommend the restaurant. They will take great pride in making such a recommendation, and you will be assured of a quality location.

Because Turks are extraordinarily hospitable, you can expect multiple invitations to eat and drink.

Allow yourself to enjoy this attention and accept it graciously.

For lunchtime gatherings, prepare to enjoy three courses consisting of a soup, salad, and main course. While eating will be the focal part of the meal, business can be discussed over coffee, which will be served following the meal.

When you extend a dinner invitation, be sure to include spouses, because this meal should be of a social nature. Business should not be discussed unless your Turkish contacts initiate it.

Turkish meals are served by course rather than "family-style." They typically include an appetizer, followed by a soup, salad, and entrée. Lamb or mutton is commonly eaten, accompanied by a rice dish. This meat is also served in shish kebab form. While chicken, fish, and other meats will also be enjoyed, you will not encounter pork, as it is forbidden by the Muslim religion.

Following the main course, get ready for a tasty pastry, such as baklava, which is made of phyllo dough, nuts, and honey. This rich dessert will be served to you with Turkish coffee.

The continental-style of dining is observed in Turkey, with the fork kept in the left hand and the knife retained in the right hand at all times.

Most foods in Turkey are eaten with utensils. However, play it safe by following your Turkish contact's manner of eating. When you are offered food, begin with a small portion, because it is certain that you will be offered second and third helpings. Part of being perceived as sociable is accepting another helping when it is offered to you.

Turkish etiquette encourages that you leave the table only after everyone at the table has completed the meal. You should be sure to extend a compliment to the host and hostess about how much you enjoyed both the food and their company.

Conversation

Turks enjoy conversing with individuals from other countries. Although many Turks have a command of the English language, making an effort to know a few words will be appreciated and will help in establishing rapport.

Turks are well-versed on a variety of subjects. They enjoy conversing about their travels and also enjoy hearing about yours. Because family is an integral part of their culture, sharing information about your immediate family, as well as asking about theirs, is a good topic of conversation. Other appropriate topics include art, current events, and sports.

As in most other countries, avoid discussing religion and politics, especially the Cyprus-Greek conflict. Discussions on international affairs should also be avoided.

Gestures and Public Manners

Although Turks are hospitable individuals, they make a point of not displaying affection with the opposite sex in public settings.

Avoid blowing your nose or yawning in public without covering your mouth, as these gestures are considered to be rude.

Your hands should be showing at all times. Do not put them in your pockets or under the table.

When you want someone to approach you, do not use a waving motion. Instead, extend your arm with your palm facing you and move your fingers back and forth.

Take care about interpreting gestures that indicate "yes" and "no." In Turkey, a subtle nod of the head means "yes" while a "no" is demonstrated by moving the head more fully in an upward motion.

As in Greece, avoid using the U.S. signal for "okay" (the thumb and index finger forming a circle), because this is considered an obscene gesture in Turkey.

Be sure to keep your shoes on the ground. It is considered rude to have the soles of your shoes showing.

Gift-giving Etiquette

While gifts should be exchanged at the beginning of an initial meeting, wait to open them until you are alone. The gifts you give should be related to the office, rather than the person. Acceptable gifts include paperweights, quality pens, and the like.

Most Turks are Muslim, so avoid giving wine and other alcohol as gifts.

Greetings and Introductions

Meeting and greeting is an important part of establishing relationships with Turks. Appropriate greetings should be extended during the initial meeting and any that follow. Be sure to shake hands first with the most senior person, based on age and/or hierarchy.

After you have established a comfort level with your Turk contact, you will be greeted with a kiss on each cheek and you should reciprocate accordingly. By mastering a few words such as the Turkish hello, "*Merhaba*," followed by a handshake, you will greatly impress the individuals with whom you will be meeting. When departing, a handshake or a kiss on the cheeks should take place.

You will note that Turks call each other by their first names. However, when first meeting your new contact, prepare to use the person's first name, followed by the following equivalents:

- *Bey:* Sir.
- *Hanim:* Ma'am.

Hierarchy Is Important

There is a definite pecking order in Turkish companies. Because decisions are made by the person at the top level, it is important to understand the structure within the organization.

How Decisions Are Made

Decisions are made by the head of the company, rather than by a group of people. If you are able to identify that person, be sure to focus your attention on this decision-maker.

Be patient and don't expect fast decisions. As in many countries, time is fluid and deadlines may be extended rather than met.

Meeting Manners

When first entering a Turkish company, be respectful of all the people you meet. This includes acknowledging them with a handshake as you make eye contact with them. Eye contact should also be maintained when you are delivering your presentation and when you are answering questions.

The meeting will likely begin with a beverage and light conversation about who you are, your personal background, and so forth. This is an important part of establishing rapport.

Punctuality

Punctuality is very much respected in Turkey. You can depend on your Turkish contacts to be prompt, and they will also expect you to arrive by the scheduled time. This also applies to social engagements. If you find that you are going to be even slightly late, call ahead to explain.

Seating Etiquette

As in many other countries, the host and hostess will sit at opposite ends of the table. The most senior female guest is offered the seat to the left of the host, while the most senior male guest is given the seat to the left of the hostess.

Tipping Tips

Although most restaurants will add a 10- to 15-percent service charge to your bill, if you have been extremely pleased with the service, you may leave extra to display your appreciation.

While the locals do not add a gratuity to a taxi driver's fare, individuals traveling from abroad are expected to do so. The amount given can range between 10 and 15 percent. When a porter has assisted you with your bags, tip the person $1 per piece handled. Both washroom and coatroom attendants should be acknowledged for their assistance with a small tip.

Toasting Etiquette

Most Turks do not consume alcoholic beverages because of their religious beliefs. For that reason, you should take your cue from your host as to what kind of beverage you can or should consume.

Besides beer or wine, a Turkish beverage you may be offered is called *Rake*. If alcohol is offered, one beverage that you may be served is called *ra*. Another popular Turkish drink is *raki*, which is an anise-seed-flavored drink.

When your host says, "*Serefe*," that means a toast is being proposed to you and others at the table.

You will impress your Turkish contacts following the meal if you lift your goblet toward the host and propose your thanks in the form of the following Turkish toast: "*Ziyade Olsen.*"

Toilet Etiquette

While you will find modern commodes at many leisure and tourist sites, you may encounter squat toilets in other locations. For instance, most train stations and restaurants will have modern facilities, but squat toilets still exist elsewhere.

It is wise to carry your own supply of tissues, as toilet paper is not always provided. You may also be charged to use the restroom.

When You Are Invited to a Turkish Home

Entertaining business associates at home is becoming more common in Turkey. When you receive an invitation, expect your hosts to treat you like royalty.

You should give a small gift to the hostess and children when you first arrive. Items that are considered good gifts include flowers, candy, or fine chocolates.

If your host's shoes are removed, be sure you do the same. Prepare to eat heartily and enjoy the company of your Turkish contact.

Women in Business

Women traveling to Turkey from abroad will be treated with respect. However, it will be important to understand the do's and don'ts of appropriate behavior in this different culture. For instance:

- Women should abide by the rule that they should speak to a male only after he has spoken to her.
- When possible, it is important to travel with another person in public; women should not be seen alone.
- Women from abroad should recognize that no matter how well-educated Turkish women are, many of them place their families before their careers and elect to stay home to raise their families. For that reason, very few women are in upper-level management.

Whatever You Do...

- Don't be surprised to see men accompany women to the restroom and wait for them outside the door.
- Don't wear shorts. Showing off one's legs is frowned upon and may provoke comments from the locals.
- Don't pick up food with your left hand. Traditionally, Turks see this hand as unclean.
- Don't travel to Turkey during the summer months, as this is the time when most Turks go on holiday.
- Don't plan on drinking alcohol with dinner. The majority of Turks are Muslim and do not consume alcoholic beverages.
- Don't be afraid to bargain with a hotel clerk about the price of your room. Haggling is acceptable in this case.
- Don't be surprised if you see people holding what may look like a rosary in various situations. They are actually holding worry beads, which are a way of relieving stress.

Conclusion

You have now read that it takes more to successfully conduct business outside your own country than merely greeting contacts and exchanging business cards. You have probably also learned that there is a unique art to doing business in Europe. I hope that you will make this book one of your travel companions when visiting this part of the world.

Do you have a question about European business etiquette that was not addressed in any of the chapters of this book? You can e-mail me at ateaseeurope@etiqu.com or contact me by writing to At Ease Inc., 119 East Court Street, Cincinnati, Ohio 45202, or by calling 800-873-9909. I can assure you of a prompt response.

Bibliography

Ash, David. *Essential Bulgaria.* Passport Books, 1994.

Axtell, Roger. *Do's and Taboos Around the World.* John Wiley & Sons, Inc., 1993.

Axtell, Roger. *Do's and Taboos of Hosting International Visitors.* John Wiley & Sons, Inc., 1990.

Barkow, Ben and Zeidenitz, Stefan. *The Xenophobe's Guide to The Germans.* Ravette Publishing Limited, 1993.

Berlin, Peter. *The Xenophobe's Guide to The Swedes.* Ravette Publishing Limited, 1994.

Bilton, Paul. *The Xenophobe's Guide to The Swiss.* Ravette Publishing Limited, 1995.

Bosrosk, Mary M. *Put Your Best Foot Forward—Europe.* International Education System, 1994.

Braganti, Nancy L. and Devine, Elizabeth. *The Traveler's Guide to European Customs & Manners.* Meadowbrook, 1984.

Cotsell, Michael and Warrender, Annabel. *France.* Passport Books, 1987.

Dresser, Norine. *Multicultural Manners.* John Wiley and Sons, 1995.

Eu-Wong, Shirley. *Culture Shock: Switzerland.* Graphic Arts Center Publishing Company, 1996.

Fiada, Alexandra. *The Xenophobe's Guide to The Greeks.* Ravette Publishing Limited, 1994.

Flamini, Roland. *Passport Germany.* World Trade Press, 1997.

Flower, Raymond and Falassi, Alessandro. *Culture Shock: Italy.* Graphic Arts Center Publishing Company, 1995.

Gioseffi, Claudia. *Passport Italy.* World Trade Press, 1997.

Graff, Marie L. *Culture Shock: Spain.* Graphic Arts Center Publishing Company, 1993.

Harper, Timothy. *Passport United Kingdom.* World Trade Press, 1997.

Hofer, Hans. *Insight Guides: Finland.* Hofer Press (Pte) Ltd., 1996.

James, Louis. *The Xenophobe's Guide to The Austrians.* Ravette Publishing Limited, 1994.

Joseph, Nadine. *Passport France.* World Trade Press, 1997.

Jotischky, Lazlo. *The Simple Guide to Customs and Etiquette in Hungary.* Global Books Ltd., 1995.

Kenna, Peggy and Lacy, Sondra. *Business France.* Passport Books, 1994.

Kenna, Peggy and Lacy, Sondra. *Business Germany.* Passport Books, 1994.

Kenna, Peggy and Lacy, Sondra. *Business Italy.* Passport Books, 1995.

Kenna, Peggy and Lacy, Sondra. *Business Spain.* Passport Books, 1995.

Launay, Drew. *The Xenophobe's Guide to The Spanish.* Ravette Publishing Limited, 1993.

Let's Go: Eastern Europe. St. Martin's Press, 1998.

Levy, Patricia. *Culture Shock: Ireland.* Graphic Arts Center Publishing Company, 1996.

Lord, Richard. *Culture Shock: Germany.* Graphic Arts Center Publishing Company, 1996.

Martin, Alex. *The Simple Guide to Customs and Etiquette in Greece.* Global Books Ltd., 1995.

McNamara, Aidan. *The Simple Guide to Customs and Etiquette in Ireland.* Global Books Ltd., 1996.

Miall, Antony. *The Xenophobe's Guide to The English.* Ravette Publishing Limited, 1993.

Mole, John. *Mind Your Manners: Managing Business Cultures in Europe.* Nicholas Brealey Publishing, 1995.

Morrison, Terri with Wayne A. Conway and George A. Borden, Ph.D. *Kiss, Bow, or Shake Hands*. Adams Media Corporation, 1994.

Morrison, Terri with Wayne A. Conway and Josep J. Douress. *Doing Business Around the World*. Prentice Hall, 1997.

Nollen, Tim. *Culture Shock: Czech Republic*. Graphic Arts Center Publishing Company, 1997.

Novas, Himilce and Silva, Rosemary E. *Passport Spain*. World Trade Press, 1997.

Nwanna, Gladson I. *Do's and Don'ts Around the World: A Country Guide to Cultural and Social Taboos and Etiquette [Europe]*. World Travel Institute, 1998.

Rawlins, Clive L. *Culture Shock: Greece*. Graphic Arts Center Publishing Company, 1997.

Robinson, Danielle. *The Simple Guide to Customs and Etiquette in France*. Global Books Ltd., 1998.

Shankland, Hugh. *The Simple Guide to Customs and Etiquette in Italy*. Global Books Ltd., 1996.

Short, Dave. *The Simple Guide to Customs and Etiquette in the Czech Republic*. Global Books Ltd., 1996.

Solly, Martin. *The Xenophobe's Guide to The Italians*. Ravette Publishing Company, 1995.

Star, Nancy. *The International Guide to Tipping*. Berkeley Books, 1988.

Strange, Morten. *Culture Shock: Denmark*. Graphic Arts Center Publishing Company, 1996.

Syrett, Michel and Yapp, Nick. *The Xenophobe's Guide to The French*. Ravette Publishing Limited, 1993.

Tan, Terry. *Culture Shock: Britain*. Graphic Arts Center Publishing Company, 1992.

Taylor, Sally A. *Culture Shock: France*. Graphic Arts Center Publishing Company, 1990.

About the Author

Ann Marie Sabath is the president of At Ease Inc., a 13-year-old Cincinnati-based company specializing in domestic and international business etiquette programs. She is also the author of *Business Etiquette in Brief* and *Business Etiquette: 101 Ways to Conduct Business With Charm and Savvy*, as well as executive editor of the European Etiquette Video Series focusing on England, France, Spain, and Germany.

Sabath's international and domestic etiquette concepts have been featured in *The Wall Street Journal*, *USA Today*, and Delta Airlines' *Sky Magazine*. They have also been recognized on *The Oprah Winfrey Show*, *20/20*, and *CNN*.

Since 1987, Sabath and her staff have trained more than 30,000 people representing the business, industry, government, and educational sectors in how to gain the competitive edge. Her 10 Key Ways for Enhancing Your Global Savvy, Polish That Builds Profits, and Business Etiquette: The Key to Effective Client Services programs have been presented to individuals representing Deloitte & Touche LLP, Fidelity Investments, General Electric, Procter & Gamble, Arthur Andersen, MCI Telecommunications, The Marriott Corporation, and Salomon Brothers, among others.

In 1992, At Ease Inc. became an international firm by licensing its concept in Taiwan. In 1998, the firm also established its presence in Egypt and Australia.

Her forthcoming books, *International Business Etiquette: Latin and Central America* and *Dress Rules for the 21st Century* will be released in 2000.

Index